THE WIZARD IN MY SHED

THE MISADVENTURES OF MERDYN THE WILD

ILLUSTRATED BY CLAIRE POWELL

SIMON FARNABY

HODDER

First published in Great Britain in 2020 by Hodder and Stoughton
This edition published in Great Britain in 2021 by Hodder and Stoughton

5 7 9 10 8 6 4

A CIP catalogue record for this book is available from the British Library.

PB ISBN 978 1 444 95438 8
Waterstones ISBN 978 1 444 96428 8

Typeset in Archetype
Printed and bound in Great Britain by Clays Ltd, Elcograf S.p.A

The paper and board used in this book are made from wood from responsible sources.

Hodder Children's Books
An imprint of
Hachette Children's Group
Part of Hodder and Stoughton
Carmelite House
50 Victoria Embankment
London EC4Y 0DZ

An Hachette UK Company
www.hachette.co.uk

www.hachettechildrens.co.uk

For Claire and Eve.
The magic in my life.

CHAPTER ONE

FOUL SMELLS AND MAGIC SPELLS

To begin our story, I need you to cast your fertile imagination back to a time that history forgot. No, not the dinosaurs, that's too far . . . no, not the Vikings, that's not far *enough*, and besides, libraries are full of books on those hooligans. No. I want you to imagine THE DARK AGES. The year 511 to be precise, right in the middle of the Dark Ages, which makes it a contender for the darkest year in all of history.

The Dark Ages were called the Dark Ages not because it was always dark (like Iceland in winter) but because nobody REALLY knows what happened during this time. Nobody wrote anything down or took photos (obviously). The Dark Ages were a time full of menace, mystery and, crucially, magic.

Having said all that, one fact I can tell you is that on

a crisp spring night in 511, King Paul and his justice chiefs gathered at a clearing in a forest near the village of Hupton Grey – a place now known as the Oldwell Shopping Centre, near Bashingford, just off the M3 – for the trial of a notorious criminal. The forest looked a lot different back then, of course. The trees were still there for a start, large and imposing, especially when the makeshift court's lanterns cast flickering shadows upon them.

A crowd of around two hundred people had gathered to watch the spectacle about to happen. The smell would have been intolerable to modern noses, as even noblemen didn't bathe for months on end, and most of the audience were peasants, who rarely bathed once in their lifetimes. They elbowed each other and stood on their tiptoes to see the action. You must remember, there was no TV, and no laptops or iPads in those days. For the local folk, this was the equivalent of going to the cinema. Some even brought snacks. Not popcorn of course, but smoked pig snouts and pickled eggs. A trial of a famous criminal such as this was blockbuster entertainment. And what's more, it was in 3D.

"Will the defendant pray riseth!" boomed the

master of ceremonies.

Gasps rippled through the crowd as the defendant rose all right, but not using his feet! Instead he rose, cross-legged, until he was floating some two metres above the ground. His chains tightened around the huge boulder they were fastened to, making a chilling sound: CRINK! And there the famous felon bobbed, like a human-shaped balloon at a birthday party, eyes closed, a playful smile stretched across his filthy face like a schoolboy who knows he's done wrong but couldn't care less. This is the hero – or should I say the *anti*-hero – of our story. His name? Well, you probably read it on the cover of this book, but just in case you missed it, his name is . . . Merdyn the Wild.

King Paul and his chiefs shook their heads. They had hoped that the presence of Evanhart – the King's daughter – might temper Merdyn's mischievous nature. The two had been friends at the School of Alchemy (Magic School to you and me) until, in adulthood, Merdyn chose the path of darkness. Now Evanhart barely recognised the man floating before her, his robes grubby, his beard long and straggly and his hair matted and adorned with stolen

trinkets. He looked more like a pirate than a wizard.

"For the prosecution, I calleth Jeremiah Jerabo," boomed the MC.

The smile quickly fell from Merdyn's face. Jeremiah Jerabo had also been at the School of Alchemy, but

Merdyn's memories of *him* were very different from his memories of Evanhart.

Evanhart had been Merdyn's best friend and confidant. Jerabo, however, was a jealous snitch. Every time Merdyn had engaged in anything fun, such as turning the teacher's apple into a toad just as he was taking a bite, Jerabo would tell on him. And here he was, at it again, telling teacher! Except this time it was the King, and there was more at stake than a cane on his backside.

Jerabo swaggered to the centre of the court and cleared his throat like an actor preparing for his big moment. He'd waxed his blond bouffant hair into a point and shaved his yellow beard into a goatee, making his head look not unlike an ice-cream cone.

"Merdyn the Wild!" he piped with great pomposity. "Thou standeth accused of multiple crimes against the Alchemist's Code. Thou art a thief, a vandal and a mischief maker who knoweth no bounds. Very few of us are born W-blood . . ."

This is probably not a blood group you're familiar with, but in those days, it was quite common, and basically meant being born a wizard or a witch with magical abilities.

". . . and those of us who art, must use their powers for good, like myself and Evanhart. But thou, *Merdyn the Wild* . . ." Jerabo had reached fever pitch – "I putteth it to THEE that thou have become the worst W of all – a *WARLOCK*!"

And I put it to YOU that you're probably wondering why there are so many thees and thous in that sentence. Well, it was the old way of saying you, yours etc. So thou had better get used to it.

The crowd gasped when it heard the word "warlock". Some felt lightheaded, while one or two even fainted and had to receive medical attention. A warlock is basically a bad wizard, times a thousand. They use their magic for nothing but mayhem.

"That's right," Jerabo hissed. "Do thou have anything

to say for thyself, Merdyn the Warlock?"

This was where Merdyn was supposed to defend himself. This was the moment he could have told them where he had put the giant rock he'd stolen from the ancient Magic Circle (he'd carved the face of Evanhart into it and shrunk it to fit in his pocket). He could have pointed out that the gold he had stolen from the royal war chest had actually prevented the King from starting wars, and wasn't that a good thing? He could have made the case for all his actions, but in truth Merdyn didn't care what anyone thought of him any more. So instead, he slowly lowered himself, put his feet upon the ground and announced in a gruff, powerful voice:

"I AM MERDYN THE WILD!
THE GREATEST WARLOCK OF ALL TIME!
DESTROYER OF ENEMIES!
ALL WHO KNOWETH ME DO
BOW DOWN BEFORE ME!

THOU THINKETH THOU CAN CAPTURE ME?"

He let out an almighty howl of laughter.

"THOU MIGHT AS WELL TRY TO SHACKLE THE WIND!"

Never mind gasps, the crowd was now at the part of the movie where they felt genuinely frightened. If there had been a sofa available, they would have hidden behind it. But sofas wouldn't be invented until 1465, so they just closed their eyes instead. It was testament to Merdyn's powers that they felt so scared, even with him chained to a rock the size of Wales.

"Now," said Merdyn in a quieter voice, "if thou will excuseth me, I'll be off." And with that, he opened his tunic to reveal a belt with little leather pouches tied to it. In a flash he took a pinch of herbs from one of the pouches, slapped his hands together – CLAP! – and chanted:

"LYCIUM BARBARUM! GRABACIOUS! THUNDARIAN!"

Thundarian was the name of Merdyn's staff. It had been taken from him upon his arrest, and his plan was to summon it with this spell.

The plan seemed to be working. A great wind swirled around the court and, from behind the chiefs, Thundarian came floating towards Merdyn's outstretched hand. It was a wonderfully gnarled piece of oak around two metres in length, with an intricately carved eagle perched on top.

It was almost in Merdyn's outstretched hand. Had he grasped it at that moment, he would have unleashed all measure of heinous magic on his captors. He would have turned Jerabo to stone, then shattered him into a million pieces with one flick of his finger. He would have turned the King and his chiefs into stinking goats in a thrice. He would have turned on the crowd and magicked their eyes – which were now as big as saucers – into *actual* saucers.

These revenge fantasies were swirling in Merdyn's warped mind as Thundarian got to within millimetres of his straining fingers. But suddenly . . . CRIIINK! Merdyn hadn't realised that there was also a chain attached to his staff. The chain pulled tight, the staff came to a standstill and Merdyn collapsed in a heap, his energy and chance of escape gone.

In the silence that followed came a hearty laugh.

Jerabo had been watching all this with great pleasure.

"I thought thou might try that," he said, and pulled an ornate black and gold spellbook from his tunic. Each witch or wizard had their own way of casting spells and Jerabo, being a stickler for tradition, liked to use a spellbook.

"CASIAN WALLAT FLOATABOAT!"

he muttered, thrusting his hand out, causing Thundarian to drift towards him instead. Then he grabbed Merdyn's precious staff and snapped it over his knee. **CRACK.**

"Nooooooo!' yelled Merdyn.

Even Evanhart winced at this cruelty. She'd seen Merdyn lovingly whittle that staff over hundreds of hours at the School of Alchemy. Merdyn's heart might have closed off over the years, but Thundarian was the one thing he obviously still cared about.

"Curse thee, Jerabo!" Merdyn wailed. "Thou art a scurrilous coxcomb*!"

Jerabo merely chuckled and threw the broken staff

---

*In case you're wondering, *scurrilous* meant vulgar in the Dark Ages. *Coxcomb* referred to a cockerel whose 'comb' is a bright red crest on top of its head. Basically, it's a very long-winded way of calling someone a show-off.

pieces down the stone well that stood in the forest clearing. *Tonk, tonk, tink, tonk, tink, tonk, splosh*, went the broken timber. Then he turned to the King.

"I hope this final act of defiance will convinceth Thy Majesty that we must mete out the very harshest of penalties to this warlock." With great fanfare, Jerabo licked his finger and used it to turn the pages of his spellbook slowly. "The prosecutor recommendeth to the court –"

FLIP – "that he be sent to the Rivers of Purgatory –"

FLIP – "for *eternity*!"

The crowd murmured, for they were truly out of gasps by now. Finally, someone was compelled to speak for Merdyn, and that someone was . . . Evanhart.

Everything about Evanhart said 'mellow'. If she were living in the present day, she would no doubt be a yoga teacher, horse whisperer or your favourite auntie. She had long flowing red hair and silver-grey eyes like still pools of calm water.

"Father," she said to the King now. "Please have mercy upon this man. His powers are great. Perchance he could learn to use them for good?"

"'Tis too late for that, Evanhart," spoke the King. "Thy pleas are wasted here."

"Do thou not remember, Father?" Evanhart persisted. "How he did fighteth for thy army in the great war? Brave and fearless was he. Thou said so thyself."

"But Evanhart, that was a long time ago. Since then, he has shown himself a villain time and time again."

"Show him mercy then, dear Father," Evanhart pleaded. "Send him to the Rivers of Purgatory but for a short time only, five years or so . . . Maybe then he will reflecteth and changeth."

"He will never changeth!" bellowed Jerabo. "Why, only last week I was riding my horse and he did turneth it into a chicken! Imagine what a fool I looked riding around on a chicken!"

The crowd couldn't help but laugh when they thought of this. But the King wasn't laughing. He was lost in his daughter's pleading eyes, the goodness radiating from them and clouding his better judgement. Eventually he spoke.

"I have decided," said the King, "that Merdyn be

sentenced to *seven* years in the Rivers of Purgatory."

"Wha—?" Jerabo swallowed before beginning again. "Very well, Thy Majesty," he seethed through his pursed lips. "Seven years in the Rivers of Purgatory it is." With that he turned the pages of his spellbook once again – FLIP, FLIP – and read out the sentencing spell.

"FRANDALIN, BUGANTI, RIVERO. CLOCKASHOCK!"

The court shook for a few seconds before the ground in the centre of the clearing opened up like a giant mouth. A green light shot from the gaping hole and lit up the sky like the aurora borealis. The crowd oohed and aahed as if watching a firework display on Bonfire Night.

On seeing the green light, Evanhart's expression turned even graver. "Father!"

"No more, child!" snapped the King. "Sentence has been passed!"

"But the light. It should not be gr—"

"I said no more!"

The King's men walked Merdyn to the edge of the great hole. For a second, he looked back at the princess.

"Worry not, Evanhart. I shall be back sooner than they knoweth," he said, with a charm that Evanhart recognised at last. But before she could reply, Merdyn was pushed into the glowing green mouth and it snapped shut, causing a mini-earthquake to pulse through the wood.

In the silence that followed, a villager said to his wife, "I'm *definitely* coming to the next one of these."

Evanhart, however, was in no mood for pleasantries. She marched up to Jerabo and grabbed his spellbook.

"Hey! Snatchy Sue!" Jerabo protested.

"Why was there a green light above the mouth of the Rivers of Purgatory?" Evanhart asked, flipping through the book. "It should have been red!"

"How should I know?" said Jerabo. "I don't maketh the rules."

The King looked at his daughter with exasperation. "Why must everything be a *crusade* with thee, Evanhart? *Women are equal to men. Donkeys have the same rights as horses. Rivers of Purgatory should be red and not green!* Must everything be questioned?"

But at that moment – FLIP, FLIP – Evanhart

found what she was looking for. It made her usually rosy freckled cheeks lose their colour entirely.

"'*Clockashock*?' I knew it. 'Twas the wrong spell! Jerabo didn't sendeth Merdyn to the Rivers of Purgatory!"

Voices in the crowd rang out with confused exclamations: "What?" "Another twist?" "I can't take it no more!" All eyes turned to Jerabo, who squirmed like a worm on a hook.

"Oh, didn't I? I'm sure I did," he said. "Although my Latin is a little rusty . . ."

"So, where did he sendeth him?" asked the King.

"To the Rivers of *Time*," said Evanhart softly, her heartbreak obvious to all.

"But what does that mean?" asked the King.

"It means Merdyn is lost. For ever." And Evanhart cast her wide, glistening eyes up to the heavens in despair.

Oh gods, hear Evanhart
plead like a child,
begging for mercy
on Merdyn the Wild.

CHAPTER TWO

MISSING GLASSES AND NASTY LASSES

"*Please welcome to the stage, Rose Falvey!*" boomed a very different Master of Ceremonies, for the stage in question was that of Mountford High School, Bashingford (just off the M3), and we are no longer in the sixth century but the twenty-first (when YOU live).

Mountford High School was having its very own version of the TV programme called *Britain's Got Talented People*, imaginatively entitled *Mountford's Got Talented People*. There had been qualifying heats throughout the spring term, and now there were only two chances left to reach the grand final next term.

Rose Falvey didn't want to wait for the last heat, the last chance – that would be too much pressure. She was pumped for this, NOW. So pumped, in fact, that on hearing her name from the wings, she sprang on to the stage like a gazelle and overshot her spotlight mark. The spotlight then had to try and find her again, while Rose ran around in a panic trying to find the spotlight in return.

None of this was helped by the fact Rose was without her much-needed glasses. She'd decided that they didn't go with her outfit: a skin-tight leopard-skin onesie like one she'd seen Beyoncé wearing in a YouTube video. In hindsight, this was a bad decision, as now she couldn't see a darn thing. She dashed around the stage, glimpsing nothing but a blur of faces and the occasional blinding light. By now, the crowd were giggling loudly.

It wasn't a good start.

By the time Rose finally found her light, she was breathing heavily. She still felt positive, however, of giving a fantastic rendition of Beyoncé's "Crazy in Love".

Rose had inherited her dad's endless positivity. He had always told her that as long as you tried your best, it was impossible to fail. She had practised for this moment in front of a mirror every night for three weeks. If what her dad said was true, which it usually was, this was bound to go well.

The music started.

"O-oh O-oh O O O O wah O-oh-O-oh -oh -oh -oh -oh!"

From the moment she began to sing, Rose felt something was wrong. When she sang at home it was within the muffled confines of her bedroom, her only audience her yellow guinea pig, Bubbles. After merely an hour of rehearsing, her older brother Kris had insisted she closed the door and wore headphones so he didn't have to listen to the song over and over again and go crazy himself. Now, onstage, singing out loud for the first time, she felt strangely exposed, like one of those dreams where you end up at school with no clothes on.

"Oh yeah you got me so crazy in love, yes I'm crazy in love! O-oh o-oh etc."

Rose started her dance moves. She figured that if her singing voice didn't wow the crowd, she could always rely on her superb dancing.

In her room she had quickly realised that she couldn't dance like Beyoncé. Who could? Therefore, Rose had invented her own routine. Her signature move, the one she was most proud of, was 'the high kick'. It was as it sounds: a super-high kick that almost went higher than her block of frizzy red hair that sat atop her head in bunches.

She let loose some high kicks now, followed by some 'spins'. Rose was proud of these too. They were really just an extension of the high kick. When the elevated leg came down, she would swing it across and behind her standing leg, using the centrifugal force to send her upper body into a spin.

Getting into the spin was easy. Getting out was always problematic, however, even in her bedroom. And as Rose now couldn't see very well, she kept finding herself exiting the spins facing the BACK of the stage, then having to track down the audience again in time for the next bit.

It gives me no pleasure to tell you, reader, that eventually, the combination of out-of-tune singing, manic high kicking and wonky spins took their toll on the audience. Soon, loud gales of laughter began to spread through the auditorium. "HEE HEE! HA HA, HA HA HA HA HAAAAA!" When the song finally ended, even the three judges (three fully grown adult teachers, mind!)

couldn't keep straight faces.

"If that had been a comedy act, you'd have got top marks, Rose," said Mr Culkin (head judge and maths teacher) eventually. The other judges were too busy laughing even to speak.

Rose made her way from the stage and into the schoolyard, feeling completely embarrassed. You could have fried an egg on her cheeks, they were so hot and red. She tried to pull herself together. What did Mr Culkin know about music anyway? He thought Stormzy was a type of weather front. She'd endured embarrassment before. She would get through this blip.

The last thing she needed to see, however, were the CATs walking towards her.

Catrina, Andrea and Tamsin were three of the most odious twelve-year-olds you'd ever wish to meet. They were collectively known as the CATs, because of their names and because they had claws. Nasty ones. Metaphorically speaking, anyway. And now they had made their way out of the auditorium specifically to get those claws into poor Rose.

"Hey, frizzpot," said Catrina, who wore too much make-up. "Nice moves!" She then did her own little high kick by way of parody. Rose couldn't help noticing that it wasn't even knee height, never mind hair height.

"Your audition from hell just went viral," Tamsin sneered. Tamsin had brains, but didn't like to use them.

She shoved her brand new smartphone in Rose's face and pressed 'play' on a video.

Rose saw the grainy footage of herself high kicking and singing in a voice which seemed even worse than she remembered. The video had been liked over seven hundred times already.

Andrea (Andie for short) joined in. She was the muscle behind the CATs, looking more like a wrestler than a schoolgirl and towering head and shoulders above even the boys. "You need singing lessons, you frizzy-haired freckle-mouse."

"Sticks and stones may break my bones, but names will never hurt me," reasoned Rose. This was another lesson her dad had taught her. He'd told her to say this to bullies to stop them in their tracks, or at least confuse them long enough to make her escape.

"Have it your way," replied Andie, before casually picking up a stick and hurling it at Rose. The stick struck Rose square on the forehead. THUD!

"OW!" yelped Rose.

But even in her agony, she had to give Andie some respect. Of all the times she'd used her dad's 'sticks and stones' line, Rose had never once realised she was actually giving her enemies a useful piece of advice.

Mind you, why am I surprised? she thought, a hot soup of anger and sadness bubbling inside her. Hadn't her dad also told her that as long as you tried your best, it was impossible to fail? He'd been wrong about that too.

Suddenly every piece of advice her beloved dad had ever given her seemed to be crumbling into dust beneath her feet.

And then Rose ran,
speeding through the gears,
she fled the cackling CATs
so they could not see her tears.

CHAPTER THREE

TWO INQUISITORS AND STRANGE VISITORS

Rose was still running when she passed the Oldwell Shopping Centre.

Now, if you will permit me, I must just add an aside here. You see, the Oldwell Shopping Centre has a very interesting history relating to our story. Were you to step through its vast electronic sliding doors on to its gleaming marble-effect floor and carry on past the neon signs of Guccio and SportsDirectly, just before Accessorize This, you would find yourself looking at a fake ornamental garden. This fake ornamental garden has fake flowers, plastic trees and synthetic grass. The only thing that's real about the fake ornamental garden is a very real . . . OLD WELL.

And if you are thinking, *Aha! I bet it's the old well from Chapter One, the one that mean old Jeremiah Jerabo threw Merdyn the Wild's broken staff, Thundarian, down approximately one thousand five hundred years ago*, then you'd be . . . WRONG. It was a different old well and—

I'm JOKING. Of course you're right. You're obviously very clever and deserve a gold star or a trophy. It was the *exact* same well, but now surrounded not by a forest of trees, but by a forest of gleaming shops. The company which had built the sprawling shopping centre several years earlier had only got permission from the council on the condition that they preserved the historic well. And so, they had turned it into a feature.

Today, like every day, two security guards, Jim and Alan, stood guard over the ornamental garden. In the olden days the well had been used as a wishing well, and people were invited to throw in coins in exchange for their dreams coming true. However, in more recent times, people had realised that you could also take coins *out* of the well, presumably to make their dreams of having 50p or £1 come true. So the shopping centre management had decided to put a fence around the well and guard it. This is where Jim and Alan came in.

Guarding the ornamental garden was one of the least demanding jobs in the world, so it was surprising that neither Jim nor Alan noticed when a huge hole opened up in the fake grass behind them and an ethereal green light shot out. A few of the shoppers noticed, but no sooner had the hole opened up than it closed again, so they quickly dismissed it as a publicity stunt and carried on shopping.

But as the light disappeared, it left behind it on the fake grass the crumpled figure of . . . sixth-century warlock Merdyn the Wild.

Merdyn opened his eyes. His pupils grew huge as they adjusted to the strip lighting and neon signs of the shops. Remember, in the Dark Ages the only light sources were the sun, fire and the odd candle. Now he had flashing lights, mirror balls and all sorts of other luminescence assaulting his peepers.

"Heaven forfend!" he exclaimed. "Hell is worse than I thought!"

This statement brought him to the attention of Jim and Alan, who could scarcely believe their eyes when they turned around. Of all the vagabonds and thieves they'd had to turf out of the garden (a whole six in eleven years!), this was the most impudent yet.

"Oi!" said Jim. "What you doin' in there?"

"Trying to fetch yourself some coins from the well, are you?" said Alan, pleased with his powers of deduction.

"Who do you think you are?" added Jim.

This was the sort of question that didn't require an answer, but Merdyn sought to give him one anyway.

"I AM MERDYN THE WILD!"

he boomed.

"THE GREATEST WARLOCK WHO EVER LIVED! DESTROYER OF ENEMIES! BOW DOWN BEFORE ME, DEMONS, OR FEEL MY WRATH!"

There was a pause as Jim and Alan looked at each other.

"You what?" said Alan, finally.

The two guards stepped over the little garden fence and moved menacingly towards the sixth-century warlock.

Merdyn reached instinctively for Thundarian in order to blow them away with a fireball. But he just ended up grasping at thin air, for of course he was without his loyal staff. He would have to use the herbs around his belt to perform magic. Herb spells were primary-school alchemy compared to more advanced staff spells, and much less spectacular, but he had no choice.

"Feel my wrath?" said Jim. "You'll feel my bloomin' handcuffs in a minute, mate." With that, he pulled out his handcuffs and went to make a citizen's arrest on Merdyn, grabbing hold of his wrists.

"Unhand me, thou fopdoodle*!" Merdyn cursed and, having no time to mix a herb spell, resorted to poking Jim in the eye with his finger, an undignified move for a warlock, but an effective one nonetheless. SQUELCH!

"Waaahaa! He's blinded me!" Jim cried.

Now it was Alan's turn to try. He got a fist in his ear for his troubles. CRUMP!

"Ow! He's broken my earlobe!" Alan wailed as he

---

*Meaning a limp dawdler. Not the most devastating insult but a great word in my opinion. As a further note of interest, there are many people who think that *fopdoodle* slowly morphed over time into the Americanism dude, meaning an extremely carefree person.

rolled around on the floor.

BOOT! Merdyn kicked him hard in the backside.

"Right! That's it!" roared Alan. "NOW you're in trouble!"

As one, Jim and Alan grabbed Merdyn's legs and pulled him to the ground.

The ungainly scuffle in the garden was now gathering the attention of shoppers, who stopped and stared at the strange sight. As the men tumbled around on the fake grass, Jim's security-guard hat fell off and Alan's wig was dislodged, revealing his shiny bald head. This just added to the anger they felt towards this intruder, and they tried even harder to cuff him.

Then, just as it looked as though Jim and Alan were besting him, Merdyn pulled a fake tree out of the ground and expertly cracked Jim's knees with a branch and knocked Alan out cold with a root. BISH BOSH. The great warlock didn't like to be reminded of his time as a soldier in the King's army, but here was an occasion where his training came in useful.

His antics had by now attracted the attention of a

local police officer, Sergeant Murray. Sergeant Murray came from a long line of police officers. He took the job so seriously that he'd grown a moustache, simply so he could look like a stereotypical policeman. When he spotted the strange man in a pointy hat fighting with the shopping centre security guards, Sergeant Murray felt his moustache bristle. It was like a radar for trouble, that moustache, and here was trouble with a capital 'T'. He immediately called for back-up through his police radio.

Merdyn heard the crackle of the radio as the sergeant's back-up answered: "ROGER ROGER. WE'RE ON YOUR TAIL!" But having never heard a police radio before, Merdyn assumed instead that this was the call of the Giant Ravens rumoured to patrol the burning skies of Hell looking for prey. He definitely didn't want to be giant bird food, so he set off running as fast as he could. Thinking he had spotted an exit, he bolted for it . . . and ran smack bang into the glass window of Accessorize This.

DOINK.

Remember, there wasn't any clear glass in the

Dark Ages either, so to Merdyn, he'd just run into a wall of hard air.

"What sorcery be this?" he wondered aloud. But he had no time to sit and think. He pulled himself up off the ground, rubbed his sore nose and took up his search for the exit again. This time, he ran straight into a Donuts-R-Us stand. Dozens of sticky circles shot up into the air and scattered across the floor.

The doughnut-stand worker assumed Merdyn was trying to steal his doughnuts. He picked up a broom and bonked Merdyn on the head with it.

BONK! BONK!

"AARGH! What demon art thou?" screamed Merdyn as the blows rained down upon him.

Somewhere, a whistle blew. Merdyn looked up to see a whole gang of black-and-white Giant Raven-people (or police!) headed his way. He picked up the closest weapon to him, a doughnut, and pelted it. POOF! The doughnut hit Sergeant Murray straight in the moustache, stopping him in his tracks and allowing Merdyn to escape

once more, shocked shoppers scattering as he ran.

Finally, the befuddled warlock found the vast electric sliding doors of the exit, but to him, they were like the giant snapping jaws of a dragon. Bravely, Merdyn ran at the crunching mouth. But each time he misjudged his charge, so that he smacked into the doors –

WHACK! CRUNCH! CRACK!

On his final attempt, he nearly made it, only to be caught in the jaws of the door like a sausage in a pair of pincers. Eventually he managed to throw himself clear, and finally he was OUTSIDE.

But his horrors weren't ending there. They were just beginning.

For he had run straight into a busy main road.

Imagine seeing a car, bus or lorry for the first time EVER. Imagine the fastest, loudest transport you'd ever experienced up to that moment was a horse. Then imagine a wall of vehicles coming towards you, screeching their brakes and beeping their horns all at once.

BEEEEEEEEEP BEEEEEEEEEEP!!!

SCREEEEEECH!

HOOOOONK!!! HONK

Merdyn stood, frozen in fear. Then he heard an ear-piercing noise from the *sky*.

SHHHWEEEEEEYAAAAAAAGH!

He looked up. His eyes could not believe what they were seeing.

"Gadsbudlikins*! 'Tis a metal eagle!"

It was, of course, an aeroplane. But Merdyn had seen nothing flying through the air but birds and butterflies his whole life. And now a Boeing 747 was shrieking past like a giant silver bird.

At this moment, Sergeant Murray popped out of the shopping-centre doors like a champagne cork, a spray of officers behind him. Merdyn looked desperately around and spotted a wood in the distance. Real trees! *Something* he recognised! He hitched up his cloak and ran straight for them, before diving into the undergrowth and disappearing from sight.

To all he passed,
I must confess,
he was just a bloke
in fancy dress.

---

* *Gadsbudlikins* literally means *God's little body*. The closest translation for today would be oh my god or, if you really must, OMG. But isn't *Gadsbudlikins* so much better?

CHAPTER FOUR

MUM TROUBLES AND A PIG CALLED BUBBLES

Rose trudged glumly past the little red-brick houses on her street, Daffodil Close. The audition was a new low, even for her.

She'd thought she couldn't get any lower. Four years earlier, she'd been part of a happy family with a happy school life. But then her dad had died suddenly. Her mum became permanently sad and they ran out of money. They'd moved to a smaller house, and Rose had had to move to a different school where she didn't know a single soul. Everything had changed for the worse.

Starting her new school had also coincided with Rose needing glasses, her red hair turning frizzy and her freckles breaking out like a meteor shower all over her cheeks. The only thing that kept Rose going was her father's belief that one day she was destined for greatness. He'd always told her she was going to find something she loved and be the BEST at it. He wasn't sure what that something was, but he'd had complete and utter faith that she would find it.

I'm just glad he wasn't there today, Rose thought. *He would have been so ashamed.*

Finally, she got to her house. Dion, her next-door neighbour, was in his driveway polishing his special Pontiac Firebird car.

Dion was a postman, but his real love was the movies. He finished work at 8.30 a.m. and spent most of the rest of his day watching films. His car was his pride and joy because it was THE ACTUAL CAR used in his favourite EVER movie, *Smokey and the Bandit*. The car had come up for sale ten years earlier, and Dion had paid $23,000 for it (plus shipping). It was now worth nearly $100,000, as it was considered a piece of classic movie memorabilia. Dion hoped that if he looked after it well enough, it might be worth a million dollars by the time he retired from the post office. Then he'd sell it and spend the rest of his life watching movies in his own private cinema.

Now, Dion was not a man of many words. He

preferred the company of movie characters to real human beings. But on this occasion, as he saw Rose marching towards him like some traumatised soldier at the end of a war film, he was compelled to speak.

"Cheer up, sweetheart. It might never happen," he offered.

"It already has," countered Rose, as she swept past him. "It's called life."

Walking down her little garden path was like wading through a jungle, so overgrown was the front lawn. Inside the house, things were as they always were. The red carpet was a faded pink and covered in crumbs, and the walls and shelves were curiously empty. After Rose's dad died her mum, Suzy, had decided she didn't want any reminders of the past, and so had hidden away all the smiling photographs of the whole family.

Suzy was sitting in the lounge watching television, working her way through a box of Congratulations assorted chocolates as usual.

If you had to describe Suzy's face you would say it was ninety per cent lips. She had an enormous mouth with

large white teeth like piano keys. She had a slender nose, large hazel eyes and scraggly brown hair that she used to keep in a trendy 'bird's nest' style, but now resembled an *actual* bird's nest, complete with the odd chocolate wrapper.

Rose's brother Kris was looking in the mirror and plucking his eyebrows.

"Oh, here she is!" Kris announced as Rose walked in the door.

Kris had major vanity issues. He couldn't pass a mirror without checking that his eyebrows were correctly plucked or his hair perfectly styled. It wasn't that Kris wasn't good looking, he was, the problem was that he thought the only thing going for him was his symmetrical face, so he needed to make the most of it at all times.

More than anything, it was the fact that Kris insisted on spelling his name with a K that told anyone all they needed to know about him. Appearances were everything.

"Have you seen this?" Kris said. He shoved his phone in Rose's face just long enough for her to see that her audition video had now reached three thousand views.

"I don't need to see it, do I? It WAS me. I was there!" Rose snapped back.

"What are you going to do about it? It's embarrassing!" rasped Kris krossly – sorry, crossly.

Rose frowned. "It's embarrassing for me, not for you."

"But what if people find out that you're my sister?" her brother whined.

Kris had a long list of ways that his sister embarrassed

him. She didn't seem to care what she looked like, she tried to be good at things that she wasn't, her best friend was a guinea pig – those sorts of things. Rose was a little confused by his embarrassment. She could sort of understand it while they were briefly at the same school, but he had left now and worked in the men's fashion store Top Boy in the Oldwell Shopping Centre. So what was he worried about?

"Why don't I just change my name then?" Rose offered, sarcastically. "Or maybe I could move somewhere else. Disappear altogether. Would that suit you?"

"You'd do that for me?" Kris said, hopefully. He wasn't good at picking up on subtle things, like sarcasm. He was even worse at irony. He thought that irony was something you did when you wanted to get the creases out of your trousers.

Rose huffed loudly and went to sit next to her mum on the couch. Perhaps she was looking for some words of comfort, but they were not forthcoming. Instead, mother and daughter sat together in silence.

Suzy was watching a re-run of last Saturday's *Britain's got Talented People*. She was currently viewing the favourite to win, a hot new magician who had come from nowhere to blow away the judges, but she liked the behind-the-scenes sob stories the best. She liked them because she felt like she was a sob story herself.

Suzy had been a singer in a band called The Mondays. They'd had a few hit records in the nineties, but their star had faded. She then had a decent career as a solo singer, but after Rose's dad died, it wasn't the same. Rose's dad, Barry, had loved to hear her sing. He'd never missed a performance. Seeing an empty chair where he should have been every night was too much for Suzy. So she'd stopped singing altogether.

"You get used to disappointment, darling," Suzy said suddenly now. "You want my advice? Give up."

"Give up singing?" said Rose, stung. She had decided that being a singer was her call to greatness. She'd seen her mum on stage when she was little and thought how cool it would be, to be up there, rocking out for all she was worth. And if her mum saw how good Rose was, then she might not be so sad any more. Maybe it would get her off the couch and singing again too?

"I mean, look what happened to me," Suzy grumped, chewing a coconut Congratulation. She was still wearing her pyjamas, which helped her case. "And *I* had talent."

Rose bit her lip. She knew her mum was sad and angry. But to say Rose had no talent? To say that to her *face*?

"That's just plain rude!" cried Rose.

Suzy just thrust her hand into another box of chocolates. Then she appeared to remember something. Something very important. "Ooh!"

Rose wondered if her mum was about to apologise for saying she had no talent . . .

"It's half price fish and chips tonight." Suzy stuffed a ten-pound note into Rose's hand. "Here, go to the chippy after you've done your homework."

Rose stomped upstairs to her bedroom, buried her head in her pillow and sobbed for Britain. If she'd been on a talent contest for the best at crying, she would have won hands down. She would have been Eurovision champion, Olympic champion, World Cup winner, the lot, if only those prizes were awarded for crying instead of singing, athletics or football. But they weren't. So instead she was just the winner of the Little Girl Sobbing in Her Room on Her Own contest, for which there were no prizes but a wet pillow.

Just as her tear ducts had been pumped dry, Rose heard a familiar, comforting *squeak squeak* from the floor. It was Bubbles, her ever faithful guinea pig. She immediately popped his cage open, pulled him out and gave him an almighty cuddle.

Bubbles was always there for Rose. He never criticised her, said hurtful things about her, or posted embarrassing clips of her on YouTube. Not yet anyway. Rose loved Bubbles right down to his fuzzy yellow fur and big black eyes, and Bubbles loved Rose right back. He showed her as much by pushing a small, oblong poo from his bottom into her lap. Rose was used to this. Guinea pigs pooed approximately every twelve seconds, and there was nothing you could do about it, except be glad they were dry and easy to dispose of.

Rose watched the poo bounce off her knee and on to a map of the world

that she had opened up on the floor the night before. She'd been trying to puzzle out where she was going to live when the world finally realised what a brilliant singer she was. London? New York? Tokyo? But now Bubbles's poo had fallen on Paris, could it be a sign?

Bubbles started nibbling at the case of Rose's smartphone that was sitting on her bedside table. Surely this was another sign. But a sign of what?

Rose switched the phone on. She didn't hear the familiar sound of pinging texts because she didn't use her phone to text her friends. She didn't really *have* any friends except Bubbles, and it was no use texting him as he didn't read or write. Or have thumbs. But Rose had bought the phone with money she'd saved up after her dad had died.

Suddenly Rose realised WHY the phone was a sign. Her dad!

Her dad used to tell a story about being in a situation exactly like hers. Except without the talent show, and YouTube video, and guinea-pig poo. But other than that, really similar. When her dad was a kid, he'd told his family that he wanted to be an inventor. They'd all laughed at him and told him to forget such lofty ideas. The Falveys had been sheep farmers for generations, and that was his destiny too.

"Get back to shearing sheep!" they told him.

But Rose's dad never gave up on his dream. When he was sixteen years old, he ran away from the farm and didn't come back until he was a doctor of engineering. And from the moment he returned with an invention to shear sheep without giving farmers bad backs and sore knees (he called it the EasyPeasyShear – perhaps you've heard of it?), his family were so proud of him, and so ashamed of themselves for doubting him.

YES! thought Rose, a plan crystallising in her head. This was what was going to happen to her! She was going to run away and prove herself, become a famous singer, come back and hand out big bags of cash – and then her mother and brother would be happy and proud at last.

Plus, she had ten whole pounds in her possession. Surely that would get her to Paris? She could walk to London and get some kind of cut-price bus the rest of the way there.

"Bubbles, you're a genius!" said Rose.

She put the guinea pig on her bed and got to work packing. Bubbles responded by laying another oblong poo on Rose's duvet as if to say, "I wouldn't be too sure, Rose, would a genius do that?"

But alas
Bubbles could not
do a jot
to stop her!

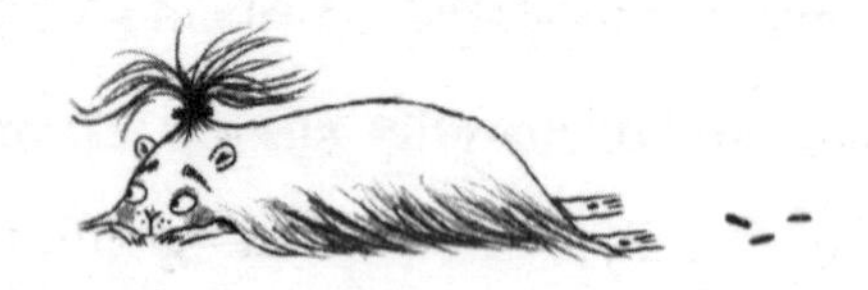

CHAPTER FIVE

ONE LOST CHILD AND MERDYN THE WILD

Packed and ready to go, Rose skipped down the stairs past her mother and brother and to the front door.

"Don't forget extra scraps!" shouted Suzy.

"Get me some for when I get back from work!" Kris said as he checked that his quiff was still straight. "And I want the low-fat batter!" he added. He knew full well the chip shop had no such thing, but asking made him feel better about himself.

Rose took one last look at her mum sprawled on the couch and Kris staring at himself in the mirror. *Don't worry*, she thought. *I'll save you.*

She imagined for a second that it was a normal household once more. One where Kris wasn't looking in a mirror twenty-four/seven and her mum could bear to hang up old pictures of the family without bursting into tears.

Then she straightened her shoulders, stepped outside and closed the door behind her.

If her mum and brother had paid Rose any attention instead of being wrapped up in themselves, they'd have seen her bulging backpack and Bubbles being pulled along behind her on an extra-long dog lead – though this was less unusual than it sounds. Rose would often take Bubbles for long walks. They were good for his immune system.

Rose stood on the front doorstep and took a deep breath. She felt like Dick Whittington, except with a guinea pig instead of a cat. Now, which way? She knew that London was *east* of Bashingford and used the compass on her smartphone to orientate herself.

Paris, here we come! she thought.

Now Bashingford is a funny old place. It has the most roundabouts of any town in the world. Plus the whole place is carved out of woodland, so that as soon as you veer off a path, road or roundabout, you are suddenly thrust into woods. And sure enough, it wasn't long before Rose came to the end of a pavement, and the trees began.

She looked down at her guinea pig.

"We'll just keep going east, Bubbles," she said with determination.

By way of reply Bubbles laid another tiny poo. He'd been doing this since they left the house; partly because he was frightened to death, and partly in the hope that should they get lost, Rose could follow the poo-trail back to the house, like Hansel and Gretel.

Bubbles knew about Hansel and Gretel because he'd spent many a night sitting on Rose's shoulder reading her books with her. Rose liked fairy stories, but Bubbles usually found them too far-fetched, and seriously lacking in guinea-pig characters.

As they walked on, the wood became more and more dense and the path became more and more *not* a path. The sun was going down and the sky had turned grey. The birds, who had been happily tweeting away, were falling silent. The ground was growing damp and Bubbles was getting wet feet, which were his least favourite kind of feet. It reminded him of when Rose hadn't changed his sawdust for a while, and it had ended up soggy with his own wee. He was very much regretting Rose's decision to run away.

As Rose walked into her fifth invisible spider's web, she began to regret running away too. Maybe her mum was right. Maybe being a singer was a silly dream. Maybe her dad was wrong. Maybe she wasn't destined for greatness. Maybe she was just going to be normal like everyone else. And what would be so wrong with that?

Well, she answered herself, *then everyone will stay unhappy. So keep moving!*

The sun was completely gone by now and the wood shrouded in shadows. Rose was getting cold and, to make matters worse, she kept remembering things she'd forgotten, like Bubbles's vitamin C powder. Rose prided herself on always making sure Bubbles was well looked after. He'd never once been to the vet. And now here she was, on the road without his medication. How could she have been so irresponsible? There was no other conclusion; running away had been a *terrible* idea.

Rose was just about to turn back when she heard a noise behind her.

CRACK.

Her heart stopped beating in her chest, then started

beating again moments later in her ears. She had seen enough scary films to know the sound of a twig cracking under someone's foot.

CRICK.

Another sound. Rose bent down to scoop Bubbles into her arms. As she did so, she saw, out of the corner of her eye, a dirty piece of cloth darting behind a bush. Who or what was following her? Was she being hunted by a child-eating dishrag?

Rose turned away from the cloth creature and tried to tiptoe quietly in the other direction. She was chilled to the bone to hear the noise now close behind her.

CRISH, CROSH, CRISH.

Rose figured she had two choices.

1. Run as fast as she could.

2. Turn and face the creature in the hope of scaring it away.

She looked at Bubbles for advice, but he just stared back at her with his wide, vacant eyes and did a poo. Finding Bubbles no help whatsoever, Rose went for option 2.

Quicker than a flash she turned and . . .

WHUMP!

She bumped straight into the cloth creature.

A hand shot out and grabbed her wrist. It was a grubby hand with dirty fingernails. It was like something from *Dawn of the Dead* or *Night of the Dead* or one of the many other such films with 'dead' in the title that Kris liked to show her to give her nightmares.

Rose screamed. "Aaaaaaaaaaaaargh!"

Given the circumstances, Bubbles would ordinarily have pooed himself again, but it had been a scary day and he had no poos left to poo.

"Child!" shouted the cloth creature, in a low, gruff, man's voice. "I meaneth thou no harm!" He released Rose's wrist and held both hands up in the universal 'I meaneth thou no harm' gesture.

Rose backed away. "Who . . . who are you?" she said. "What do you want?"

At this point, Rose noticed the man's shoes. They were very peculiar moccasin-type things with layers and layers of strapping that went all the way to his knees. His trousers were . . . cowhide? Or leather? And he wore a cloak of multicoloured rags.

He raised his arms slowly and stepped into a ray of moonlight that was now poking through the trees. He had a long scraggly beard and matted dark hair with silver bits in it. His hat was pointy on top, and floppy at the sides. And . . . black? Purple? It was hard to tell. It looked like it had NEVER been washed.

The same could be said for his face. Rose could make out high cheekbones and a long thin nose. His features had a quiet dignity. And then there were his piercing blue eyes. You could hardly look at them, they were so dazzlingly blue, like police lights. They were made even more striking by the dirt caked around them, so it looked to Rose like he was wearing dark make-up or eyeliner.

"My name is Merdyn," said the strange man. "This land be Purgatory?"

"What does 'purgatory' mean?" asked Rose.

"'Tis another word for Hell."

Rose blurted out a nervous laugh. "Yeah, you're in the right place. But we call it Bashingford."

Merdyn tilted his head in a perplexed fashion, much like a dog does when trying to understand a basic command. "Ba-shing-ford," he said slowly, stressing each sound like it was a foreign word.

Rose thought him a very peculiar man indeed, but reckoned he meant her no harm. He looked lost. Confused. Perhaps he was homeless or something.

"Where are you from?" she asked.

"I did cometh through the Rivers," he said, a hint of sadness in his voice. "Sent here against my will. But then, who goeth willingly to Hell?"

"Well, yes. Most people come here against their will," mused Rose. "Relocating from London mainly. A lot of businesses find it cheaper to . . ."

Merdyn's eyes started to glaze over as she talked. He was looking at something. What was it? Rose stopped talking and tried to follow his blue-eyed gaze.

He was staring at Bubbles.

Merdyn licked his lips. "Thou have bellytimber!" he said.

"Belly . . . what?" said Rose.

"Bellytimber," Merdyn repeated impatiently. "Food. I am very hungry." He snatched the guinea pig out of her arms. "Build a fire while I killeth it, we can have it with parsley and sage."

He was about to dash Bubbles's head against a tree when Rose grabbed the traumatised animal back and pulled him to her chest.

"This is my pet!" she shrieked. "His name's Bubbles. You can't *eat* him!"

"All right then, what be this?" Merdyn reached over her shoulder and snatched a plastic bag sticking out of Rose's backpack. It was Bubbles's food pellets. He opened it and started shoving the contents in his mouth. "Hm. 'Tis a little dry but . . ."

"That belongs to Bubbles!" Rose said, seizing it back.

"Fine," said Merdyn, irritated. "Then take me to thy lodgings. We will feasteth there. I shall taketh refuge with thee while I endeavoureth to escape this dread place and get back home."

"Erm, excuse me. You're not staying at my house," said Rose, alarmed. "I don't even know you!"

"Worry not, little one, I have monies. Much monies." He dived into a pouch around his belt and flung some dirty old lumps at Rose. They looked like . . . pebbles?

"Right," said Rose. "For a start, that isn't money. And for a finish . . ." She wasn't sure where to finish. "Look, I wish I could help you, but I've got problems of my own, OK? So. Goodbye."

She lowered Bubbles to the ground and set off in what she hoped was the direction of home. But Merdyn blocked her path.

"Youngling, please. I have other things to trade with," he said. "I could help thee with thy 'problems'."

"How can *you* possibly help *me*?" asked Rose. "You look like you can barely help yourself."

Merdyn pulled a highly offended face. "How DARE thee? I am Merdyn the Wild, destroyer of enemies. The greatest warlock who ever liveth!

ALL THOSE WHO KNOWETH ME, KNEEL BEFORE ME!"

he finished with gusto.

"What's a warlock?" asked Rose.

"A warlock, I ought not to have to tell thee, is capable of great and powerful magic."

"Oh," said Rose. "Like a wizard?"

"Pah!" spat Merdyn. "Wizards be woolly-hearted fools. A warlock serveth only the powers of darkness."

"Like a bad witch?" offered Rose sensibly.

"Nay!" cursed Merdyn, even more annoyed at this suggestion than the wizard one. "Bad witches be ugly, smelly, uncouth hags!"

"You don't smell so great yourself," said Rose, wafting her hand under her nose to illustrate. "And why do you speak in that weird way?"

"What meaneth thou?"

"That for example. What's with the thous and thys? Are you an actor?"

"An actor?" Merdyn was stunned at the insolence of this child. (Actors were considered the lowest of the low in the Dark Ages, quite rightly in my opinion. But I digress . . .) Did the child not know the dangers that could befall a person who insulted a warlock? Then Merdyn realised something terrible.

"Thou believeth me not," he said quietly. In his land, EVERYBODY knew Merdyn the Wild. Everybody feared him. But now, here, he was . . . a nobody.

Rose shrugged. "Of course I don't believe you." Then she had an idea. "Tell you what. If you're some kind of magician or whatever, then show me something."

Merdyn looked downcast. Without his lovingly crafted magical staff, Thundarian, he could not perform his most spectacular spells.

"Thought so," said Rose, reading his body language. "Come on, Bubbles." She tugged on Bubbles's lead and they set off.

"Wait!" cried Merdyn, suddenly remembering that he didn't need his staff for basic magic. All he had to do was recall his first year at the School of Alchemy. "There is something I can show thee. A morsel. A crumb. A shrew*."

And with that, he grabbed what looked to Rose like some leaves or herbs from pockets around his belt. Then he began scurrying around the wood collecting bits of shrub, mushrooms and spiders' webs and crushing them in his

---

*Not literally, reader, he just means a small thing.

hand. To Rose, he looked like a complete lunatic, crawling around on his hands and knees, getting excited about grass and rubbish.

Finally, he stood upright, held a pinecone in the air and whispered a bizarre incantation.

"PRIMULA VERIS, SPEAKINSIDEOUTSIDE VIBERNUM OPULUS!"

Bubbles looked at Rose as if to say, "Who is this nut job?"

"SAMBUCA NIGRA FRUCTUS!"

Merdyn continued much louder. Then with great fanfare he threw the crushed mixture over the pinecone and held it proudly aloft.

"Well, thanks for that," said Rose, thinking that was the end of the trick. "Very, er, impressive."

But Merdyn wasn't finished. He snatched Bubbles from her once again.

Rose lashed out with her fists. "What are you going to do? Try and eat him again?"

But Merdyn simply held her back by her forehead

while she flailed wildly. "Cease thy protestations, girl. And listen . . ."

Merdyn pressed the pinecone gently against the guinea pig's head.

A strange sound began to emerge. At first, it sounded like someone talking on a distant radio. Then it became louder. Intrigued, Rose leaned into the pinecone. And when she did, she could hardly believe her ears.

"What's happening?" said a tiny voice. "Hang on. Why is my voice sounding outside my head? Ooh, I'm freaking out. I knew this was a mistake! I wanna be home in my cage! I wanna be home in my cage!"

Rose's mouth fell open like a goldfish. "Whose voice is that?" she asked.

"Why, thy rat's. 'Tis his inner voice," said Merdyn.

"'Rat'? Who are you calling a rat?" complained Bubbles's inner voice. "Oh, I'm so confused. I feel a poo coming on. I'm-gonna-poo-I'm-gonna-poo-I'm-gonna poo-I'm-gonna . . ." Then, of course, Bubbles did a poo.

Rose was astonished! It was Bubbles's voice all right. This was *exactly* what she imagined he'd sound like. She looked at the strange, smelly, scruffy man with the bright blue eyes standing in front of her. "OK. So . . . you're a wizard," she said slowly.

"Warlock!" snapped Merdyn. "Now, listen to me. I must get back to my world. Thou art from this hellish place, thou can help me navigate it. What I have just shown thee is but the pips of an apple. If thou helpeth me, I have the power to give thee thy heart's desire. Believe me, I can do it. I am no hufty tufty*."

"Hm. Could you make me a great singer?" Rose asked, excited suddenly.

"Of course," replied Merdyn. "If that really is what thou wanteth."

"Being a singer *is* what I wanteth! I mean, want."

"So be it. If thou helpeth me, I shall make thee a singing spell. Thou shall sing like an angel. No one will ever have heard the like!"

"Then we have a deal," said Rose. She grasped Merdyn's outstretched, dirty hand – albeit reluctantly –

---

*A person who likes to talk up his or her abilities: a show-off. Next time you feel like someone is bragging, try calling them a *hufty tufty* and see what happens. Although don't be surprised if he or she calls YOU a *hufty tufty* back, for being so clever as to have read this book!

and shook.

"Just to be clear," Bubbles jabbered as they set off home, "nobody's going to eat me?"

"No, rat," Merdyn replied. "Not yet anyway."

And at that, Rose suddenly remembered why her mum had sent her out in the first place.

"Oh blimey!" spoke poor Rose's lips:
"I forgot the fish and chips!"

CHAPTER SIX

HORSELESS CARRIAGE IN MY GARAGE!

It was slow going on the main road, because every time a car went past, Merdyn jumped into the hedgerow or behind a bin.

"What be these foul beasts?" he wailed as he picked himself up from the floor for the tenth time.

"Beasts?"

"Aye." Another car roared past, making Merdyn leap behind a lamp post. "There be another. They have wheels instead of legs and emitteth a rancid stench from their back pipes."

Rose looked at him. Now what was he on about? "Don't you have cars where you come from?" she asked.

"Caaars?" said Merdyn, stressing the word weirdly again.

"Yes. People use them to travel around."

"Ah. 'Tis a carriage!" Merdyn deduced. "But has no horses?"

"Horses?" Rose laughed. "Well, no. It has an engine though, you know . . . you start it. With a key?"

"Huh," said Merdyn quietly to himself. "Purgatory gets stranger and stranger . . ."

A moment later, Rose's smartphone went off in her bag, playing Beyoncé's "Crazy in Love" as usual.

"Ye gods!" cried Merdyn, slamming his hands over his ears. "What be that caterwauling?"

Rose stopped walking and pulled out her phone. Her mum's face appeared on the screen.

"Where's the fish and chips, love?" Suzy complained immediately.

Merdyn could not believe his eyes. He stared at the tiny woman, trapped in the little black square before him. "What black magic be this?" he whispered in horror.

"Yeah. Sorry, Mum, I got a bit . . . er . . . delayed," said Rose, blissfully unaware of Merdyn's mounting terror.

"Well, hurry up, will you? I'm starving here!"

"OK, I'll—"

Rose had barely begun her sentence when Merdyn GRABBED the phone from her hand and THREW it on to the pavement with great force. The screen smashed instantly. CRACK!

"Wha—? Stop!" Rose screamed.

But the wizard-warlock wasn't finished yet. He JUMPED and STAMPED on the phone for all he was worth, breaking it into tiny pieces. Then he threw himself to the ground and sifted frantically through the shattered glass and plastic with his fingers.

He looked up at Rose, bemused. "Where did she go?"

"Where did WHO GO?" yelled Rose. She couldn't remember a time she had been angrier. That phone was expensive! She NEVER took it to school in case something happened to it, and now this IDIOT had smashed it to smithereens.

"Why, the wicked witch in the box?"

"That was my mum! She was just at home!"

"Thy mother *liveth* in that tiny box?" said Merdyn, aghast. "What happened? A hex? A curse? Did she fall foul of another wicked witch?"

"What? No! Stop talking about witches!" said Rose. "She wasn't IN the box, you idiot. It's a smartphone."

"Even I knew that," Bubbles chimed in squeakishly. "And I'm a guinea pig."

Merdyn looked at Rose, dumbfounded. "A . . . startfoam?"

"Smartphone," Rose repeated.

"Startfoam," he said again, stubbornly.

"Smartphone," Rose tried again. "And it cost a LOT of money."

"I told you. I have monies."

Merdyn threw some more dirty pebbles at the livid Rose, which did NOT help. Rose threw the stones right back at him. Merdyn couldn't help pondering how odd it was that he had fought marauding murderers and crusading conjurors, but that was nothing compared to the wrath of this twelve-year-old girl. She must have really liked that startfoam.

"This singing spell had better make me REALLY famous!" Rose yelled, before picking up the broken phone pieces and putting them in her bag.

They walked in silence the rest of the way to the fish and chip shop. Rose got some for herself, her mum and Kris and, her anger finally subsiding, for Merdyn too.

She wondered how she was going to explain her new companion. It would be OK, she figured. As long as Merdyn didn't smash Mum's phone, or hog the TV, or eat her chocolates, she imagined she'd be fine with a warlock staying in the shed for a while. *Though I won't say* warlock, thought Rose. *I'd best say* wizard. *Sounds less, erm . . . kill-y.*

When they arrived back at Daffodil Close, Rose tiptoed down the little path between her house and Dion's garage, with Merdyn behind her.

"Now listen. I need to persuade my mum to let you stay for a while," she whispered. "Are you happy to sleep in there?"

She pointed at the little shed in the Falveys' garden.

It was a basic affair with a peeling green roof, small door and window.

"It is a paltry abode but, being in Hell, I suppose I cannot expect a castle," said Merdyn.

"Er . . . exactly," said Rose. "So, just wait here."

Inside the house Rose found her mum exactly where she had left her. The talent show had finished and now she was watching a documentary about Marilyn Monroe.

"You took your time," Suzy said, barely looking up.

"I bumped into someone," said Rose.

NOW Suzy looked up. "I thought I heard another voice when I called you! Who was it? Not a stranger? What did I tell you about talking to strangers?"

"He's not a stranger," said Rose. "Well, he is quite strange. And kind of full of himself. But he's nice at heart, I think. Well, I'm not sure about that but . . . the thing is, he's . . . he's a . . ."

"Spit it out, Rose," said her mum, impatiently.

"He's a . . . he's a wizard," Rose managed, finally.

Suzy was so shocked she even paused the documentary about Marilyn Monroe.

Outside, Merdyn saw Rose's next-door neighbour, Dion, emerging from the side door of his garage, having finished tinkering with his beloved car for the night. Dion jumped out of his skin when he saw Merdyn, but he didn't want to get into a conversation with an extra from *The Lord of the Rings*, so he just nodded and dashed into his house.

As he did so, Merdyn saw something drop from his pocket and lie among the paving stones, shining in the moonlight. Merdyn liked shiny things, so he bent down to pick it up.

It was a small black box. As Merdyn studied it, pressing and prodding, he heard a muffled noise from inside the garage. BOOP BOOP!

The clever reader, which I think we have already established you are, will recognise this sound as the noise made when unlocking a car remotely. But to Merdyn it sounded like a bird call.

Being a curious type, the warlock opened the little side door of the garage and went in. Once inside, he could see that it wasn't a bird at all, but a *caaar*. Since Rose had explained that they were just horseless carriages, Merdyn wasn't scared of them any more. In fact, he found this carriage rather beautiful. It had a picture of a huge eagle on its front, and the moonlight streaming through a window made it gleam like a giant gemstone.

Merdyn ran his hand down its side. *So shiny, so smooth, so cold.* He noticed a handle and instinctively pulled it. A door popped open. The leather seat inside looked very inviting, so he sat in it.

There was a round thing in front of him. Weirdeth. Why have a wheel *inside* the carriage? Then he remembered Rose saying something about a key. Could the silver shard chained to the little black box be a key? Merdyn held it up in front of his face.

'Tis a small and dainty key, but a key nonetheless, he thought. *Now where does it go . . .?*

In the lounge, Rose was still fending off questions from her irate mum.

"You met a vagrant in the woods? And you want him to live in the shed? Have you gone completely potty?"

"But Mum, he can do magic! He made Bubbles talk! Listen . . ."

Rose pressed the pinecone against her guinea pig's head. There was a long silence.

"Come on, Bubbles. I couldn't shut you up five minutes ago!" Rose begged. Bubbles just stared at her with vacant eyes. "He was talking earlier," Rose told her mum, smiling desperately. This was going even worse than she had expected. Suddenly the possibility that she would soon have a magic singing spell and transform everyone's lives for the better seemed very remote.

Rose's mum had seen Rose do some eccentric things in her time, but this behaviour was on another level. "I knew this would happen," she said, shaking her head. "You've gone mad. I've read about it. This can happen to children who've suffered sudden changes . . ."

Rose was about to interject when they were interrupted

by the sound of a revving car engine.

VROOM-VROOOOOOOM.

It was an odd noise. Dion never revved the engine of the Pontiac Firebird so loudly. He knew that such high revs per minute would damage the pistons. Was this . . . something to do with Merdyn?

No sooner had this worrying thought entered Rose's head than it was confirmed. She heard a crank of gears, followed by a loud explosion that sounded not unlike a car crashing through a garage door. SMASH!

Rose and her mum rushed to the front window just in time to see Dion's beloved $100,000 Pontiac Firebird hurtling backwards across the road, swerving and snaking and screeching as it went.

As it whizzed past, Rose glimpsed Merdyn at the wheel looking sick and screaming at the top of his lungs. The car swerved one last time, then thumped into a lamp post. CRUNCH!

The boot (or 'trunk' as they call it in America) crumpled up like an accordion.

Two seconds later, Dion's front door flew open. The postie had bare feet, and he was wearing nothing but a dressing gown. He'd been in the bath watching *Titanic* on his iPad when he'd heard his car fire up. Now he was pelting across the road leaving foamy bubbles in his wake, screaming, "My car! My beautiful car!"

He reached the car-wrapped lamp post and yanked open the driver's door. Merdyn, who looked very green, was instantly sick all over poor Dion's naked legs.

"What the . . . Oh my GOD!!! That's it! I'm calling the police!" Dion screamed.

Rose and her mum watched the whole thing unfold like a – well, like a car crash, from behind the window of their front room. Eventually, Suzy turned to Rose.

"Is that your wizard, by any chance?" she said.

"Actually, he's more of a warlock," replied Rose, meekly.

A phone and now a car,
crushed like a toy.
How many more things
could Merdyn destroy?

CHAPTER SEVEN

BROKEN CARS AND LONG LOST STARS

By the time Sergeant Murray arrived, Rose was outside and trying to coax Merdyn out of the driver's seat. The warlock was gripping the steering wheel tightly and had yet to let go. Her mum was comforting a near hysterical Dion.

Sergeant Murray took one look at Merdyn and his moustache formed a big, upturned, banana-shaped smile. "Well, well, well," he said, with no effort to avoid clichés. "If it isn't my doughnut-throwing friend." He clicked his handcuffs on to a still shell-shocked Merdyn's wrists and dragged him out of the crumpled car.

"Where are you taking him?" Rose wailed. She wasn't a hundred per cent sure she hadn't imagined the whole magic pinecone incident, but she wasn't yet ready to let go of her dreams completely. And if Merdyn was thrown in jail, there was NO chance he'd be whipping her up a singing spell any time soon.

"What's it to you? You know this man?" the policeman asked.

"Yes," replied Rose. "Sort of. And I don't think he meant to steal the car. I think he was just . . . curious."

"Curiosity killed the cat," said Sergeant Murray with a smirk, as if he was the first person ever to say that line. "And this cat has already pelted me with assorted doughnuts in the shopping centre." He licked his top lip. "I still haven't got all the icing off my moustache. This cat's going to prison for a loooong time!" And he started marching Merdyn towards his squad car.

"Wait!" cried Rose's mum suddenly. Now Merdyn was out of the car, she could see his face properly for the first time, and she was staring . . . Rose thought she looked pale and confused, as though she'd seen a ghost. "I'm sorry but . . . I think I know this man!" Mum said now, much to the surprise of everyone. Especially Rose. "Those cheeks. That nose. Rose, I think it's . . . your father . . ." She trailed off, almost overwhelmed with emotion.

Rose was totally baffled. She knew her mum hadn't

been herself these last few years, but she'd never actually forgotten her husband was dead before. "Mum," she said. "Are you OK?"

"It is, it's your father . . .'s brother!" Suzy gasped. "It's Uncle Martin! Rose, don't you recognise him?"

Rose had hazy memories of Uncle Martin. She knew he was her dad's brother and that he became a racing driver. She'd heard her mum on the phone to Auntie Eileen, her dad's sister, whispering about 'problems' he was having one time. But he certainly was not a warlock slash wizard who could (maybe) make animals talk.

Rose quickly surmised, however, that this "Uncle Martin" mix-up was a perfect cover story for Merdyn to stay at the house. Certainly long enough for him to potentially create a spell to make her the best singer in the world anyway . . .

"Ah yes, of course!" she said now, in her best acting voice. "*That's* where I knew him from. It's Uncle Martin!"

"Why did you say he was a wizard?" asked her mum, quite understandably in the circumstances, don't you agree?

"Sorry, I er . . . thought that's what he said," said Rose. "I must have misheard him."

Merdyn hadn't yet recovered enough of his wits to cotton on to Rose's plan. "I am a warlock!" he insisted now. "I am NOT *Un-cle Mart-in*! I am Merdyn the Wild, the finest warlock who ever liveth! Destroyer of enemies. All those who knoweth me er . . . something something." He petered out, still too traumatised to finish his usual intro.

"I'm confused," said Sergeant Murray. "*You* say he's Uncle Martin, *he* says he's a blimmin' warlock. What's going on?"

"I can explain," Suzy whispered, lowering her voice so that "Martin" couldn't hear. "A few years ago, he had a bad car crash. In a race. He was in a coma for a while. Never been the same since. I didn't realise it was so bad. You'll have to let him go. I need to phone his sister Eileen, she'll know what to do with him."

"All right then," said Sergeant Murray, much to Rose's relief. "I'm releasing him into your charge."

Up to this point, Dion had been kneeling by his crashed car, gently weeping and stroking its bashed bumper. "Hold on," he said now, as Sergeant Murray took the handcuffs OFF Merdyn's wrists. "Are you telling me you're NOT arresting this man?"

"I don't get involved in family matters pertaining to comas and the like, sir," said the sergeant. "Leads to nothing but headaches and paperwork, not necessarily in that order. This will have to be settled internally."

"But – what about my car?"

"You've got insurance, haven't you? Use it," said Sergeant Murray. He turned to Merdyn and tapped his nose. "Suffice to say, I've got my eye on you, mate."

"Come on inside, Martin. This way . . ." said Rose's mum gently, walking ahead to the house and beckoning Merdyn to follow.

"Yes, come on, *Uncle Martin*," said Rose.

"Child, thou knoweth I am not Martin!"

"SHHH!" Rose hissed. "You want to stay with us? You're Martin. OK?"

Merdyn shrugged. He couldn't claim to understand *every* word these strange people said, but he guessed "prison" meant the same as it ever did. Sticking with Rose and her deranged mother seemed like his best hope of getting home – for now.

Ten minutes later, they were all eating fish and chips in the kitchen. It turned out that Merdyn the Wild *really* loved fish and chips. Rose watched him eat with a mixture of wonder and disgust. He had no regard for whether bits of food went into his mouth or on to the floor. He just grabbed handfuls of fried potato, batter and cod, flung them in the general direction of his face and hoped for the best.

When Suzy finally got off the phone, she was also a little taken aback by the mess Merdyn had made. "Someone's hungry," she said with a wink to Rose. "He's a messy pup. Your father was the same."

"'Tis goodly bellytimber, this!" Merdyn replied, smattering the table with chips and scraps as he spoke. "Thou must think me a terrible raggabrash*. But I have

---

*Very messy person. Next time you encounter someone who is disorganised and horrifically grubby, try calling them a *raggabrash* and see what happens. They'll probably be very confused, unless they've read this book, in which case they have good taste and you can cut them some slack.

not eaten in a long time." (Literally centuries, if you think about it.) "And these *fish and ships* are a delight."

The warlock stuffed the last of the battered fish into his mouth. By now his robes looked like the floor of a fish and chip festival after everybody had gone home.

"Erm, perhaps you'd like to clean yourself up?" offered Rose's mum. "The bathroom is at the top of the stairs."

"Aye. Thank ye," said Merdyn, and shuffled off.

As soon as he'd gone, Suzy turned to Rose. "I couldn't get hold of Auntie Eileen. I've tried every number I know. I left a message with two of the cousins, hopefully someone will tell her . . ."

"So Merd—" Rose remembered the ruse just in time. "I mean, Uncle Martin can stay with us in the meantime?" she asked, hopefully.

"He'll have to," said her mum, much to Rose's relief. "He's worse than I thought he'd be. Why does he talk so weird? I can't understand half of what he's saying. And what's he on about Purgatory and wizards for? He's stark raving mad!"

Upstairs, Merdyn had found the bathroom. Or at least he *thought* he had. There was a bath-shaped object there for sure, but no water pump. He tried to lever the taps. Then he hit them with his fists, pulled them, pressed them. Nothing. (Remember, he's from 511 AD. Screw taps wouldn't be invented for another twelve hundred years.) He grabbed a shower head and tried that too. Again, nothing.

"Aha!" he exclaimed finally. For in the corner of the bathroom he'd spotted a little bowl with a small pool of water in it. Now, we would recognise this object as a toilet, but in Merdyn's time, toilet activities were done outside in a hole in the ground. It would be unthinkable to do your number ones and twos in your own home. So, to Merdyn, this little bowl of water looked like just the sort of place you could easily wash your hands and face – and perhaps slake your thirst too, with a nice cool drink.

At this exact moment, Kris returned from his shift at Top Boy in the shopping centre.

"I'm back!" he shouted as he came through the front

door. "Dion's car's wrapped around a tree outside, FYI. He's out there weeping like a baby. What's the story there then?"

He received no reply, as Rose and her mum were still deep in conversation in the kitchen. So he headed upstairs to his room.

He skipped up the short flight of stairs as usual. But as he passed the bathroom, he heard a strange sound. He leaned his ear against the door. Someone . . . a man . . . was humming to himself in there.

A man? "That's odd," he thought. There hadn't been another man around since Dad died.

Finding the door ajar, Kris felt within his rights to push it a little. It swung open. So did Kris's mouth. For there, before his very eyes, was a scruffy, bearded pirate with dirty clothes, kneeling down and splashing his face and hair with water from the toilet bowl. And not only that, but the man was cupping the water in his hands and *drinking* it, too!

Now, do not be alarmed. The thought of washing our precious faces in the toilet obviously appals us, but hygiene

in the Dark Ages was so terrible that this may well have been the cleanest water Merdyn had ever tasted.

However, let's leave Kris and our toilet-drinking warlock for a moment. Rose is still downstairs, and you're probably wondering what she's up to.

In the kitchen, mother and daughter were in the midst of a heated debate about where Uncle Martin/Merdyn would sleep.

"I think the shed will be OK," Rose was insisting. She wanted to keep the wizard/warlock close, but not TOO close.

"The SHED? You can't make a former world rally champion sleep in a SHED!" her mum was insisting in return.

"But he *wants* to go in the shed!"

"He doesn't know what he wants. He's not in his right mind!"

As they argued, they barely noticed Kris enter the room. The colour had completely drained from his pretty face.

"You all right, sweetheart?" asked Suzy, when she finally noticed him.

"Erm . . . yeah. I think so," said Kris. "Just wondering why there's a tramp in the bathroom, drinking from the toilet bowl?"

No sooner had he said this than Merdyn entered the

kitchen, looking very refreshed.

"Say what thou liketh about Purgatory, the water is as fresh as the morning dew!" he said cheerfully.

"Kris, this is Uncle Martin," explained Mum. "He's visiting from Scotland, he'll be staying with us for a while."

Merdyn held out his hand to be shaken. Kris just stared at it.

"I'm not touching that, bruv," he said.

"Kris, don't be rude!" Rose snapped.

"No offence, mate," said Kris. "It's just not that normal to wash in the toilet."

"What is '*toilet*'?" asked Merdyn.

"You know," answered Kris, squirming with embarrassment. "Where we do our . . . you know . . ."

"A *privy*?" Merdyn bellowed in horror. "Who in the name of Vanheldon has a privy IN THEIR HOUSE?"

"Mate, what world are you living in?" said Kris. "This is the twenty-first century, not the Dark Ages. Now where are my fish and chips? You'd better have got the low-fat ones, sis."

But Merdyn's eyes had widened. A firework had just

gone off in his brain. "What sayeth thou, fellow?"

"I said, you'd better have got the low-fat ones because I'm on diet, see, and . . ."

"No, before then!"

Kris rolled his eyes. "I said it's not the Dark Ages, it's the twenty-first century, and guess what? We have toilets in our houses now."

Merdyn's darting, panicking eyes landed upon a calendar pinned to the wall. He slowly approached it, his heart pounding. Because, of course, up to this point the great warlock had presumed he was in Purgatory. That's what he'd been sentenced to, so that's where he was. He could handle Purgatory. If worst came to worst, he would be there for seven years; fewer if he found an escape route, or if Evanhart persuaded the King to grant him clemency. And then he'd return home. But now he stared at the calendar in disbelief.

There it was. In black and white.

He wasn't in Dark Ages Purgatory any more. He was fifteen hundred years in the FUTURE, and everyone he had ever known would be dead. Evanhart included.

"How . . .? Why . . .? I shouldn't be here," he said softly to himself.

Something about the way he said this struck Rose's heart like an arrow. Merdyn's usually booming voice was suddenly fragile, and moistness gathered in the corners of his large blue eyes.

Suzy picked up on this too. "Don't you worry, Uncle Martin. We'll look after you 'til Eileen comes," she said, trying to comfort him.

Merdyn wasn't listening. His sadness was turning to anger. He flung open the back door and stomped into the garden. Then he looked up to the heavens, searching for something.

There they were.

The same stars.

The same moon.

He had probably stood in this very spot nearly fifteen hundred years ago. The expression on his face turned from despair into a scowl as he realised this was the work of one man. The man who had been jealous of him since their School of Alchemy days. And now, finally, he had beaten him. Merdyn was trapped out of time – probably for ever.

"A pox upon thee, Jeremiah Jerabo! Thou crooked nose knave*, thou fusty-lugged bespawler**, thou wax-nosed hufty tufty***!" Then Merdyn stretched his arms out wide and howled at the heavens like a wolf,

"CURSE THEE, JEREMIAH JERABO!!!"

And the stars themselves
shook like jelly
when Merdyn the Wild
yelled with such welly!

---

*/**/***Low class, mouldy, slobbering, fickle show-off! Safe to say, Merdyn didn't like Jerabo much.

CHAPTER EIGHT

TIME FOR BED/ THERE'S A WIZARD IN MY SHED!

Rose was putting Bubbles to bed in her room. She had the smallest room in the house, but she didn't mind. It was cosy. Posters of her favourite singers adorned the walls. Beyoncé of course. Amy Winehouse. Florence and the Machine. Even her mum, in a poster from when Suzy was in The Mondays. She was stunning and wild, all blonde hair, lipstick and tons of attitude. Any other free space was taken up with pictures of animals: dogs, cats, hamsters, horses and, of course, guinea pigs.

Rose carefully measured out Bubbles's vitamin C powder, a bowl full of pellets and some hay to chew on. She looked at the enchanted pinecone next to his cage. Had she imagined Bubbles's voice? What happened in the wood already felt like a dream. And what about the singing spell? Was Merdyn even really a wizard, or a warlock, or whatever he said he was? And why had he been in such a terrible mood since the calendar incident?

She picked up the pinecone and pressed it against Bubbles's fuzzy head.

"Bubbles?" she said softly. "You still there?"

There was a long pause as Bubbles continued chewing. Rose was about to turn away in disappointment, when he suddenly stopped munching, stared into the middle distance, then looked up at Rose, his nostrils flared.

"Did you say something?" he squeaked. "I couldn't hear, I was chewing on this stuff."

Rose let out a HUGE sigh of relief. She *hadn't* imagined the whole thing! "Why didn't you say something before?" she asked, irritated suddenly.

"When?" asked Bubbles. He started chomping loudly on his hay again.

"When I was trying to prove to Mum that Merdyn could—" MUNCH MUNCH

"What?" interrupted Bubbles. "I can't hear you."

"I *said*, I really could have done with your help earlier when I was talking to Mum."

"When were you talking to a nun?"

"What?"

"You said you were talking to a nun?" Bubbles said, nibbling again.

"My MUM. Stop chewing your hay!" complained Rose, barely comprehending that she was losing patience with her own talking pet guinea pig. *If all guinea pigs are as annoying as this, it's probably best they* don't *talk,* thought Rose. She forced herself to return to a calm voice. "When I was talking with Mum. Why didn't you speak?"

Bubbles shrugged. "Dunno. Couldn't think of anything to say." Then he paused, twitched his nose, and added, "Can I go back to eating my dinner now?"

Rose nodded, put the pinecone on the windowsill and looked out of the window. She saw Merdyn sitting alone in the middle of the garden. Her mum had tried to persuade him to sleep in the house, but he was having none of it. He said he couldn't bear to sleep under the same roof as a privy. So Suzy had eventually given up and made him a bed in the shed with a little lamp next to it.

It was strange how happy her mum seemed since

Merdyn had arrived. Usually Suzy sat on the couch as if nailed to it, even resenting having to get up to go to the toilet. But now she was plumping Merdyn's pillow and fetching him glasses of water and bedtime snacks as if she were the most accommodating person in the world. Rose had missed this side of her mum. Suzy had even offered Merdyn a pair of Rose's dad's old pyjamas, but he said they weren't woolly or scratchy enough for him, and that wearing them would be like wearing nothing at all.

Rose thought Merdyn looked so sad, sitting there all alone in the moonlight. Rose certainly knew how it felt to be alone. She put on her dressing gown over her pyjamas and went downstairs.

Opening the back door, she felt the cold air around her ankles as she approached the cross-legged warlock. She sat down on the damp grass next to him.

"Are you OK?" she asked.

"No, I am not *okaay*," he grumped. "And your promise to help me go home just becameth a sight harder."

Rose frowned. "What do you mean?"

"Because I AM home, child. I am from this very place.

Fifteen hundred years ago. Last time I did looketh, it was the year 511."

Rose's mind started exploding. Surely that was impossible. But it DID explain a lot. The incident with the phone. The car. The annoying thees and thous. "But then . . . how did you get here?" she asked, after a long pause.

"There was a trial. I was sentenced to the Rivers of Purgatory. But my arch-enemy, Jeremiah Jerabo, sent me to the Rivers of Time instead!"

"A *trial*? What did you do?" Rose enquired nervously, thinking how cross her mum would be when she realised she'd invited a criminal to live in their shed.

"Oh worry not, child. 'Twas nothing." Merdyn waved his hand disparagingly. "Just treason, arson, witchcraft, sorcery, petty theft, grand theft. Mere trifles."

Rose's eyes widened. It didn't *sound* like trifles. It sounded like a whole pudding tray, followed by rhubarb crumble and custard. And this was the man she'd entrusted to make her dreams come true?

Just then, Rose noticed that Merdyn was holding something in his hand. It was a strangely perfect oblong stone, about the size of a large matchbox, with the face of a beautiful woman etched into one side.

"Who's that? Your wife?" she asked.

The warlock smiled fondly. "A wife? Nay. Warlocks have no time for wives. Thou can't handcuff the wind."

This struck Rose as a rather sexist opinion, but he was *literally* from the Dark Ages, so she let the comment slide. Instead, she raised her eyebrow inquisitively.

"What?" said Merdyn uncomfortably.

"You don't have to pull that rubbish with me."

"I speaketh no 'rubbish', child! How dare thee? I am Merdyn the Wild, the finest—"

". . . warlock who ever liveth, blah blah blah, yeah yeah. I know a defence mechanism when I see one," said Rose. "I practically invented them."

"A whaty-what what?" asked Merdyn.

"You pretend you don't care so you never get hurt. Except it doesn't work, does it? Because you still feel hurt. In here." Rose pointed to her heart. "She must have meant a lot to you, to want to carve her face. It's very beautiful."

Merdyn spoke slowly. "Her name was Evanhart. She is

. . . *was* a very powerful and good witch. A heart the size of Albion* and a brain the size of a mountain ox. There WAS a time when I thought we could marry, have younglings. But our paths did divergeth . . ."

"Why?" asked Rose.

"Zounds! Thou asketh a lot of questions!" Merdyn snapped. But his eyes softened into sadness again as he stared into the distance. "If thou must know, a great and terrible war did cometh. The King ordered every man to join the fight. Evanhart did beggeth me not to go. She said wars change people. How right she was." He swallowed. "Something did happeneth. Something unspeakable. And it was then I found out who I really was. Not a wizard, not a family man, but a warlock. Destined for greatness yes, but not goodness."

"What happened?' asked Rose breathlessly.

Merdyn frowned. "What aspect of 'unspeakable' do thou not comprehendeth?"

Rose was undeterred. She had plenty of other questions. "What was it like then, in the Dark Ages? It

---

*An old name for the island of Great Britain. Merdyn's not literally saying her heart was that big, because that would be ridiculous. But she was obviously very nice.

must have been very different from now."

"Ha!" Merdyn snorted. "'Tis like comparing flower and fowl. The air here, it stinketh. There is no nature. When I am from, yes, there was turmoil and war. But we did believeth everything was one: the trees, the birds, the grass beneath our feet. All was connected, from one edge of this great flat earth to the other."

Rose felt she ought to pick him up on the 'flat earth' thing, but now maybe wasn't the time. It made her think, though. There had to be so much that Merdyn didn't know. That the earth was round for a start. The Big Bang. E=MC squared.

Suddenly, Rose had a brilliant idea. Of course! Why hadn't she thought of this before? "Merdyn, we should go to the library tomorrow!" she said. "They've got loads of old history books there. Maybe you could find out what happened to Evanhart?"

"Yes, child!" Merdyn looked excited now. "Thou could look me up. Then thou will see how famous I once was!"

"Yes! And maybe we'll even find out how to get you

back home. I'll meet you at the church near my school at three-thirty."

"Right. What be *three-thirty*?" Merdyn asked.

Wow, hanging out with someone from the Dark Ages was going to be hard work. "Sort of halfway between lunch and dinner time?" said Rose.

"Ah. When the sun passes over the yard arm?"

"Er . . . if you prefer that, yes."

"I'll be there." Merdyn frowned. "But tell me, why not meet *at* thy school?"

Rose blushed. "Oh, it's just, well – to modern eyes you look like . . . someone who has fallen on hard times . . ."

"You mean a mumblecrust?" demanded Merdyn. "I look to you like a toothless beggar?"

"Just a little bit, yeah," admitted Rose.

"Well, I would hide THEE away if thou were in MY time!" Merdyn barked defensively. "I mean, look at thee! Thy bizarre clothing made from scratchless wool. Thy fuzzy hair. The way thou speaketh. People would think I was friends with a rock elf!"

Rose didn't know what a rock elf was, but she

recognised an insult when she heard one and it suddenly reminded her too much of school. She tried to stop it, but her eyes filled with tears.

"You're not the only one who's had a bad day, you know," she said. "You might have been in a medieval war, but I've had an audition from hell go viral on YouTube. I'll . . . I'll see you tomorrow." She jumped up and rushed back into the house, slamming the door on her way in.

BANG.

Merdyn the Wild, the greatest warlock who has ever lived, knew he had been mean. When would he learn? Here he was, fifteen hundred years in the future, all alone in a strange land, and he'd just managed to insult the only person who had shown him an inch of kindness. How Evanhart would have disapproved. He looked at her image in the stone once more and sighed.

Merdyn didst hide his love away,
oh, how the girl was right!
He didst regret it sore today,
with all his warlock might.

CHAPTER NINE

RETURNING THESE PAGES TO THE DARK AGES

"I . . . I . . . I just don't knoweth what happened. Perchance the pages did sticketh together?" Jeremiah Jerabo was jabbering in front of King Paul like a naughty schoolboy before a headmaster.

That's right, gold star again to you, we're back in the Dark Ages – although the chapter heading rather gave the game away, so don't go feeling too clever. After Merdyn had been sucked into the Rivers of Time – as opposed to those of Purgatory – Evanhart began an inquest, and Jerabo was ordered to the Great Room of the King's castle to explain what had gone wrong.

The King's home wasn't quite as grand a castle as you might have seen on school outings. Those wouldn't be built until 1200 or so. Early castles were a crude mixture of stone and wood, glued together with mud, hay and horse poo. Nevertheless, the Great Room was decorated with huge tapestries depicting the great battles that King Paul had won, and there were gold goblets and silver ornaments everywhere so, yeah, it still looked pretty Great.

The King was sitting on his throne, feeling increasingly exasperated. Evanhart was pacing the stone floor, shooting angry looks like daggers from her grey eyes at the flailing Jerabo. His coiffured golden hair, slicked into a point with candlewax, was annoying her more than ever.

"Ah yes, see?" Jerabo said as he held up his black and gold spellbook. "The pages WERE stuck together! LOOK! Wax, perchance? Thou knoweth how wax can be. It sticketh terribly."

"Can't we just open the Rivers of Time again and bring him back?" asked the King. He had no REAL desire to bring Merdyn back, but he hated to see his only daughter so upset.

"The Rivers of Time are just that, Father," said Evanhart. "They floweth through the centuries like water. There is no knowing where Merdyn did landeth. One hundred, two hundred years from now? A millenia?

Forward or backward." Evanhart gasped. "What if he did goeth backward? To the dangerous time of the sabre-tooth tiger?"

"Well, lucky for him if he did," said Jerabo. The King and Evanhart glared at him. "I'm just saying. Magnificent beast, the sabre-tooth," Jerabo spluttered on. "Until we did wipeth them out. We must remember to conserve our native species, do thou not thinketh . . .?"

"So, thee see, Father," Evanhart turned her back on the rambling wizard , "we could enter the Rivers of Time with magic. We have Jerabo's spellbook, after all. But then, where would we get out? It's like asking where a grain of sand did landeth on the shore. So . . . let us put all our most wondrous scientists to this task instead. Perhaps they knoweth how to locate Merdyn."

"Very well," said the King tiredly. "Thou will see to this, Jerabo."

"With respect, sire, why me?" said Jerabo. "If 'twere up to me, I'd leave the skelpie-limmer* whensoever the Rivers did spitteth him out. Evanhart appears to be the one

---

*From old Scots dialect, *skelpie* means someone who deserves to be smacked and *limmer* means thief or scoundrel. If you ask me, Jerabo is talking more about himself than Merdyn – but that's just my opinion.

who has the most affection for Merdyn. Let her find the vagabond."

The King and Evanhart looked shocked.

"I beg thy pardon, Jerabo?" asked Evanhart. "What art thou insinuating?"

"Yes, speak Jerabo! What meaneth thee by 'affection'?'" said the King.

"Oh, I'm sorry," Jerabo simpered. "I did assumeth Evanhart had *some* sort of feelings for Merdyn? I did presumeth this is why she has refused to marry anyone else? Including myself. The Lord knoweth, I've asked her enough times. I . . ." Then he actually thrust a hand to his forehead. If there had been soap operas in the Dark Ages, Jeremiah Jerabo would have made a great actor in one. "Oh! What am I saying? Hush thy mouth, Jerabo! Hush now!"

The King looked sternly at the wizard, then at his daughter, whose cheeks had turned a deep shade of crimson.

"Would thou excuseth us, Jerabo?" said the King. "I wisheth an audience in private with my daughter."

Jerabo bowed, turned on his heels and left the Great

Room, a smirk playing across his thin lips.

Once alone, the King turned to Evanhart, being careful to subtract the anger from his voice. "Is it true, Evanhart? Do thou have feelings for Merdyn the Wild?"

"Oh, Father," Evanhart replied. "Thou do not knoweth him as I do."

"The man is a criminal!" the King bellowed angrily.

"He was not always that way," cried Evanhart. "Before the war he was charming, he did maketh me laugh so. Lord knows, we needeth to laugh in these dark times!"

Outside the Great Room, Jerabo had cast an eavesdropping spell (made from eavesdrops, a flower similar to snowdrops but more ear-shaped) and was listening through the large wooden door.

"He most likely casteth a spell on thee!" reasoned the King from within. "Did he giveth thee a love potion?"

"No!" cried Evanhart, before smiling at a memory. "Although we madeth a love potion together once. We madeth a sparrow fall in love with a hedgehog. 'Twas most amusing."

"I findeth nothing amusing about this entire

farrago*!" **BOOMED** the King. "Thou thinkest I will ever let thee marry Merdyn the Wild? On my birthday last year, he did turneth my wine into parsnip soup!"

Evanhart's smile dropped. "But—"

"Silence!" bellowed the King. "I have had enough of thy nonsense! Thou will do two things from this day forward. Number one: thou must cease thy pleading for Merdyn's return. He is where he is and let time have him. And number two: thou will be *married* before this year is out."

On the other side of the door the eavesdropping Jerabo's ears were aflame.

The King's demand left Evanhart speechless. She gathered her breath before asking,

"Married? But . . . to whom, Father?"

"Whomsoever thou liketh," said the King. "There are plenty of eligible gentlemen around. How about Jerabo? I knoweth he can be a little annoying at times. But he is a loyal servant. And, more importantly, of noble blood. Why, his father owneth half of Wessex! Whereas Merdyn

---

*A word still used a lot today, meaning a confused mixture of things. It originated from Latin words meaning mixed-up grains. Loaf of farrago bread, anyone?

was an orphan. His parents could have been mumblecrusts, for all I know."

Behind the door Jerabo did a little jig.

"Marry Jerabo? Never!" thundered Evanhart. She clenched her fist so hard that the stone floor cracked beneath her. She WAS a witch, after all.

"Thou will do as thy father ordereth you!" thundered the King in response. "I have humoured thee for too long, daughter! A woman thy age should be married and having children. Thou must produce an heir to the throne! After all . . ." At this, the King became quiet. "I will not live for ever. One day thou will be Queen. Do thou not wanteth our family name to carry on? To ring throughout the ages?"

Evanhart was angry at her father, but the thought of him dying one day made her pause. She paced up and down the room a few times in silence as he watched.

"Very well, Father. I will marry Jerabo if it pleaseth thee," she said eventually, to the King's, and I'm sure your, amazement. Behind the door, Jerabo was cock-a-hoop. He performed several fist pumps as if he were a footballer who'd just scored a goal. Even the cleaning lady, who was sweeping up at the far end of the Great Room, dropped her brush in astonishment.

"However, I have one binding condition . . ." Evanhart continued.

"Which is?" asked the King, with trepidation.

"That we find Merdyn the Wild and bring him safely home."

Behind the door Jerabo's face turned to thunder. *Why must that wretched Merdyn be a constant nail in my shoe?* he thought. Surely the King would not agree to this?

The King, however, knew better than to argue with his daughter. It was a hard bargain, but it was a bargain all the same.

When the King called him back into the room and told him of the pact that had been reached, of course, Jerabo pretended he was hearing it for the first time.

"Thy Highness, I would be honoured, nay *flattered*, to join thy prestigious family," he said, with all the oiliness of a snake dipped in oil.

"Very well," said the King. "Here is thy Royal Engagement Ring." And he handed over a gold ring set with a ruby, which Jerabo eagerly slid on to his finger. Evanhart shuddered, but held her tongue.

"Just one teeny thing, sire. A mere shrew, if I may," Jeremiah piped, smarmily. "What if we findeth Merdyn but he be dead, not alive? Just for clarity's sake, thou understandeth. After all, who's to say he didn't endeth up in the time of the great crocodiles?" (I think he means dinosaurs, don't you?) "Or in some future warring country?"

At this point, as a curious reader, you may be wondering why he would ask such a question. And you would be right to wonder. What was Jeremiah Jerabo up to?

The King looked to Evanhart for help.

"Dead or alive, I shall marry," Evanhart said, swallowing her pride. "Just find him."

That was precisely the answer Jerabo wished to hear. And so, as he was wont to do, he started a speech. "Dear King Paul, I cannot help but feel responsible for what has happened to Merdyn the Wild—"

"Thou ART totally responsible!" Evanhart cut in.

"Well, yes. 'Twas what I was saying," agreed Jerabo.

"So, given that fact, I do solemnly swear that if we tracketh Merdyn down, I shall PERSONALLY go through the Rivers of Time to retrieve the poor fellow myself, where'er he may be! I am sure this can be done much quicker than thou imagines."

"In that case," declared the King, "alert the finest scientists in the land. We have a warlock to find!"

Evanhart holds out hope
for her rescue wish,
but why does Jerabo seem
slippery as a fish?

CHAPTER TEN

WARLOCKS AREN'T COOL IN SCHOOL, THAT'S THE RULE!

With all the excitement of the night before, Rose had almost forgotten about her disastrous audition the previous afternoon. But as she walked into school the next day, she was met with cries of "Hey, Beyoncé!" and "Show us some moves!" There were roars of laughter from every pupil she passed.

Be calm, Rose, she told herself throughout the day. *They'll soon be grovelling at your feet for an autograph. When you're a famous singer, thanks to Merdyn's singing spell, the CATs will be clamouring for a selfie with you as your bodyguards beat them away with sticks.*

She woke with a jolt, some unsightly drool dribbling from her mouth. She'd been having her revenge fantasy during her last class of the day: history.

"I'm sorry, did I wake you, Rose?" the teacher was

saying. The class tittered.

The teacher in question was called Mr Watson – or Mr Onetone, as he was nicknamed, because he only ever spoke in one tone of voice, somewhere around an E-flat. He'd been in the middle of talking about an upcoming field trip when he'd spotted Rose dozing off.

"So, to recap, the end-of-term field trip this year will be to . . . Stonehenge." Mr Onetone waited for some show of excitement from his pupils, but it was not forthcoming. Undeterred, he pulled down the window blinds and started a slideshow.

The class groaned. A *slideshow?* Every pupil's worst nightmare! Mr Onetone, however, was made of stone himself, so carried on regardless.

"Thought to date from around 3000 BC, Stonehenge is a marvel of Bronze Age architecture," he droned. "Many aspects of Stonehenge, such as such as how and why it was built, remain subject to debate. We can have some fun with that once we're there . . ."

CLICK. Another slide appeared, this one showing two stone pillars.

"For example, these pillars would have had a stone on top,' Mr Onetone said. "But it vanished. Where did it go? *How* did it go? The druids believed that shortly after it disappeared, somewhere around the sixth century, the gods became so angry that they cursed the earth by beginning to take away its magic. This heralded the end of ancient mysticism and the dawn of modern cynicism."

Catrina, Andrea and Tamsin exchanged looks and twirled their fingers in circles around their temples, signalling that they thought Mr Onetone was cuckoo.

"And looking around the room, I'd say the druids were bang on," Mr Onetone added with a sigh.

Suddenly the class was interrupted by a loud

BANG BANG BANG!

Someone was thumping on the window from outside. Rose glanced at the clock on the wall. 3.25pm. Surely this wasn't . . .

Her heart started beating faster as Mr Onetone jogged to the window and lifted the blinds. The class let out a collective gasp. There, waving his arms around like a loony, was a strange-looking dirtily dressed man in a battered pointy hat – or Merdyn, to Rose, you and me.

"*There* thou art!" he shouted when he saw Rose through the window.

Mr Onetone turned to Rose. "Rose Falvey? Do you know this man?"

"Never saw him before in my life," she said automatically.

"ROSE! It is I!" yelled Merdyn. "I have been waiting for thee for three thumbs*!"

The class looked at Rose.

"Maybe I do know him a bit," she admitted.

Thankfully, the bell rang for the end of the day. Rose's classmates giggled and whispered to each other as they filed out. This was *all* Rose needed. Merdyn may have been the greatest warlock who ever liveth, and perhaps all who knew him *had* bowed down before him, but in modern Britain, he looked like a complete weirdo.

Rose trudged across the playground to the school gates. "Please don't let Merdyn be there, please," she whispered to herself. "Oh boy . . ."

---

*That's around three hours, in case you were wondering, measured by how many thumb lengths the sun moves across the sky.

Alas. There he was.

"Youngling! Over here!" Merdyn cried out when he saw her, as if she could miss him. "I did waiteth by the church but thou did not cometh."

"I said three-thirty!"

"We did sayeth when the sun climbs over the yardarm," Merdyn pointed out. "'Tis well over by now. 'Tis nearly at the tree tops. Come! I wanteth to see how my fame has endured through the years!"

Merdyn seemed to have no other setting than "extremely loud" when he was in full flow. The mums and dads at the school gates hurried their children into the waiting Volkswagens and Minis and drove away as fast as they could.

Then the CATs appeared.

"Who's this then, Rose?" hissed Catrina. Her make-up was even more garish than usual today. "Your *dad* finally made an appearance?"

The others high-fived Catrina and howled with laughter. Rose had never told anyone that her father had died. She didn't like people feeling sorry for her. So the

CATs weren't to know, but their words cut even deeper than usual.

"Like father like daughter, going by the smell!" said Andie, waving a meaty hand under her oversized nose.

Rose had to admit, Merdyn did stink to high heaven. But so would you if you were from the sixth century. Also, he'd washed himself in the toilet the night before, which never helps.

"Let's get out of here, he's giving me the skeeves!" said Tamsin.

Merdyn had watched all this like a hawk, including Rose's face as she tried to steady her bottom lip.

"I am pitch-kettled*. Why do these hens vexeth thee so?" he asked as the CATs disappeared round the corner, hissing and cackling to themselves.

Rose looked up from the ground. Merdyn had managed to clear the entire school playground of parents and pupils in record time. "Look," she said. "Maybe magic made the world go around in your day, but it doesn't any more. Now it's all about how cool or famous you are, how

---

**Pitch-kettled* means deriving from pitch or glue, meaning Merdyn was stuck and confused – just in case YOU were *pitch-kettled* too.

much money you've got—"

"I told thee, I have monies," said Merdyn, once again dipping his hand into his purse and throwing some dirty-looking stones at Rose.

"Stop throwing pebbles at me!" she cried, losing her temper. "It's about how pretty your nose is and where you get your clothes from and how many followers you've got on Instagram and . . . I don't have any of those things. This world is for winners and I'm not a winner. I'm a loser."

Rose's voice cracked. Her belief in herself had collapsed like a giant Jenga tower, and lay scattered about the floor in tiny wooden bricks. Her dad was wrong. She wasn't ever going to be any good at anything. Her eyes filled with tears and she sobbed.

Just then she felt something cold press against her cheek. She looked down. It was an old cup. A sixth-century cup, to be precise. And it was being pressed against her cheek by Merdyn the Wild.

"What the heck are you doing?" said Rose, almost forgetting, for a second, the unimaginable pain she was in.

The warlock looked surprised. "Hm? Oh, just

collecting thy tears," he explained casually. "A child's tears be one of the most precious ingredients for spells. They may be of use to me in my quest to get back to my time."

Rose stepped backwards, leaving Merdyn holding the cup in mid-air.

"Oh. Have thou finished crying?" he said in disappointment. "I was hoping for a few more drops."

"You're such a selfish, horrible man!" Rose yelled. "Don't you care about anyone but yourself?"

"Well," Merdyn began, "I understandeth how it might *look* that way, but—"

"Yes, it does look that way! Very much so!"

"But thou art forgetting something," said Merdyn. "I have promised to fulfil thy heart's desires. The singing spell? Will not that help thee get monies or followers on 'instantgrannies' or whatever thy currency be? Hm? Yes? But first, thou must help me find a way home. That was the deal. Therefore, I AM helping thee by THEE helping ME. See? Now, more tears please."

He went to press his cup on to her cheek once more. Rose batted his hand away.

"I don't feel like crying any more. I'm too angry!" she said, before taking a deep breath. This warlock was going to drive her crazy, but he was right. She had to help him in order to help herself. For all her dad had stood for, she'd put up with Merdyn a little longer.

Poor Rose, poor Rose –
her temper ran hot.
Today this warlock
she enjoyeth not.

CHAPTER ELEVEN

INTERESTING BOOKS AND DISPARAGING LOOKS

Rose sensed trouble as soon as they entered the usually silent library. Merdyn walked straight up to the very stern-looking librarian and shouted in his loudest speaking voice, "A COLLECTION OF THY FINEST BOOKS UPON THE SO-CALLED DARK AGES, PLEASE! ALTHOUGH I CAN INFORM THEE THAT IT WAS QUITE SUNNY MOST OF THE TIME!"

The poor librarian nearly fainted. She'd never heard anyone raise their voice above a whisper in her precious library before, and now here was someone shattering her eardrums without a care in the world. She recovered her senses and looked daggers at Rose, who quickly marched Merdyn to a table and sat him down.

"Don't worry, he'll be quiet from now on, I promise," she told the librarian as she did so.

"Why must I shusheth?" Merdyn complained.

"Because you have to be quiet in libraries."

"Why?"

"Because you just do!"

Merdyn finally brought his voice to a whisper. "*Fine. But 'tis a nonsense.*"

"I'll get you some books on the Dark Ages while I find out about these Rivers of Time," said Rose. "Just sit there and be quiet."

A few minutes later she plonked a pile of books in front of Merdyn. He attacked them hungrily as Rose tried to find out what she could about advances in time travel. Unsurprisingly, very little.

This was the quietest Rose had ever known Merdyn, as his eyes darted from page to page, sentence to sentence, scouring for some mention of himself or anyone he knew. How odd to be in the future looking back to see if anyone mentioned your name. Did you make your mark? Or did you disappear without a trace?

After an hour, Merdyn lifted his head from the pile of books. He had his answer.

"Bah!" he shouted and banged his fist on the table. A move which got a nasty look from the librarian. "Not one mention of me. Not a shrew of King Paul or Evanhart either. Nothing until this *King Arthur* fellow in 535!"

"Well, I suppose that's why we call it the *Dark* Ages. We don't know that much about it," Rose whispered comfortingly, giving the librarian another apologetic look.

"How did thou fare?" asked Merdyn, calming for a second. "Any clues how to get me back in time?"

"Nothing, I'm afraid."

The great warlock's head dropped. "I must return to rectify this tragedy. The only magical figure the history books speaketh of is this *Merlin* character."

He pointed to a book called *Wizards, Witches and Warlocks of Auld.* There was an illustration of Merlin inside, in his classic look of grand flowing robes, long silky beard and pointy hat. He was holding a sword – most likely Excalibur, Rose decided. She looked closer. There were some Latin words inscribed on the sword blade. She tried to make them out, but Merdyn *slammed* the book shut.

"It's all Merlin hither, Merlin thither! Merlin was the

best wizard who ever liveth, blah, blah, blah!" he whinged.

"I guess he *is* the most famous wizard we have," said Rose. "Apart from Harry Potter."

This was too much for Merdyn.

"HARRY POTTER? WHAT KIND OF NAME FOR A WIZARD IS HARRY POTTER?"

In an instant, the librarian was at their table.

"Will you PLEASE keep your voice down," she hissed. "Or I will have to call security."

Before Rose could stop him, Merdyn was on his feet. "I will not, madam!

I AM MERDYN THE WILD! THE GREATEST WARLOCK WHO EVER LIVETH!

Silence indeed! Books should be celebrated with laughter and tears! It is not I that should be silenced, but YOU!"

To Rose's horror, Merdyn thrust his hand into his herb pouch and launched a cloud of greenery in the librarian's direction.

"FINCANTUS! SILENCIO! LIPSEALUS!"

In a flash – *ZZIPP! – the librarian had NO MOUTH. It just . . . disappeared.

The poor lady immediately began to freak out.

"Merdyn, give this woman her mouth back! Right now!" shrieked Rose.

The librarian launched herself in a frenzy at Merdyn, hitting him with the nearest weapon to hand: a large *Encyclopaedia Britannica*.

Merdyn was so shocked by the attack that he fell backwards into a shelf of books. WHUMP. The shelf toppled backwards, hitting another shelf. WHUMP WHUMP. That shelf hit another, and before Rose could utter the words, "Here we go again" . . . shelf after shelf toppled like dominos the whole length of the library.

WHUMP WHUMP WHUMP WHUMP WHUMP

(You get the idea.)

I will spare you the unseemly events that followed

immediately after Merdyn destroyed the entire library. Suffice to say that a few minutes later, Merdyn the Wild was forcibly ejected from Bashingford Library by (yet another) angry security guard.

"And don't come back!" shouted the librarian, her mouth now fully restored.

Merdyn lay in a crumpled pile on the pavement as Rose ran out of the library behind him, a copy of *Wizards, Witches and Warlocks of Auld* under her arm. She helped the luckless sorcerer up.

"Ye gods," he said, painfully clambering to his feet. "The hedge-borns here have no respect for their betters. So much for the library. We have gained nothing from it! What a pair of saddle gooses*!"

But no sooner had Merdyn dusted himself down from one drama, did he fling himself straight into another as something caught his eye on the road in front of him. He grabbed Rose and pulled her down behind a parked car.

"What are you doing now?" Rose asked crossly.

---

*Someone who is wasting one's time, like by putting a horse's saddle on a goose. Which IS a total waste of time – unless you're tiny like, say, a leprechaun, in which case it could be a good way of getting around.

"Shhh! It is him!"

"Who?"

"My arch-enemy!" hissed Merdyn. "Jeremiah Jerabo himself. He is here!"

How many shocks
can poor Rose handle?
For drama, no other
could light a candle!
(To Merdyn the Wild, that is)

CHAPTER TWELVE

WHERE EYES ARE DECEIVED AND STORIES ARE WEAVED

"Where?" Rose's eyes darted around for a sign of another Dark Ages person. From experience, they didn't exactly blend in.

"Right there!" insisted Merdyn. "Just beyond this horseless carriage! He has come to do battle with me and finish what he did starteth. Damnation. I cannot face him without Thundarian!"

"I can't see him!" Rose complained.

Merdyn was breathing heavily, his eyes as wide as hula hoops. He raised his head above the car roof to look into the road. "Ah," he said more calmly. "He's gone."

Rose rolled her eyes. "Then can we get off the floor now, please?" She was beginning to think that, however magical he was, Merdyn was also completely bonkers.

Right on cue, Merdyn flew into a panic once more.

"There he be again! He's flying!"

This time Rose saw what he was looking at. It was an *advert* on the side of a bus for the magician who had just won *Britain's Got Talented People*. Rose let out a giggle.

"Thou mocketh me, Rose?" Merdyn roared. "This be my arch-enemy!"

But Merdyn realised his mistake as he watched the bus drive away, revealing yet another poster for the magician stuck to the bus stop. Rose marched him over the road to show him the picture at close range.

"It's an advertisement. For a show."

Merdyn felt a twinge of embarrassment. However, had Rose read the first chapter of this book, as you have, it would have been *she* who felt embarrassed. For she would have recognised the face that beamed out from the poster. The blond hair, the sly, narrow eyes, the air of arrogance. She would have been even more red-faced when she read the name emblazoned across the front of the poster: *Jerabo the Great.* But alas, Rose hadn't read the first chapter of this book. How could she? She was IN the book. She didn't come into the story until chapter two. But if she *had* read it, she would have seen that the two faces were identical in every way.

As it was, she just said, "Merdyn, that guy isn't a sixth-century wizard. He's just some cheesy magician. He was on TV weeks before you arrived."

"Never underestimate Jerabo!" exclaimed Merdyn. "Is he a rakefire*? Yes. A smell-feast**? Yes. A hufty tufty***? Yes, thank you, sir!" Rose hoped he would stop using words she didn't understand very soon. "But a piece of cheese? No. Look here." Merdyn pointed to a tag line

---

*Someone who outstays their welcome by keeping the fire burning needlessly at the end of the night.

**An opportunist. Someone who smells a feast from miles away and arrives uninvited.

***Show-off. Ah, you remembered this one from last time, did you? All right, don't get big-headed, you hufty tufty!

for the show: *Are you brave enough to enter the Magic Circle?*

Rose shook her head. "The Magic Circle is just a weird members' club for magicians."

"Nay. The Magic Circle is where we settleth our disagreements. Where we do battle!" replied Merdyn, his blue eyes ablaze like sapphires. "Believe me, Rose, these *adverts* – they are a sign that he wanteth to settle this with a duel! He is telling me he is here. The Rivers of Time are imperfect. He could have set out after me, but arrivethed several months ahead. What more do you know of this man?"

"He has sort of come from nowhere in the last month," Rose admitted.

"Aye! That maketh sense," enthused Merdyn. "He hopeth that I shall come to him! I knoweth it! Tell me, this magic show – it playeth soon?"

Rose looked at the date on the poster. "This Saturday night, in London."

"Pah! London?" Merdyn spat the word out. "Who would want to go to that sewer?"

"It's not that bad. I love London, actually."

"Love London?" echoed Merdyn. "'Tis not possible. 'Tis a place for peasants who cannot afford to live elsewhere."

"Errr," said Rose, doubtfully. "London *might* have changed a bit since you were last there."

"Fine!" proclaimed Merdyn. "I will do battle with Jerabo in London and make him return me home with his spellbook. But first I needeth to restore my full powers, or else I standeth not a chance. I needeth my staff, Thundarian."

Rose thought seriously for a second. Jeremiah Jerabo WAS an unusual name. She supposed it was *possible* that this guy was from the sixth century too. And if this *was* Merdyn's rival, this could be a genuine way home for him, and a way to Rose's promised singing spell.

"OK. I'm in. So where is your wand?" asked Rose.

"Staff," Merdyn corrected. "It was broken in two and thrown down a well. I can only hope that the well is still intact. 'Twas situated where Crondike Wood meets Alderly Forest. Thou knoweth of these places?"

"I know Alderly Forest but there is no Crondike Wood

. . . wait." Rose stopped. "A well? You mean the old well?"

"No," said Merdyn. "'Twas a new well . . ." He paused to correct himself. "But I supposeth by now it would be considered old. Fifteen hundred years have passed, after all."

"Then I know where it is," said Rose, "it's in the Oldwell Shopping Centre."

"Let us go at once!"

"It'll be closed by the time we get there," said Rose. "The show is on Saturday, right? Which means we've got tomorrow to get your wand . . ."

"Staff," corrected Merdyn again, even more emphatically this time. "And he has a name. Thundarian."

"Well, we'll get . . . er, Thundarian tomorrow. After school. I think we've had enough excitement for one day."

Now they had a plan, this would all be over soon, Rose reflected as they headed home, and she would be a singing sensation with a happy family at last.

When they got home, Rose saw something she hadn't seen in a long time. Her mum was cooking. Suzy had made roast chicken with roast potatoes, peas and carrots and a jugful of gravy. Merdyn was ecstatic and gobbled it up in no time. It was all Rose's mum could do to stop him eating the bones as well.

"Fine bellytimber, Mistress Susan, fine bellytimber," he said with a beam when he'd finished.

After dinner, Rose decided to show Merdyn the first Harry Potter film. It turned out not to be such a good idea. First of all, he kept trying to climb into the television to talk to the characters. Then he kept leaping off the sofa every ten seconds to complain about how inaccurate a depiction of W-blood life it was. Here are a few examples of his outbursts.

"Is this 'Hogwarts' supposed to be a School of Alchemy? 'Tis nothing like it!"

"Quidditch? A W-blood has no time for sport!"

"They can all fly already, can they? Ten years! It taketh *ten years* to master the flying spell!"

"Call that a staff? 'Tis tiny! A staff must touch the

ground, find its power from Mother Nature."

"This Harry Potter is piffle. It won't catch on."

Rose's mum and brother found his interruptions and leaping about very amusing, though Suzy kept asking Rose where Uncle Martin had gathered his knowledge of wizards and warlocks.

About halfway through the film, Merdyn kicked the TV over out of sheer anger and it stopped working. Suzy found this LESS amusing. Then he dragged everyone into the shed, lit a candle and demanded they each told a story from their lives.

"Where I am from, we didn't watch TeeVee," he said. "Of an evening, we would sing songs around the hearth. Pluck chickens. Tell stories."

"I had no idea they were like that in Aberdeen," said Rose's mum.

Rose just smiled awkwardly.

No one wanted to kick the storytelling off, but in the end Suzy agreed, on the basis the sooner they started, the sooner they'd be done and could go to bed. And the story she told was about Rose's dad.

It had been a long time since Rose had heard her mum talk about her dad, as she found it all too difficult. But now Suzy started to smile as she told a tale from the time they were dating. Apparently, one night they had been driving home down a country lane when they hit a rabbit. Rose's dad had felt so bad that he put the poor rabbit's body in the boot of the car to take home and give it a proper burial. But when they got back to the house, her dad opened the boot and BOOSH! The rabbit leaped out.

"It jumped right up in his face and kicked him hard with its back foot!" Suzy laughed. "Your dad had a black eye for a week."

Rose had never heard this story before and she liked it. Most of all because it showed her that her dad had loved animals just as much as she did.

When Rose headed to bed, she told Bubbles all about their unusual evening.

"Sounds good. Nice to get an invite," said Bubbles sulkily, twitching his nose.

Rose felt bad. She hadn't thought to invite Bubbles. "Why don't you come to school with me tomorrow instead?" she suggested.

"That sounds boring. Poo."

"Yes, but after school we're going to the Oldwell Shopping Centre!"

"Even more boring. Double poo."

"Yes, but while we're there Merdyn's going to get his magic staff from the well so he can do battle with Jerabo the Great on Saturday, give me my singing spell and go home!"

"Now it's getting interesting," Bubbles conceded. "Count me in."

And that night,
no one wept (makes a change!).
The family Falvey
were well slept.

CHAPTER THIRTEEN

CUNNING PLOYS AND TOP BOYS

The next day Rose gave Merdyn strict instructions to meet her at THE CHURCH, not THE SCHOOL. Then she put Bubbles in her backpack with some hay and food pellets. She had attached the pinecone to his collar so that he could speak whenever he wanted. It was too big to hang underneath the collar, so Rose tied it on top and it stuck up like a Mohican or a Cherokee headdress. Bubbles thought a guinea pig in a pinecone headdress looked ridiculous.

"That's the price you pay for being able to talk, I'm afraid," Rose told Bubbles with a shrug as they walked to school together. "Speaking of which, don't talk to anyone. The world isn't ready for a chatting guinea pig. Besides, we can't share Merdyn's secret yet. I don't want him giving away my singing spell to anyone else."

"I don't get it," Bubbles groaned, squeezing another

poo from his bottom. "First you want me to talk. Then you don't. Then you do, then you don't. I'm getting mixed messages here, Rose."

"Be quiet!" Rose hissed. "And stop pooing in my bag!"

As luck would have it, the CATs were passing just at that moment. And it looked to them like Rose was talking to herself. Or to her school bag. Rose wasn't sure which was worse.

"Weirdo," sneered Tamsin.

By the end of the day, Bubbles had done approximately thirty-seven poos and ten wees in her bag. Rose vowed she would NEVER bring him to school again.

After school, the meeting with Merdyn didn't quite go to plan either (of course). Granted he hadn't turned up at school, which was an improvement on yesterday, but he *was* an hour late. Apparently, it was because it was cloudy and he couldn't see the sun properly to tell the time. Rose pointed out this proved maybe not EVERYTHING was better in the Dark Ages.

Once inside the shopping centre, they took up a position behind the Donuts-R-Us stand and observed the ornamental garden beyond. Merdyn recognised the place at once. This was where he'd arrived through the Rivers of Time two days earlier. And sure enough, there was the old well, exactly as it had been fifteen hundred years ago – barring a few missing stones and all the plastic flowers. It was only thirty feet from where he had found himself. He could have got Thundarian from the well there and then, had it not been for the guards.

No sooner had Merdyn thought these thoughts than the guards themselves – named Jim and Alan, if you recall – marched into view. They were stalking the perimeter of the ornamental garden like a couple of panthers, eager not to get caught out again.

"We have a problem," said Merdyn to Rose. "Those two guards. When I did landeth here the other day, well, I may have attacked them a shrew."

"What?"

"In self-defence, I might add! I was confused. I did

not know I had landed in the future," said Merdyn, his tone turning melancholy. "This was once a beautiful forest full of great pines and oaks, the most magnificent herbs and plant life. Now look at it. A gaudy monstrosity! 'Tis enough to make a person weep. Anyway, as soon as they clappeth eyes on me, they will try to retain me again, I have no doubt."

Rose racked her brains for a solution. Her eyes, quite by chance, rested on the Top Boy shop where Kris worked. He should be on his shift right now, she remembered. Then another genius idea grew in her cranium, and she dragged Merdyn into the men's fashion store.

Kris was leaning against a cash register, flirting with his co-worker Shakia. Kris had fancied Shakia for ages. She had curly Afro hair and a nose ring, which was absolutely the very height of cool in Kris's mind.

Suddenly Kris saw Rose and Merdyn coming across the shop floor towards him. The shock caused his elbow to slip off the cash register, sending his body crashing to the ground like a character in a cartoon.

"You all right?" asked Shakia, picking him up

off the floor.

Kris tried to style it out. "I dropped a fifty pence, I was looking for it, that's all. I'll just go see to these customers." And with that he hurriedly made his way over to his sister.

Rose saw Kris coming and waved enthusiastically.

"Don't wave at me!" her brother snapped. "What are you doing here? I thought we had a deal. No meetings in public spaces."

"Kris, shut up. We need your help!"

Her brother looked around anxiously. Shakia was staring at him, her face a portrait of curiosity. Kris smiled in return, then spun back to his sister.

"Certainly, madam!" he said loudly, with a false grin in Rose's direction. "The changing rooms are this way, if you'd like to follow me?"

He ushered Merdyn and Rose across the shop floor and into a cubicle.

"What do you want?" he hissed now. "I could get fired for having him in here. This is a FASHION store, for FASHIONABLE men! Uncle Martin drinks from toilets and he stinks. No offence, Uncle Martin."

"None taken," replied Merdyn. And he meant it too. A powerful aroma was seen as a good thing in the Dark Ages.

Rose grabbed her brother by the shoulders and looked into his eyes. He was her big brother, and it was time to be honest with him. Surely he would come through for her in her hour of greatest need.

"Kris, listen to me very carefully," she said. "This man is not Uncle Martin. He is *actually* a wizard—"

"Warlock!" shouted Merdyn for the twentieth time since arriving.

"Warlock, sorry, from the sixth century. He needs a disguise so he can get his magic wand—"

"Staff," Merdyn interjected again, wearily.

"Staff, sorry. But will you stop interrupting please?" said Rose.

"Get it right, then!" the warlock snapped back.

Kris's head bobbed back and forth between the bickering pair like he was watching a demented tennis match.

"He needs to get his staff from the old well," Rose

went on, trying again. "So he can go back in time. But we need to get past the security guards first. With a disguise. Provided by you."

"These guards and I have history," Merdyn said, with a grimace.

"You're both insane," said Kris, calmly. "Please leave the shop, thank you." And he swished open the curtain of the changing room to let them out.

Rose's shoulders slumped. "Come on, Merdyn," she said with a sigh. "Let's try something else."

Merdyn didn't move. Instead, he fixed Kris with a knowing gaze and said, "What if I could make her fall in love with thee?"

"What? Who?" Kris spluttered, his face turning a deep shade of pink.

"Why, the object of thy affections," said Merdyn, and gestured towards the girl at the cash register.

NOW Kris was interested. He ushered Rose and Merdyn back into the dressing room and shut the curtain once more. "How?" he said, quickly.

"Why, a *love potion* of course. 'Tis a simple recipe.

Thou will find the ingredients in any forest or wood – if there are any left in this godforsaken place."

Kris still looked sceptical. They were losing him again. Then Rose had an idea.

"He really can do magic. I'll show you," she said.

She got Bubbles out of her backpack and held him up. Bubbles twitched his nose as if to say, *I am not a performing monkey*. But he didn't *actually* say it, because he was REALLY ANNOYING.

"Bubbles? What is wrong with you?" Rose screamed, exasperated. "All right. Kris, you'll just have to trust me. Will you help us?" She fixed him with a pleading look, as only an annoying little sister can. "Pleeeeeeeease? For once just trust me on this! Pleeeeeee—"

"All right!" said Kris finally. "She'd better fall DEEP in love with me. Like you hear about in songs and stuff."

"Oh, she will," replied Merdyn, with great confidence.

Kris smiled. "Then it's time . . . for a makeover."

"What's a makeover?" Bubbles whispered to Rose after Kris had left to get some clothes.

"Shut up. I'm not talking to you," Rose huffed at her

furry friend. But really, she was too excited to be annoyed. After all, what does a warlock look like after a makeover?

Ten minutes later Rose found out. Merdyn was transformed. Kris had gone for a 'street' look for the sixth-century sorcerer. Gone were his flowing robes and pointy hat – replaced by skinny jeans, big trainers and a blue bomber jacket. On his head he wore a garish orange trucker's cap and huge wrap-around sunglasses. Now Kris gathered Merdyn's matted hair in a bunch at the back of his head and tidied up his beard with a hair bobble, which made him look like he had a ponytail on his chin.

"What do you think?" asked Kris, turning the warlock to face the mirror.

"I don't know," said Merdyn. "I cannot see a wretched thing in these absurd eyeglasses."

"Well those guards won't recognise you," said Rose. "And that's the main thing."

Rose gathered Merdyn's old garments into a bag as she was sure he couldn't stay in those jeans for long. They

looked VERY tight.

Kris, however, was pretty pleased with Merdyn's look. "I think this will catch on," he said, proudly.

Suddenly the curtain of the dressing room flung open – SWISH – and there stood . . . Shakia.

"What are you up to, Kris?" she said, in a firm voice. "We're not supposed to let homeless guys in here. And who's this?" Shakia gestured toward Rose.

"That's my, er . . . that's my sister," said Kris, reluctantly. "And this . . . this is . . ." Kris didn't know what to say about Merdyn. He felt he couldn't say 'Uncle Martin' any more. "He's a . . . friend of my sister?"

"He needs our assistance," Rose said, helping her brother out. "He just wants to get something that belongs to him that someone threw down the old well a long time ago." It was the best she could do without using the words 'wizard', 'warlock', 'wand' or 'staff'.

Shakia eyed them suspiciously. "OK," she said after a pause, much to everyone's surprise. "But who's paying for these threads?"

Kris hadn't actually thought about who would pay for

Merdyn's clothes. And he wasn't usually the fastest thinker in the world, but on this occasion, he managed to come up with something pretty quick.

"Me," he said, with a nod. "Out of my work allowance. We all get an allowance, right? To spend on clothes. Well, I can pay for these clothes out of mine."

Shakia looked at him in astonishment. So did Rose.

"You'd blow your *entire* allowance to help a friend of your sister?" she asked.

Kris nodded. Strictly speaking, it was to get Shakia to fall in love with him, but yes, he'd blow his entire allowance to help a friend of his sister (to help him).

Then something amazing happened. Shakia HUGGED Kris. Actually HUGGED him. Not in his dreams, but in *real life*.

Dear reader, this was a momentous moment in Kris's short, anxious life. He had never felt so ecstatic. His heart was pounding so hard he thought there was a mixed martial-arts fight going on in his ribcage. He was sure Shakia would notice, but she didn't. Instead she stopped hugging him, looked into his eyes and said softly,

"Sorry, Kris."

"That's OK," Kris said automatically, before adding, "What for?"

"I misjudged you. I thought you were just another bloke obsessed with his hair and clothes and shallow stuff like that," said Shakia. "But I was wrong."

Rose raised an eyebrow. No, she wasn't, that was *exactly* what Kris was really like. But she wasn't going to bring that up at his moment of accidental triumph.

"Hey, that's OK, we're cool," Kris said, trying to hide his happiness.

"All right then," said Shakia, turning to Merdyn. "Can I help too?"

'Tis not a dream,
it would seem
Rose now has
a fledgling team...

CHAPTER FOURTEEN

THE FASHIONARIAN GETS THUNDARIAN

Merdyn, Rose, Shakia and Kris walked briskly through the mall towards the ornamental garden. Rose had to guide Merdyn by the arm because he kept bumping into things. He'd never worn sunglasses before, and his tight jeans were cutting off the circulation to his feet.

Bubbles was watching Merdyn through a hole in Rose's backpack.

"What's wrong with him?" he said, only loud enough for Rose to hear. "He looks like he's trying to crack a nut between his butt cheeks."

Rose had to admit that Merdyn was an odd sight. However, his pony-tailed beard combined with his colourful skater clobber and cool shades were quickly gaining more positive attention from the fashion-conscious young men they passed. Rose could have sworn that by the time they reached the ornamental garden, she'd already seen two teenagers dressed *exactly* the same as the warlock-cum-dude. Kris had been trying to become a fashion icon for years; Merdyn had managed it in a matter of minutes.

"Hoooold up, there!" said Alan, as Merdyn, Rose, Shakia and Kris finally reached the ornamental garden. "Where do you think you're going?"

"Yeah! Where do you think you're going?" repeated Jim, unnecessarily.

"We just wanted to have a little look at the old well," said Rose, as innocently as she could.

Alan and Jim laughed heartily.

"We'd *all* like to have a little look at the old well . . . er . . . little girl!" said Jim, losing confidence halfway through the sentence because he remembered that this wasn't actually true. Most shoppers couldn't give two monkeys about it. "But we can't!" he continued, regardless. "So clear off!"

Alan, meanwhile, had noticed something familiar about the oddly dressed gentleman in front of him. He peered a little closer.

"Do I know you, sir?" he asked.

Merdyn stared back. "Er . . . *okaay*!" he said, thinking of the only modern word he could remember.

Rose was panicking. It hadn't occurred to her that they needed a plan BEYOND disguising Merdyn. They didn't let any old person get near the Well, not since the Great Wishing Well Coin Thefts of 2011. You'd need to be a visiting royal or some other famous person to get past security.

Hang on. That was it! Rose had a plan. Another one.

"You should recognise him!" she announced. "This is MC Wizard – I mean, Warlock. He's a famous rap artist."

"*MC Warlock?*" said a baffled Alan.

Merdyn glared at Rose from beneath his glasses. *Now* what was she talking about? Shakia was thinking the same thing. She leaned into Kris's ear. "What's going on?"

Kris decided to come clean. "She thinks this guy is some sort of wizard and he's lost his magic wand down the well," he whispered. "I know. It's embarrassing."

He shook his head. This could be the end of his and Shakia's minutes-old relationship. But Shakia just laughed.

This was exactly the sort of madness she loved. She turned to the security guards.

"Yes! This is MC Warlock. He's promoting his new album *Well . . . Good Tunes?*, and to promote it, we're taking photos of him next to various famous wells. Get it? I'm the photographer." Shakia held up her smartphone and engaged the camera as proof, then winked at Rose. Rose could have hugged her. "And this is his stylist," Shakia added, pointing to Kris.

"All right," said Alan, suspiciously. "You can go through." But before the gang could move, he added, "On ONE CONDITION. We'd like to hear a little song."

Jim got what Alan was doing immediately. "Yes! If this is this *MC Warlock,* the FAMOUS rapper, let's hear one of his songs, shall we?"

And with that, Jim and Alan both folded their arms, ready to listen.

Merdyn leaned towards Rose's ear. "What is happening?" he asked.

"They want to hear a rap," she hissed back, in a blind panic.

"What be a *rap*?"

"It's a sort of spoken song that rhymes. It has a lot of attitude and, well, you could never—"

Before Rose could finish, Merdyn strode forward with great gusto.

"A *rap*, thou sayeth, sirs?" he announced. "Very well. Behold for your pleasure."

Then, to Rose, Shakia and Kris's horror, Merdyn started to dance in his own unique way, hopping from his left to right foot and back in a most peculiar manner. Shoppers stopped and stared as his spindly legs took on a life of their own. He danced with complete abandon, as if no one was watching, which in my opinion is the best type of dancing. The sight was bizarre enough. But then he began to sing. Well, it was *sort of* singing . . .

"THE HOGWHISTLE ROOT
WILL MAKE A GRUMPY OWL HOOT,
NEVER SIP CATNIP
BEFORE A LONG TRIP,
AND THE PEPPER SEED AND MACA WEED
WILL MAKE THEE FEEL THE NEED TO FEED."

Remarkably, because of its quick delivery and staccato rhythm, and if you forgot the subject matter, it did sound a little bit like a rap. Merdyn flung his arms around like a madman trying to catch flies with his hands, then launched into a second verse.

"THE JUNIPER SHIGGLE
WILL GET THEE IN GIGGLE,

BE BUSY WITH THIN LIZZY
IF THEE WANT TO FEEL DIZZY,

BUT THE GROUND IVY TRICK
WILL MAKE THEE FEEL SICK."

Merdyn built with speed and energy to a crescendo, like he was headlining Glastonbury.

"AND THE GUMTREE BUSH
WILL GET THY MUSH IN A HUSH,

THE WHITE WILLOW BARK
WILL HAVE THEE UP WITH THE LARK,

LET IT NEVER BE FORGOTTEN
THAT TORMENTIL MAKES THEE ROTTEN,

OR I'LL MAKE THEE FORGET-A
WITH MY GROUND-IVY-HERB-NEPATA!"

And with that, Merdyn sank down on one knee, head bowed and breathing heavily due to the physical exertion of the performance. It was like watching Michael Flatley at the end of a particularly vigorous River Dance.

Rose, Shakia and Kris weren't entirely sure what they'd just witnessed. Jim and Alan were gobsmacked too. But when a round of applause spontaneously broke out among the shoppers who had gathered to watch, they all joined in.

"That was, er . . . very *interesting*, Mr Warlock," said Alan, a little bashfully.

"I agree," said Jim. "More artists ought to promote the power of organic produce in their songs. I'll download that when I get home."

"Good," said Rose quickly. "Now if you don't mind, we'll just get our photo and be on our way." And MC Warlock and his three assistants then stepped over the fence and walked towards the old well.

"That was great. Where did you pull that from?" Rose asked Merdyn in a low voice.

"Folk song," Merdyn said, matter-of-factly. "Songs are songs. Words. Rhymes. 'Twas ever thus."

"What's everyone talking about? That was the worst rap I've ever heard!" Bubbles piped up from Rose's bag. Rose zipped it shut. "*Er, hello? Hello*?" came a muffled cry shortly afterwards.

The eager warlock reached the old well first. He opened his jacket to reveal his herb belt with its row of little leather pouches which he'd put on under his puffer jacket. He stuffed his right finger and thumb into three pouches in quick succession. Then he started the incantation, with a look of dire seriousness on his face.

"LYCIUM RISEARIUM ANGELICA FLOATISIS! ZEA MAYS, THUNDARIAN!"

he bellowed.

Shakia grabbed hold of Kris's elbow. "Is there *really* a magic staff down there?" she said. "I thought you were joking."

Merdyn clapped his hands together, sending a puff of mixed herbs and greenery over the well like a magical cloud. But it wasn't a normal clapping sound. It was more like a roll of thunder.

BOOM!

It was so loud, the ground shook briefly. He clapped his hands again. KABOOOM!

This time it was more like a nuclear explosion. The glass in the windows of Accessorize This shattered, scattering shoppers in a panic. In a supermarket on the other side of the mall, a giant pyramid of baked bean tins collapsed, causing pandemonium in aisles six and seven.

Everybody except Merdyn dived to the ground and clung on for dear life. Rose finally understood why Merdyn had kept saying, *All those who know me bow down in fear*. Seeing him like this it all made sense. He. Was. Awesome.

Merdyn clapped his hands a third time.

KABOOM - BOOM - BOOM!

The earth shook again. This time, it continued shaking as debris from inside the old well started shooting out of it in jets. WHOOSH! At first, old cans of Coke and lemonade. Then coins, thousands of coins, remnants – no doubt – from the well's wishing days. They blasted into the air as if from a burst water pipe, then rained down on the stunned shoppers like a thunderstorm of tin, copper and chrome. CLINK, CLATTER, OW! Then dirt and mud flew out of the mouth of the well at a frightening speed, splattering on the ceiling of the shopping centre and sticking to the shiny white tiles.

From his prostrate position, Alan blew his emergency whistle and Jim ranted into his emergency police radio. "Help! All agents, help!" But the sound was drowned out by the powerful rush of earth slamming into the roof. *Splat splat splat!*

Watching from the floor, his hair blown back by the sheer energy radiating from Merdyn's hands, Kris turned to Shakia and said in a loud voice, "I THINK ROSE WAS RIGHT. HE MIGHT BE A WIZARD ACTUALLY."

"YOU THINK?" Shakia hollered back sarcastically.

Finally . . .

WHOOSH!

An old gnarled bit of wood flew out of the well, darted about like an angry wasp, then thumped into Merdyn's outstretched right palm.

WHUMP!

Another into his left palm.

WHAP!

Merdyn crashed the two pieces of wood together and a blinding light strobed outwards through the mall.

Then, as quickly as it had begun, it ended.

Silence.

Rose stood up, blinking away the effects of the strobe light. Standing before her was a smiling Merdyn. And in his hand was a fully repaired staff – as noble a piece of wood as you could ever wish to see, with a proud eagle's head carved into the top.

"Thundarian," he said, as simply as if he'd just made a boiled egg.

The joy of the moment was short-lived, however, as none other than Sergeant Murray came running towards them, with at least a dozen officers. In all the chaos, Merdyn's truckers cap and sunglasses had blown off and his blue eyes, hair and scraggly beard were now there for all to see.

"And to think I was gonna buy your song!" said Jim bitterly with tears in his eyes.

Rose was terrified as the ring of police closed in. She could see her brother and Shakia felt the same, and she didn't even want to think about the number of nervous poos Bubbles must be doing in her bag right now. Merdyn on the other hand was as calm as . . . well, a warlock who had just been reunited with his beloved magical staff.

"PASSIFLORA INVISIBLATA!"

he chanted and banged his majestic staff on the ground.

Sergeant Murray pounced on Merdyn and handcuffed his wrists together.

"Gotcha . . ."

But the handcuffs jangled to the floor. Merdyn had completely vanished, taking the others with him.

The officers looked at each other and scratched their heads. Had that really just happened? Sergeant Murray's police training, however, had taught him that there was a rational explanation for everything.

"After them!" he howled. "They can't have just disappeared!"

But oh, Sergeant Murray,
yes they can.
Just open your mind,
you silly man.

CHAPTER FIFTEEN

HELL'S BELLES AND FLYING SPELLS

Merdyn and Rose reappeared outside the Oldwell Shopping Centre. Rose looked down and watched in amazement as her legs returned, materialising before her eyes. Wow! How cool had it been, turning invisible? She'd been able to feel everything as she ran through the shopping centre. She'd felt her trainers on the ground, the air against her face; she'd even felt it when she bumped into an old lady, making her wave her umbrella at nothing. And yet . . . she had been totally see-through.

Now she watched as her hand reappeared at her side, as if being coloured in by a computer animator. She checked her bag for Bubbles.

"I just had a *very* weird experience," her guinea pig said, a glazed expression on his face.

Phew, Rose thought. Back to normal.

"Rose, look!" shouted Merdyn suddenly. "The mean witches from thy school!"

Rose looked around. There, among the shoppers fleeing from the mall, were Catrina, Andie and Tamsin.

"Now I have Thundarian, I shall avenge thee," said Merdyn. A fiery mass was already collecting at the end of his staff.

But Rose grabbed his arm. "What do you mean 'avenge thee'? What with?"

"Well, I was thinking . . . a fireball?" the warlock said casually.

"What?"

"Too much?" The fiery mass at the end of his staff went out – POOF! "All right, then. I shall just give them the plague." And he went to point Thundarian again.

"No!" said Rose. "You can't just go around giving people the plague!"

"Well, thou art no fun," he sulked.

But Rose had bigger problems. Like, never mind Bubbles – where was Kris? What if he never rematerialised? What would she say to her mum?

"Kriiiiis!" she yelled.

Thankfully, at that moment, Kris and Shakia started to appear beside her. First their feet, then their knees, waists, arms and finally their heads. But her brother looked different somehow.

"Did you . . . do something to your hair?" Rose asked.

"We went via that hair salon, Hell's Belles?" said Shakia, with a raised eyebrow.

"It's Crème de la Bear Hair Fudge!" Kris protested. "Do you know how expensive this stuff is? It's not every day you become invisible."

Rose was pleased her brother was back, with or without his new hairdo, but a new problem had arisen. The police were now spilling out of the shopping centre in search of the Ornamental Garden Trespassers. It would be a matter of seconds before they were spotted.

"We gotta move quick," she said.

"I don't suppose you can make us fly?" Kris asked Merdyn hopefully.

Merdyn smiled. "Of course." He thumped his staff on the ground once more – BOOM! – then shouted,

"TRILLIUM PEUMUS LEVITATO-US!"

Suddenly Rose felt her entire body become as light as air. It was as if someone had turned gravity off with the flick of a switch. She looked down to see her feet rising off the ground. Two centimetres, then five . . . now she was fully forty centimetres off the floor.

Kris was floating too. And Shakia. From inside her backpack, Rose heard a strange retching sound.

"That was me being sick, just in case anyone was wondering," groaned Bubbles.

It may have made the guinea pig sick, but the kids were all smiles. Instinctively, they held hands and squealed in delight. First invisible, now flying!

Best. Day. Ever! Rose thought.

"Tell me, knoweth thou a forest near here?" Merdyn asked, hovering beside them. "I need to do some serious potion preparation for my battle with Jerabo tomorrow night."

"Clearwater Forest is that way!" Shakia managed to say, in between shrieks of excitement.

"Then to Clearwater Forest!" ordered the warlock

with great fanfare.

Rose braced herself, expecting to shoot off at lightning speed like they did in Harry Potter. But instead they found themselves travelling at no more than two miles an hour, barely faster than walking pace.

"Erm . . . Any chance we could speed it up, mate?" pleaded Kris.

Merdyn looked shocked. "This *is* fast," he said, as an old man trundled past them on a mobility scooter.

"Mate, this is slow," complained Rose's brother. "It's like escaping on a tractor."

"Or a steam roller," Rose chipped in.

"Fine!" Merdyn snapped. "THOU can do the next flying spell!"

Suddenly the sound of police radios filled the air. Now that they were floating, it was easier for the cops to spot them.

"Arrest them levitating layabouts!" Sergeant Murray screamed, scarcely able to believe the words coming from his mouth.

Thankfully, Shakia had an idea. "My car's over there,"

she said. "Put us down and I'll drive."

But Merdyn was having none of it, not after his experience in Dion's Pontiac. Cars made him feel as sick as a dog. It wasn't natural to go so fast.

"Merdyn, please! Put us down. We're going to get caught any second!" cried Rose. "And you haven't even made me my singing spell yet!"

I can't imagine that any child in the history of humanity has ever begged a wizard NOT to fly, can you, even if that wizard was a warlock . . .? But I'm spoiling the drama. Where were we? Ah yes.

Eventually Merdyn realised the children were right and they'd better stop flying. He reluctantly dropped them down (rather unceremoniously, Rose thought) and they ran for Shakia's car.

Sergeant Murray looked furiously around. With all the panicking shoppers trying to flee the mall he'd lost them again. Then he had a thought and a grin spread slowly, maliciously across his face.

He doesn't forget, he doesn't forgive –
this clever copper knows where they live . . .

CHAPTER SIXTEEN

WITH FRIENDS LIKE THESE, WHO NEEDS ANEMONES?

Merdyn the Wild was vomiting out of the window before they'd even got out of the car park. Rose had Bubbles on her knee, feeding him some hay, but she was worried about the warlock.

"How far is it to the forest?" she asked.

"Three miles," Shakia replied.

"I'm fine! Keep going!" Merdyn insisted before hurling up again.

Suddenly, Shakia stopped the car.

"What are you doing?" asked Kris. "He said keep going."

"Picking up my little sister."

Shakia got out of the car and – to Rose's horror – approached none other than the CATs, who were walking along the pavement. One of the CATs was Shakia's sister?

Even Bubbles looked appalled. Especially when it became clear Shakia's target was Tamsin.

Tamsin didn't look too happy about the situation either. Shakia had to drag her back to the car. Reluctantly, she squeezed in the back, next to Kris and Rose.

"Hi," she said to Kris grumpily. She just stared at Rose.

Rose couldn't believe she was sitting next to one of her arch-enemies. Out of all the CATs, Tamsin always irritated Rose the most because she had curly hair and freckles too, but somehow carried them off better than Rose ever could. She could see the resemblance to Shakia, now she saw them together.

"What have I told you about hanging out with those two?" Shakia said to her little sister, looking in the rear-view mirror as she drove.

"They're my friends!" Tamsin replied sulkily.

"I know a couple of bullies when I see them. There's other kids in the world, you know. What about Rose? She goes to the same school as you, doesn't she? She's not a bully. She's cool."

Tamsin looked at Rose, then at the guinea pig in Rose's lap with a PINECONE stuck on its head. She guffawed. "Rose? *Cool*? Give me a break."

Shakia tutted. "Well, she doesn't hang out with mean girls. SHE hangs out with wizards." She gestured to Merdyn, who was still busy throwing up out of the window.

"Warlock actually," Rose corrected on Merdyn's behalf. "Though he's not at his best right now," she added defensively.

"He just made us disappear, then fly," Shakia said.

"Flying might be too strong a word for it," Kris added.

"I don't believe any of you," Tamsin muttered.

"Then you're even more stupid than you look," said a squeaky voice from somewhere. "If that were possible."

"Who said that?" Tamsin looked around the car for the culprit.

"Me."

Tamsin looked down at the guinea pig in Rose's lap. Then she let out a blood-curdling scream.

"What's the matter? Never seen a talking . . .

hang on." Bubbles looked at Rose. "What am I again? I keep forgetting."

"A guinea pig," Rose said, delighted that Bubbles had finally come through for her and spoken at exactly the right moment at last.

"Ah yes," said Bubbles. "That's the one."

Bubbles talking was news to Kris and Shakia too. But at least they'd learned to expect the unexpected when Merdyn was around.

"Are we there yet?" interrupted Merdyn from the window.

"Almost," said Shakia. "Just hold on."

Ten minutes later they were parked in a layby next to Clearwater Forest. Merdyn was mightily relieved to be out of the car, and ran into the forest with great relish shouting, "Come, come! So many magical treats in store!"

Shakia and Kris followed, but were distracted by their mobile phones. News of "an earthquake" at the shopping centre was spreading fast.

"They've shut it down," Shakia said.

"Which is good," observed Kris. "No one'll know

we're skiving off work."

Rose was just behind them, putting Bubbles in her backpack. Tamsin was watching her every move. Rose wasn't sure what Tamsin's game plan was. Sure, she wasn't making catty remarks any more, but if she wanted to be friends, she needed to work on her mate face.

Merdyn stopped in a clearing next to a stream. The water was coming from the hills beyond Bashingford, and a small waterfall had filled a lovely pool, around which was growing some very healthy-looking vegetation.

"Aha!" he exclaimed. "All is not lost with this world. Now, help me, younglings. Get gathering." He got down on his hands and knees – no easy task as he was still in his super-tight jeans – and started grubbing about in the undergrowth.

"Gathering what?" asked Rose.

"Yeah. There's nothing here but grass and stuff," Kris added.

Merdyn looked at them in disgust. "Thou knoweth nothing of nature!"

"Hey! We know about the environment, old

man," said Tamsin.

"Good," replied Merdyn. "Then thou can tell me how many species of plant are in this clearing." He pointed to a space around four metres square. It really just looked like your average forest floor. Part grassy, part muddy.

"I dunno. Three?" voted Kris.

"Ten," suggested Shakia.

"Twenty," said Rose, sure that it was bound to be higher than expected.

"One hundred and thirty-seven," said Merdyn smugly. "And that is just giving it a cursory eye-sweep. Thou sayeth thou care for nature, but thou know not what it is! What it does! How MAGICAL it is! Thou art not *connected* to it!" He continued scrabbling around on the forest floor. "Look, foxglove – the flower of the heart," he said. "Hawthorn – each one has a story to tell. Wood anemones – for digestion. Primrose, red campion, sweet woodruff, wood sage, fern!"

"Oh my goodness!" the kids screamed in unison.

"I know. 'Tis wonderful!" cried Merdyn.

But the children weren't ecstatic about the abundance of flora and fauna. They were crowded around Shakia's phone. "We've gone viral!" They were looking at a very fuzzy video of the moment the old well had erupted, filmed by someone crouching behind the glass on the upper level of the mall.

"Now I knoweth why they call them startfoams," said Merdyn. "A sorcerer has cursed them. As soon as thou looks at them, thou *starteth foaming* at the mouth!" He was quite pleased with this piece of observational humour.

The kids ignored him.

"Now the police are saying the disturbance was caused by a giant sinkhole," Shakia read.

"What's a stinkhole?" said Kris.

Merdyn's patience snapped. He had experienced quite enough of this world's indifference to nature. He would have to adopt a more robust approach to get Rose and her friends' attention.

Quickly, he pointed Thundarian at them and chanted,

"TRILLIUM PEUMUS LEVITATO-THEM!"

which the observant among you will recognise as a variation on the magnificent flying spell from earlier (or slow-flying spell, as it was now known).

Rose, her brother, Tamsin and Shakia all left the ground at the same time. They started screaming. Tamsin was especially alarmed. She'd assumed the talking guinea pig had been some sort of magic trick, but now she was as weightless as an astronaut in space.

"Whoa, what the—!" "Hey!" "What are you doing?" "Put me down!" they all cried as Merdyn took great delight in floating them (slowly) across the water until they were above the deepest part of the pool.

"Please!" Shakia begged as she caught on to what Merdyn was about to do. "You're going to break our phones!"

"Yeah, he does that," said Rose, speaking from experience.

"I'm still in my clothes, dude!" cried Tamsin.

"I've got Crème de la Bear in my hair, bruv!" shrieked Kris.

But this just made it all the more fun for the pesky

warlock. "What was that?" he said cheekily. "I can't hear thee . . ."

"I don't know what's going on out there," came a squeaky voice from Rose's bag, "but it doesn't sound good."

"Merdyn, no!" Rose shouted. "I've got Bub—"

But it was too late. With a flourish of Merdyn's staff to end the spell, all four of them fell – SPLOOSH! – into the cold blue water: clothes, phones, hair fudge, guinea pig and all. As they wailed and scrambled to get out, Rose holding her backpack over her head and the others trying in vain to save their precious phones, Merdyn laughed to himself.

And he went back to foraging on the forest floor.

The children eventually emerged from the water and Rose pulled a saturated and very angry Bubbles out of her bag, putting him on a rock to dry. She was really beginning to understand why Merdyn had been cast out of his world now. She would gladly have sent him into the Rivers of Time herself at that moment, singing spell or no singing spell. But as they all stood on the bank now, dripping wet, their phones and rodents soaked to their circuits, something extraordinary happened.

It started when Rose looked at Tamsin and saw her hair all out of place, and Tamsin looked at Rose and saw that she, too, looked like a drowned ginger rat. And the pair of them started to giggle.

Then Rose, realising she couldn't get any wetter, decided she was going back in the water. PLOP! Tamsin shrugged, and jumped back in too. Shakia was next. And if she was going in, so was Kris. The four of them then splashed and larked and played like they hadn't a care in the world.

While Rose and her (sort of) friends were cavorting in the water, Merdyn stocked up his supplies for his battle with Jerabo the next day. He needed to get hold of Jerabo's spellbook if he was going to get home. It was the only way he knew to access the Rivers of Time. Jerabo wouldn't just hand it over however, so Merdyn collected ingredients for a special spell of his own: a disenchantment potion. This was a liquid which, once drunk, would render a W-blood powerless for ever. One drop, and nabbing the spellbook from Jerabo would be as easy as taking eggs from a bird's nest. (This was seen as OK in the Dark Ages, but now frowned upon. Do not try this at home!)

Merdyn then collected wood and set it ablaze with a fire spell. WHOOSH CRACKLE. Rose was the first to climb out of the pool and huddle by the fire to dry off. Tamsin followed.

"What else can you do?" Tamsin asked Merdyn as she took off her hoodie and spread it out beside her to dry faster. "Can you make fireballs and stuff?"

"And can you make lightning come from your fingers, like in *Star Wars*?" wondered Kris, joining them with Shakia.

Merdyn hadn't a clue what Kris was talking about. "Come see me practise for my battle in the morning!" he said. "I'll show you fireballs and lightning, the likes of which the world has never seen!"

"Will you teach ME how to do fireballs?" asked Kris in excitement.

"Only W-bloods can do real magic," said Rose, rolling her eyes. "Isn't that right, Merdyn?"

"That's right," he agreed. "Are your father or mother a warlock, wizard or witch?"

"Well, Rose can be a bit witchy sometimes," said Kris.

Rose elbowed him in the ribs for his cheek.

"OW!"

"Maybe we should show them something eh, Rose?" Merdyn put out a hand. "Give me Bubbles."

Rose passed a dry but still cross Bubbles over.

"I'll bet everyone a bag of hay this won't end well," said Bubbles. "Ooh. It's poo time. Yep. Here it comes. Oh, hang on. Not a poo. A wee. False alarm."

Tamsin and Rose clapped their hands over their mouths to hide their giggles as Bubbles did a wee in Merdyn's lap.

"Bah! Thou filthy animal," cried Merdyn. "Thou did asketh for it!" He banged his staff on the ground and threw crushed nettle leaves into the air around the guinea pig. **"ANIMA FOXILOXI,"** he intoned. And with that,

Bubbles turned into a fox. POP!

The laughter halted as everyone gasped in delight.

"Oh crikey!" said Bubbles the Fox. "What's going on here? That's not my nose. Hang on . . ." Bubbles looked at his fluffy red tail. "That's not my tail! Have I been eaten by a fox?"

Rose couldn't help it. Despite Bubbles's alarm, another snort of laughter escaped from her nose. Tamsin and her sister were clutching on to each other, tears of glee rolling down their cheeks. Even Kris had given into a cool smirk.

"ANIMA BUFFONEM TOADAMODE!"

Merdyn banged his staff on the ground again. POP! This time Bubbles turned into a TOAD.

"Ooooooh, now what?" croaked Bubbles the Toad. "What's wrong with my voice? I feel cold. So cold. Why are you all looking at me?" He instinctively flicked out his tongue and caught a fly on it, before whipping it back into his mouth and gulping hard. "Bleugh! I feel sick. Why did I just do that? I don't eat flies. That was disgusting."

"Stop!" cried Tamsin, laughing so much she was hardly able to breathe. "Please stop!"

Merdyn turned Bubbles back into himself. Rose, her brother, Tamsin and Shakia were ALL rolling around in fits of giggles by now.

"That's better," said Bubbles, relieved. "I didn't feel myself then for a minute. You know when you don't feel yourself? I didn't feel myself then." He saw everyone thumping the ground with their fists, they were laughing so hard. "Shut up. All of you." Which only made them laugh even more. Even Merdyn joined in, chuckling with mirth as the sun went down. "TEE HEE, TEE HEE, HA HA HA HA HA HA HA HA HA . . ."

"Why does everyone laugh at me?" said Bubbles to himself. "I am *literally* the least funny person I know."

Who'd have thought it?
Bubbles the guinea pig!
Some would pay to watch
his comedy gig!

CHAPTER SEVENTEEN

POTIONS AND COMMOTIONS

As it was on the way, Shakia dropped Tamsin off at their house before driving the others home. Rose waved goodbye, but Tamsin walked through her front door without waving back.

"Maybe she's just tired," Rose whispered to Bubbles. Bubbles gave her a cynical look – no mean feat for a guinea pig.

It was nearly 10.30 p.m. by the time Shakia pulled into Daffodil Close. She had driven as slowly as she possibly could so that Merdyn didn't feel sick. To pass the time the warlock was trying to teach them the 'rap' (sixth-century folk song) which he'd delivered with such success in the shopping centre.

"And the gumtree hush will get thy
bush in a mush,

The white willow lark will
have thee up with a bark—"

"Nay nay nay!" complained Merdyn. "'Tis 'The gumtree *bush* will get thy *mush* in a *hush*', and there's no such thing as a willow lark! It doesn't make sense your way!"

The jollity in the car was brought to an abrupt halt, however, for as they approached Rose and Kris's house they saw not one, but THREE police cars parked outside. Rose's mum, Sergeant Murray and several officers were waiting, all looking very cross indeed.

"Uh-oh!" said Rose, although she was also a little pleased to see her mum off the sofa again, even if it was to give them a telling-off.

"I could blast them with a fireball?" Merdyn offered.

"NO!" came the collective response.

"As far as they know, we've done nothing wrong really. They can't possibly believe Merdyn did all that with magic powers," said Rose.

"They said on the news it was a stinkhole, right?" Kris agreed.

Rose and Shakia looked at each other and decided

not to correct him.

"So, we've nothing to fear," said Rose sensibly. "We'd best just face the music."

They stepped out of the car to face said music. Or Sergeant Murray's loudhailer, to be precise.

"Put the staff DOWN!" Sergeant Murray roared at Merdyn through his loudhailer, which was totally unnecessary as he couldn't have been more than four metres away. The policeman realised this and put it away.

"Why didn't you answer my phone calls and messages?" demanded a furious Suzy. "I missed *The Making Of Britain's Got Talented People*, thanks to you! And as for you, Uncle Martin . . ." She turned on the warlock, who had almost forgotten who he was supposed to be. "I'm VERY disappointed in you! And what on earth are you wearing?" Merdyn was still dressed in his MC Warlock trendy togs.

"The whole lot of you are under arrest!" announced Sergeant Murray next.

"What *exactly* did we do wrong?" asked Rose.

Sergeant Murray laughed. "What did you do *wrong*?

How about breaking and entering a synthetic horticultural enclosure? Vandalism of an ancient monument? Resisting arrest? Pretending to fly? And the popular hair salon Hell's Belles has reported half a very expensive tub of hair cream missing. You might know something about that too!" He directed this last remark at Kris. "Officers, arrest these criminals!"

The officers moved to put handcuffs on the four felons when Merdyn issued a short plea.

"If I am to spend the night incarcerated," he said, "may I at least change into my normal attire? These youthful garments do not befit a man of my age."

Sergeant Murray looked him up and down. "You've got something right at least," he said. "Go on then. Be quick about it."

"And I've got Bubbles with me," said Rose. "You wouldn't put a guinea pig in prison, would you?"

Bubbles popped his head out of Rose's bag. "What are you on about?" he said in his tiny voice. "You keep me in a cage!"

Rose quickly shushed him.

"And I need an overnight bag," Kris said. "I'm on medication!" He meant he wanted to pick up his face cream.

"Blimey O'Reilly! All right. But hurry up!" bellowed Sergeant Murray, tutting.

"Why don't you come inside a minute, Sergeant? I'll put the kettle on," offered Mum with a sigh. "It's been a long night."

I think you, dear reader, would probably agree. But there was more drama to come.

As you may have guessed, Merdyn wanted to do more than just change his clothes. Once he had switched back into his warlock outfit, he beckoned Rose to join him in the garden, where he unveiled his plan.

"I will take all responsibility for these crimes," he insisted. "I'll say I did putteth a spell on you younglings and did forceth thee to help me."

"Merdyn, we can't let you do that!" Rose said, more than a little surprised and touched by this gesture from the usually cranky warlock.

"All will be fine. Now I have Thundarian, I shall

escape from prison without difficulty."

"And then what? Spend your life on the run?"

"I won't need to," Merdyn said in a soothing voice. "Tomorrow night I shall defeat Jerabo and go home. But Rose, thou must come with me to the theatre. I must give thee the singing spell before I go."

"I'd love to, Merdyn," said Rose. "But I checked out tickets today. They're fifty pounds each."

"Then thou must buy the whole theatre." Merdyn dipped into his pouch and threw a handful of dirty stones at Rose. She sighed.

"How many times? This isn't money!"

With Merdyn and Rose arguing outside, let us concentrate for a moment on Kris. Merdyn had snuck him the promised love potion in the car on the way home and, with his mum making tea in the kitchen, this was Kris's chance to use it.

Suzy now handed cups of tea to the supporting police officers and nodded to Kris to pour out the rest. "Those two are for Sergeant Murray and your friend, Shakia," she said, pointing at two red mugs near the kettle.

"Four and a half sugars for me," Sergeant Murray said.

Kris put four and a half sugars in the sergeant's tea, and half a sugar in Shakia's. He knew that she took half a sugar from the countless cups of tea he'd made for her at work. Then he reached into his pocket and pulled out the little bottle that Merdyn had given him, trying to remember the warlock's strict instructions. *Just one drop*, Merdyn had said. *And be careful that you are the* first person *she sees after she drinks it.*

Shakia was busy drying her phone on a radiator on the other side of the kitchen. This was his chance! Kris opened the potion bottle and tipped it towards the mug. But instead of just one drop, the entire bottle emptied into the mug in one go.

"Oh sugar!" Kris said.

As bad luck would have it, Sergeant Murray swept in behind him at that precise moment and snatched up one of the mugs. "Yes, four and a half. This mine?" he said.

Kris looked at the red mug still sitting on the side. Now in a total panic, he couldn't remember which one had four and a half sugars in, and which one contained a full bottle of love potion.

"This must be mine then," said Shakia, and she picked up the remaining mug and sipped from it. Kris made sure he stood right in front of her as she did so, just in case.

"Wow," she said, making a face. "How many sugars are in here?"

Kris started to sweat. Had he given her the wrong mug? Because in that case . . .

Sergeant Murray took a long slurp of his tea. "Oh dear," he said. "I need more sugar in my . . ."

His sentence trailed off. For at that moment, his eyes had fallen upon . . .

Rose and Kris's mum.

Now, I don't know whether you have ever had the fortune – or *misfortune*, some would say – to fall in love. But as soon as Sergeant Murray looked at Suzy, everything went into slow motion. (Or it seemed that way anyway!) Soft rock played in his head as she handed the tea out to the other officers. If you'd looked into his eyes at that moment, you would have seen a firework display in the shape of pink love-hearts going off in each iris. Up until this point in his life, Sergeant Murray had been married to the police force. Now, for the first time ever, he was completely in love with another human being.

"Is there a problem with the tea, Sergeant Murray?" Mum asked, noticing the change in his face. "You look a little sick." Which of course he was. LOVE SICK.

"Not at all, Mrs Falvey," Sergeant Murray replied woozily.

"Please, call me Suzy."

"Suuu-zeee?" He savoured each syllable of her wonderful name. "Did I mention how utterly *beautiful* you look tonight?"

Suzy blushed. "I'm not beautiful," she said. "Well, a long time ago, maybe."

The other officers were chatting about football or some such, so it was only Kris that noticed this abrupt change in Sergeant Murray. He gulped.

"Hey!" said Shakia, snapping her fingers in front of Kris's eyes. "When this is over, do you wanna . . . go to the cinema or something?"

Now Kris was confused. *Wait*, he thought, *did* she *take the mug with the potion after all*? Or – and this was his preferred option – did she like him *without* any hocus pocus?

To make matters more confusing, Merdyn and Rose now spilled through the back door.

"I should be arrested!" Rose shouted. "No one else!"

"Set Rose free and arrest ME!" Merdyn insisted.

Such was the hullabaloo that Sergeant Murray employed his loudhailer once again.

"QUIEEET! No one here is getting arrested!" he said, much to everyone's amazement. "Except maybe this lady," he added, smiling coyly at Mum. "For making a criminally good cup of tea. Three cheers for our host, team!"

The supporting police officers obediently got to their feet and cheered.

"We'll get out of your hair now, Suzy," Sergeant Murray said mistily. "Sorry to have troubled you. And you, Uncle Martin. And, of course, your wonderful children."

Rose looked at Kris. *What happened here?* said her eyes.

Kris held his hands up innocently. *No idea!* Though

he had a fair clue, as did Merdyn, who'd spotted the empty love potion bottle on the side. But neither of them felt the need to say anything, especially as the mishap had *literally* just got them out of jail.

On the way out, Sergeant Murray turned hopefully to Suzy. "Will you go out with me tomorrow night?"

Suzy was so taken aback, she didn't know what to say.

"Erm . . . Mum's busy," said Rose, coming to her rescue. "We're going to see the magician who won *Britain's Most Talented People*."

Suzy looked surprised. But Sergeant Murray's face lit up.

"Jerabo the Great? In London?" he said. "What a good idea. We can all go. I'll get us VIP tickets. My treat."

"Thanks, boss!" said a dozy-looking officer.

"Not you, you cretin!" snapped Sergeant Murray, reverting to type. "I shall pick you up at five sharp, beautiful lady," he continued, turning back to Rose's mum with a woozy smile.

"All of us?" asked Kris hopefully.

"Yep," said Sergeant Murray. "You, your friend here,

Rose, maybe even your little guinea pig." He laughed.

From upstairs Rose heard a faint voice: "I'm fine thanks, don't really like magicians."

"Pardon?" Sergeant Murray asked.

"That'd be great. Thank you, Sergeant Murray," said Rose quickly.

"Please," said Sergeant Murray. "Call me Leslie." And he kissed Suzy's hand, said "Adieu!" and skipped merrily away.

"Wow, that was lucky," remarked Kris. "We were let off AND got tickets to the theatre."

"Too right," agreed Rose. "That's what you call 'two birds, one stone'."

"Which coincidentally," said Merdyn, "is my favourite type of soup."

Rose was elated
at the end of this day.
Finally, her singing spell
was just one night away!

CHAPTER EIGHTEEN

FILTHY LIARS AND TOWN CRIERS

James Alexander De Selby was the first to find a clue as to the whereabouts and whenabouts of the missing warlock, Merdyn the Wild. He had been chosen specifically by Evanhart because he was a rebel, just like Merdyn. He had wild, white, wispy hair that he never brushed and a bizarre scientific theory that all space, time and matter were as one, and had been for ever, and for ever would be. (What a weirdo, eh? AS IF that could ever be true. He was as delusional as that oddball Einstein.) He was also a rather nice man, but sadly nobody knew that because they all avoided him and his bizarre ideas at all costs.

It was a pleasant surprise then, when De Selby received the order from the King's daughter asking him to come to the royal castle to help find a criminal lost in the Rivers of Time.

As soon as he arrived, De Selby asked Evanhart if she had anything in her possession that Merdyn the Wild had touched.

"He did maketh this for me on my birthday at the School of Alchemy," Evanhart said, sadly, passing the scientist a beautifully hand-carved squirrel. "He was always making me something or another in the old days. This object is very precious to me because it is made from the same piece of wood as Thundarian, Merdyn's staff—"

No sooner had Evanhart uttered that last 'F' sound than De Selby picked up her precious squirrel, placed it on a metal plate and shoved it, unceremoniously, in the fire that was burning in the hearth.

Evanhart could barely find the words. "What the . . . How dare thee!"

"Sorry," said De Selby as the squirrel turned to ash upon the plate. "Didn't I sayeth that it would change shape?"

"Change shape? 'Tis burned to a cinder!"

"Granted, 'tis a little less . . . *solid* than 'twas," admitted De Selby. "But 'tis still there, ha!"

He grabbed a pair of tongs, pulled the squirrel ash from the fire and placed it inside a strange contraption he'd brought with him. It looked a bit like a pizza oven, except that it was covered with dials, levers and measuring paraphernalia, and pizza ovens hadn't been invented yet.

"I have broken the wood down into ash. Or to be more accurate, '*mono-cubes*'," explained De Selby, and he gave a little giggle at the wonder of it, in the way only mad scientists who fully understand something mindblowing,that no one else gets, can. I will spare you the complex details, but it worked along the lines of what is now known as atomic tracing, whereby the tiniest fragments imaginable can be tracked to their origins, sometimes back as far as the BIG BANG, taking into account variables, high-density column constructions and bananagrams. But as I said, I'll spare you that.

Next, De Selby activated the machine by cranking a wheel on the side, much like the steering wheel of a ship. The bizarre device squealed and belched like a constipated piglet and the dials spun wildly.

SQUERCH-THHHHPPPP-WHEE!

"What happeneth now?" asked Evanhart, fascinated.

"I am not entirely sure," said De Selby. "'Tis the first time I have used it, if I'm honest."

"What—" Evanhart began.

At that moment, there was a loud DING, DING, DING. De Selby grabbed a magnifying glass and thrust it between the hot plates of his machine. Then he ran out of the door and down the corridors of the castle, shouting, "It worketh! It worketh! My mono-cubal tracing machine worketh!"

Minutes later the King and Jeremiah Jerabo were witnessing for themselves the jumping, oscillating instruments on De Selby's strange machine.

"But what does it all meaneth?" asked the King.

"It meaneth," explained the scientist, trying to contain his excitement, "that we have a trace on Merdyn the Wild. In fact, in all my testing, I have never had such a strong reading. And I think I knoweth why . . ."

"Go on," said Evanhart eagerly.

"The ornament thou did giveth me to burn was carved from the same wood as Merdyn's famed staff,

Thundarian, was it not?"

The King's daughter nodded.

"Well, that would explaineth it!" enthused De Selby. "Not only is Merdyn alive, he must be using his staff *elsewhere in time.*"

"'Tis impossible!" spat Jerabo haughtily. "I did throweth the staff down the well myself. At the court hearing."

"Ah. Then he must be somewhere in the *future*," the scientist deduced. "He must have *realised* he was in the future, returned to the well and pulled it out."

"There we are then," said the King. "He is found!"

"Not quite," warned De Selby. "He could still be fifty, a hundred, a thousand years in the future. We needeth to narrow it down much more. But I'm confident I can do it."

Evanhart felt a flutter of excitement rising within her. Merdyn was still alive!

"Well, my dear," said Jeremiah. Ever since their engagement he had taken to using endearments such as this whenever he could, much to Evanhart's annoyance. "So soon we can be married."

"After thou have used thy spellbook to go and retrieve him as promised, of course," the King added.

Jerabo forced a smile. "Nothing would giveth me greater pleasure than to put right this wrong of mine."

A delighted Evanhart squeezed the scientist's hand in gratitude. "I thank thee, good De Selby," she said. "If Merdyn is returned, we shall see thou art handsomely rewarded. Forty pieces of gold, no less." And with that, she and the King swept from the room.

Jerabo made as if to follow them, then stopped. "I'll be right there, darling!" he called after Evanhart. "I shall just talketh timings with my good man De Selby."

As soon as they were alone, Jerabo's tone changed. Gone was the false jollity, suddenly he was all business.

"Tell me, De Selby. Let us say we getteth an accurate reading. Once I landeth through the Rivers of Time, how easy will it be to find Merdyn? It's important I am not caught . . . unawares."

"If I were thee, sire, I would posteth a notice on a local billboard, advertising thy arrival," said De Selby. "Or perhaps in the future, they will have more advanced levels of communication."

"What do thou mean?" asked Jerabo, confused. "Like a pamphlet, or town crier*?"

"Oh, much more advanced than that, sire," said De Selby, becoming animated. "If my theory of mono-cubes is correct, then in the future people will sendeth messages through the very air!"

"What, like . . . by pigeon or something?"

"Smaller than that, sire!"

"By sparrow? Blue tit?"

"Sire, even smaller than that – and *invisible*," said De Selby. "They may have communication devices that enable thee to speak to the whole country all at once. The whole world, even!"

The penny dropped for the devious wizard. "I see," said Jerabo slowly. "So, if I were to advertise my arrival on whichever communication device they have in the future, I wouldn't have to find him at all . . ."

"Exactly, sire," cried De Selby, excited. "Merdyn

---

*Believe it or not, instead of twenty-four-hour news channels, in the Dark Ages, a man would simply stand in the middle of a town and "cry out" what had been happening recently. He was known as a town crier. Imagine that as a way of letting people know the latest developments on Celebrities Love Islands!

will findeth YOU!"

"Yes!" yelled Jerabo, joining in the enthusiasm. "And when he cometh to me . . . then *I will kill him*!"

De Selby froze. "Erm . . . I beggeth thy pardon, sire?"

"Oops. Did I sayeth that out loud?"

There was a split second while the two men looked at each other. De Selby made a mad dash for the door. Jerabo was too quick, however, whipping a knife from underneath his tunic and pressing it to De Selby's neck.

"What is the meaning of this, sire?" sputtered the poor eccentric scientist, frightened for his life.

"Seeing that the toad is out of the pond, dear boy," Jerabo said menacingly, "thou may as well hear it all. There has been a change of plan. From now on, thou will doeth exactly as *I* say. Not Evanhart. Not the King. ME. Do thou heareth?"

"No. NO!" De Selby protested. "I would rather dieth than goeth against the King!"

"The reward the King is offering is forty pieces of gold," said Jerabo. "I will give thee four hundred."

De Selby had a little rethink. "Go on . . ."

"On top of that, thou will become Royal Scientist to the King himself, with thy very own study and lodgings right here in the castle. How does that soundeth?"

"That soundeth . . . nice," croaked De Selby.

"Good." Jerabo let him go. "Here is the plan. Thou art going to find out exactly when Merdyn landedeth in the future. I will then goeth through the Rivers of Time and get rid of him. While I am gone, thou will telleth Evanhart that thy machine got it wrong and that Merdyn was dead all along, blah blah blah. Then when I returneth, empty-handed but heroic, Evanhart and I will be wed and we'll all liveth happily ever after. Except for Merdyn, of course. But who cares about him, eh, De Selby?"

"Right." The scientist gulped. "And the King will maketh me his Royal Scientist because . . .?"

"Because *I* will be King!" replied Jerabo gleefully, as if it was the most obvious thing in the world. "Did I not mention that after I marrieth Evanhart, I will killeth the King and becometh King myself?"

"I don't recalleth that bit," said de Selby.

"Actually," Jerabo admitted, "thinking about it, I

should have added the King to the list of people who won't liveth happily ever after, shouldn't I, ha ha!"

"Ha ha!" De Selby laughed along nervously.

"I meaneth, the 'me being King' bit is the BEST bit, really," went on Jerabo, smiling from ear to ear. "Which is why we must be *together* in this, my dear De Selby. Merdyn must die! He is the only one powerful enough to stop me, thee see? The one question left is . . . will thou helpeth me?"

Now, you must remember that the year is 511. It's the Dark Ages, OK? In those days, Kings came and went like hedgehogs in the garden. Half the time nobody even knew who was King at all, so De Selby could just have agreed there and then and we shouldn't be too harsh on him. But as it happened, De Selby was a decent fellow, and so was reluctant to get involved in regicide.

"I supposeth I'm with thee," he stammered. "'Tis just . . . I feel a shrew uncomfortable helping with acts of murder—"

SHWING! Jerabo pressed the knife against De Selby's lips this time. "Shhhhhhh, my dear De

Selby. Before thou answereth, I wanteth thee to meet somebody . . ."

The terrible wizard lifted up his tunic and showed De Selby a keychain on his belt. Except on the end of the keychain, instead of a key, was a tiny peasant man hanging upside down. He waved at De Selby. De Selby, not knowing what else to do, waved back.

"This is the last man who did turneth me down," Jerabo said coldly.

The tiny man looked up at De Selby with a sad, upside down expression.

His eyes full up with weary hate,
he spoke four words: "I'd do it, mate!"

CHAPTER NINETEEN

"PARDON, MRS ARDEN, THERE'S A WIZARD IN OUR GARDEN"

Rose was awoken on Saturday morning by a strange sound coming from the front garden. Music . Was it an ice-cream van? No. Someone was singing; a man with a very deep voice. Whoever it was couldn't sing very well. It reminded Rose of men who sang karaoke in pubs.

Bubbles was awake too, munching on some hay.

"What's that noise, Bubbles?" Rose asked.

Bubbles stared at her blankly.

"Bubbles? Hello?"

Nothing. Rose wracked her brains. Had she offended him? She couldn't think how.

She decided to deal with Bubbles later. What *was* that noise? It was getting louder by the second. She got up, walked on to the landing and looked out the front window.

Sergeant Murray was standing on the front lawn,

serenading her mother with a song. It sounded like "I Will Always Love You" by Whitney Houston, but Rose couldn't be sure. Whatever the song was, he was singing it with great passion, bordering on mania.

As he hit the last notes, Suzy leaned out of the upstairs bedroom window with an awkward grimace on her face. "Thank you, Leslie! That will do! Very good!" she shouted. While she was enjoying the attention from Sergeant Murray, she was finding it a little weird too.

"Fare thee well then! See you tonight, my sweet!" shouted Sergeant Murray, prancing merrily off down the street.

Repairing his Pontiac in the driveway next door, Dion watched the sergeant depart too, with an odd look on his face.

Rose pulled on some clothes, tamed her frizzy hair into a ponytail, grabbed Bubbles and went to see Merdyn, who was working feverishly in the shed, mixing up some kind of potion. There were bubbling pots and glass flasks on every shelf and strange mixtures stacked up in her mum's Tupperware collection against the shed's back wall.

"Are you working on my singing spell?" asked Rose hopefully.

"All in good time, impatient one. I have tonight's battle to prepare for first."

"Oh, and I think Bubbles has stopped talking and I don't know why?" Rose added.

"The pinecone spell only lasteth a few days," said Merdyn. "I suspect it has run out."

"Can you renew it? I kind of miss him."

"Heaven forfend, child!" Merdyn answered irritably. "Singing spells? Pinecone spells? I am a warlock! I have no time for such whimsy."

He shook the bottle he was holding. Inside, the liquid turned blue to red to green, then went as clear as water. The air sizzled suddenly, and Rose could have sworn she saw sparks.

Merdyn's face lit up as if he'd just created pure gold. "I've done it at last!" he announced with vigour. "The disenchantment potion – the trickiest, most feared spell in the land! I am so clever! With this, I shall rendereth Jerabo powerless, seizeth his spellbook and returneth home!

Now to practise . . ."

Rose followed as Merdyn strode out into the back garden. It was perfect timing as Suzy was just heading into town. Rose had managed to persuade her to go to the hairdressers before their night out to the theatre – if only just to get the chocolate wrappers out of her hair. The plan was to get Merdyn warmed up for tonight's wizard-versus-warlock duel while Mum was out. Rose felt a little uneasy about Merdyn's battle that evening, but she kept her thoughts to herself.

Kris had found himself a deckchair and was ready to watch the action from the patio. He would usually have been at work on a Saturday morning, but since the shopping mall had been closed down he was determined to enjoy his new-found unemployment. Merdyn, however, had other ideas.

"Get up off thy backside, thou scobberlotcher*! I needeth both of thee to assist. In fact, ideally I could do with three of thee."

"Good job I swung by then," came a voice from

---

*A lazy person, making *scobberlotcher* the ideal insult to throw at a person who is unlikely to bother looking up what it means.

the side of the house.

Rose looked up in surprise. It was Tamsin.

"Wouldn't want to miss fireball training now, would I?" Tamsin grumped, trying to be cool. Nonetheless, she crossed the lawn to stand beside Rose with a small smile.

Merdyn put them all to work straight away.

First, he made them run across the lawn with garden implements raised above their heads. Kris ran with a spade. Merdyn swished his robe, pointed Thundarian, chanted

"GELIDA GLACIA FROSTORA!"

and – *ZZZZFRING!* – cast an ice spell that encased the blade in a block of ice. It was so heavy that Kris dropped it, and the ice shattered across the patio. Rose looked at Tamsin gleefully. WOW! This was going to be FUN.

Tamsin and Rose were next. They ran in zigzags across the lawn, holding up a rake and a pitchfork. BOOSH! Merdyn hit Tamsin's rake with a fireball. She chucked it aside quickly, where it set fire to Rose's favourite pear tree.

"Worry not. Merdyn the Wild is here to save the day!" said the warlock with a grin. He pointed Thundarian at the tree, causing torrential rain to pour down around it

in a perfect circle, dousing the flames.

SHWING! Next Merdyn threw an invisible lasso around Rose's pitchfork and pulled it back towards him. He had planned to catch it in his hand, but it missed – CRASH! – and went straight through the shed window.

"Oi!" shouted grumpy Mrs Arden three doors up. "Keep it down over there!"

"Bit rusty," murmured Merdyn. "This is why I need the practice!"

Over the next two hours Rose, her brother and Tamsin ran, jumped, skipped, hid, jumped out and generally made things as hard as they could. And gradually Merdyn got sharper and sharper.

Old bicycle helmets, bowling balls and tennis rackets all got FROZEN, ZAPPED and FRIED, until there was nothing left in the garden to destroy. By the end of the morning, they were all exhausted. Even Kris had had a whale of a time – until he saw his reflection in one of the few unbroken windows and noticed his eyebrows were overgrown. He immediately ran inside to do some emergency pruning.

Tamsin flopped down on the grass, where Rose was recuperating with her notebook in her hand. She was writing down all the herbs Merdyn had used moments earlier, when he'd finally renewed the pinecone spell that made Bubbles speak. She tried to remember the incantation too. **Primula veris, speakinsideoutside vernis opulus?** Something like that. She may not be a W-blood, but if Rose could master just this one spell, that would be enough for her.

"He's not so bad after all, is he?" Tamsin admitted. "This sure beats doing homework on a Saturday morning anyway."

"You do HOMEWORK on a *Saturday morning*?"

Rose said teasingly.

"Square," added Bubbles, who had taken up a seat on Kris's deckchair to watch the action and had already deposited thirty-five poos on it.

Tamsin ruffled Bubbles's fur affectionately.

Their conversation was interrupted by the sound of Suzy's voice.

"What ON EARTH . . .?"

Rose's mum was standing in the back doorway, newly coiffured for the big night out. Rose hardly recognised her. Gone was the couch potato with cheese puffs in her hair. Suzy now looked like she did in Rose's poster of The Mondays, vivid and alive.

"You look fantastic, Mum!" Rose gasped.

Merdyn was confused. A transformation like this was impossible in the Dark Ages where there were no hairdressers. "Have thou been to see a witch?"

"What?" Suzy replied, a bit insulted. "No, just Tracy from Hair Apparent on the high street. Never mind that, Martin, what's been going on here?" She gestured to the garden.

Rose looked around her. Oops. The garden looked a bit like a bomb had gone off underneath it. There were burnt garden tools and holes in the ground, frazzled shrubs and smashed windows.

"Sorry. We'll, er . . . get tidying," said Rose meekly.

"You'd better. Good job I'm in a nice mood!"

Much to everyone's relief, Suzy went back inside. She hadn't even noticed the pear tree.

Tamsin picked up a twisted golf club from the charred grass. "Come on, Rose. I'll help you," she said.

Rose's doubts were at an end.
She'd finally made a human friend.

CHAPTER TWENTY

LOVELORN COPPERS AND SECOND THOUGHTS IN CHOPPERS

Sergeant Murray was so in love with Rose's mum that he paid out of his own pocket to privately charter the POLICE HELICOPTER to take them all to London. At Rose's insistence, Suzy had told him that Uncle Martin suffered with severe car sickness, so Murray had used his rank to pull the favour.

"Strange that, seeing as he was a racing driver," observed Sergeant Murray, but Mum put it down to his head injury and they left it at that.

The helicopter caused quite a commotion when it landed on Daffodil Close. Dion was tinkering with his Pontiac Firebird in the street. He'd almost fixed the rear bodywork after Merdyn had crashed it. When he saw Suzy emerge from the house with her new hairdo and her 'going to London' crushed velvet mini-dress, his jaw hit the floor.

She looked like a movie star – and the helicopter escort did nothing to dispel the illusion.

Shakia and Kris had got dressed up too. Even Rose had changed into jeans (Bubbles had done a goodbye wee on her other trousers anyway) and a black top with sequins all over it. And Merdyn had asked Rose to straighten his pointy hat and brush the dried mud out of his long robes. Though even at his best, he still looked like a pirate who'd got lost on his way back from an all-night party.

The ancient warlock was clearly nervous as the helicopter (or "whirly-bird" as he called it) took off, but he found it much less puke-inducing than a car.

As they flew through the late afternoon sky, Rose and Merdyn marvelled at the sights below. Kris and Shakia leaned together against the windows opposite, headphones clamped over their ears and recording everything on their phones. Sergeant Murray was giving Suzy a potted history of the police force from 1845 to the present day. Mum was trying her best to enjoy it, but they were half an hour in, and he'd only just got to 1850.

Soon they were flying over London. Merdyn could

not believe his medieval eyes.

"In the name of Vanheldon, I have never seen such a transformation! 'Twas but a sewer once. Who liveth in those giant towers?" He pointed at a tower block. "The King?"

"Erm, no," said Rose. "Lots of different people live there, in flats. THAT'S where the Queen lives, look. Buckingham Palace."

"Heaven forfend!" said Merdyn, amazed at the size of the royal residence as they flew overhead.

"And that's Big Ben." Rose pointed out the famed clock tower.

"Who is he?" Merdyn asked. "A giant? Did he eateth all the fields? And is that his cartwheel?"

"No, that's the London Eye," said Rose, giggling.

"London hath an eye now?" the warlock exclaimed, shocked.

Rose giggled again, but a wave of sorrow quickly followed. She was suddenly realising how much she would miss these baffling conversations if they succeeded in getting Merdyn home tonight. How dull it would be without him, however annoying he could be.

And what would even happen tonight? She'd never been to a wizard duel before (obviously). Might Merdyn get hurt? Might anyone else? And what would her mum say when she found out the truth?

All of a sudden, the whole plan seemed like a big mistake.

Between you and me, Merdyn was worried too. Jerabo would be a powerful opponent. He had travelled all this way to confront Merdyn, and he would not give up easily. The warlock looked at Rose, then at her crazy family, and thought how he might even miss them. Desperate as he was to return to his own time, it wasn't ALL bad in this world.

"Rose," he said eventually.

She looked up at him.

"I could have bumped into a much worse person than thee in this strange land. You have shown me great kindness. And . . ." He desperately wanted to tell her that he would miss her, but after a long pause he only managed, "And . . . I shall make sure thou get thy singing spell before

I leaveth. Thou hath certainly earned it."

Rose desperately wanted to say that she wasn't even sure she needed the singing spell any more – that she wished she could call this whole thing off and keep her wizard friend living in her shed for ever. But she didn't either. "Thanks, Merdyn," she replied instead. "It's been fun." Then she turned and looked back out of the window.

In other words, reader,
they shut off their feelings,
and hoped for a night
of successful dealings.

CHAPTER TWENTY-ONE

FORGET WHAT THOU DOTH KNOW ABOUT THE MAGIC SHOW...

At last Rose, Merdyn the Wild, Sergeant Murray, Suzy, Kris and Shakia arrived at the theatre to watch Jerabo the Great. Merdyn attracted some very odd looks from the other theatre-goers as he passed through the gold-painted foyer. Inside, they found Sergeant Murray had pulled some favours with the management too (probably by threatening them with jail) and got them fantastic seats right in the middle of the stalls. The scarlet auditorium was packed, and the atmosphere crackled with anticipation. This magician had been completely unknown until a month ago. And now suddenly he was one of the most famous people in Britain.

As they headed to their seats, an eagle-eyed usher spotted Thundarian and tried to take it off the pumped-up warlock, as it was deemed an offensive weapon. He might as well have tried to take a juicy bone from a snarling dog.

"It's OK," said Sergeant Murray, waggling his grand moustache. "He's with me." And he flashed his badge, hoping to impress Suzy with his authority.

Kris and Shakia had gone crazy at the snack kiosk and bought several tonnes of popcorn, pick 'n' mix and fizzy drinks which they now shared out. While everyone else tucked into their snacks, Rose and Merdyn stared at the stage. All the great warlock had in his mind was victory. He kept patting the little leather pouch on his belt where he'd placed his disenchantment potion. He was ready to do battle. All Rose had in her mind was panic – what on earth had she let herself in for?

The lights went down and a blanket of hush descended over the audience. Only Kris could be heard crunching on his popcorn. Shakia had to give him a little elbow to make him stop. All was now eerily quiet and dark.

Suddenly, dramatic music punctured the silence. DO-DO-DO-DOOOO!

Relieved, Kris started crunching on his popcorn again.

"BEHOLD . . . THE EAGLE!" boomed a voice over the loudspeakers.

“’Tis Jerabo all right,” Merdyn said to Rose, recognising the voice of his foe immediately.

The stage curtains flew open. A spotlight flashed on, to reveal what looked like a man-sized eagle complete with feathers and beak.

“That’s him!” said Merdyn. “Damnation! He has perfected the eagle transformation spell on himself!”

The “eagle” thrust out a wing and a puff of smoke appeared from nowhere. It spread through the theatre in waves, as drums rolled loudly. BOOM di di BOOM BOOM BOOM.

“He produceth smoke! Not an easy task,” Merdyn whispered to Rose.

Rose knew – just as the audience did – that pyrotechnics could produce pretty spectacular results in the twenty-first century, but could they really do something this atmospheric? Surely not. And that was nothing compared to what they saw next.

For out of the smoke, the eagle FLEW.

“Gadsbudlikins!” Merdyn exclaimed in awe. “With such *speed* he flyeth!”

The crowd was enraptured. Oohs and aahs rang throughout the theatre, mingling with the jaunty flute notes that now trilled through the air as the eagle soared over their heads. FLAP FLAP FLAP. Even Rose was gobsmacked. It was incredibly impressive. She couldn't see any ropes or wires anywhere. This guy was the real deal. He MUST be a wizard from the past!

On to the stage came an actor dressed as a gamekeeper, complete with tweed jacket, deerstalker and plus fours.

"Damn these pesky eagles eating my crops!" he bellowed hammily. "I'm going to shoot him dead!"

He produced a shotgun from behind his back and took aim. "BOO!" went the audience happily.

The eagle shrieked when it saw the gun. "CAW! CAW! CAW!"

BANG! The gamekeeper's shotgun rang out. Merdyn grabbed Rose's arm.

"Erm . . . like, ow?" Rose said, feeling a bruise forming already.

"He shot him with the little cannon!" Merdyn hissed.

"The little carry cannon."

The warlock was hypnotised. Above their heads, the eagle swirled in circles as if shot dead, limply spiralling downwards with the spotlight upon him . . . and then, miraculously, he sprang to life again.

The theatre lights flashed every colour of the rainbow – FLASH, FLASH, FLASH – the music reached a crescendo – DUM DA DA DUM DUM DUM! – and the bird-man reached into his own mouth and pulled from his teeth . . . a bullet.

The crowd went berserk. Merdyn almost found himself clapping too. Shakia, Suzy, Sergeant Murray and Kris were applauding wildly.

But Rose wasn't.

Because she had spotted something that made her heart sink.

She had been as entranced as Merdyn until Jerabo/the eagle had landed back on the stage – where she was sure she saw him unclip a wire from his belt, which then shot up to the gantry at lightning speed. What kind of wizard would need a wire to fly?

Rose felt the blood drain from her head to her toes as the answer came to her.

The kind of wizard that was NOT a real wizard from the Dark Ages.

That was who.

In Rose's brain,
alarms went off like a blaster.
This evening might end
in total disaster!

CHAPTER TWENTY-TWO

AN AUDIENCE IS DAZED AND THE CURTAIN IS RAISED

The audience was still cheering as Rose regained her hearing. Jerabo the Great/the eagle had thrown a smoke bomb on the floor. When it cleared, he had transformed from an eagle into a man in a normal magician's outfit of black suit, white shirt and dickie bow tie, topped off with an annoying blond quiff. He took a bow.

But Rose was watching even closer this time and saw the eagle outfit disappear through a tiny trapdoor in the stage – along, she thought sadly, with Merdyn's hopes of finding his way back home.

"Merdyn!" she whispered. "I'm so sorry, but I don't think this is your guy after all."

"Of course 'tis him! Just look at him!" Merdyn hissed back. (Reader, you would concur if you could see him, he looked EXACTLY like the Jerabo we met in chapter one!) "Now be silent! I neededth to concentrate. His powers have improved greatly. This will be even harder than I thoughteth."

"And now!" announced Jerabo the Great from the stage. "I would like to ask for a brave volunteer."

Merdyn glanced at Rose with a determined look in his eye. "Here we goeth."

He started to rise to his feet. Rose pulled him back down. "Don't do this, Merdyn. Can't we just go and talk to him later backstage?" she pleaded.

"Thou do not knoweth Jerabo," he said. "The time for whiffle-whaffle has passed. There is only one way to solve this. Wish me luck." Merdyn got to his feet and shouted towards the stage, "I SHALL VOLUNTEERETH, SIRE!"

"Lovely jubbly," enthused Jerabo the Great. He peered into the crowd to identify the brave soul. "What's your name, mate?"

Merdyn thumped his staff upon the floor and shouted,

"Trillium peumus LEVITATO-US!"

This sent whispers through the crowd like a wildfire.

Hello? Who's this weirdo in fancy dress? was the rough translation. But they'd seen nothing yet. Moments later, Merdyn started to rise off the ground. The audience was baffled.

"Uncle Martin!" shouted Suzy, in bewilderment too. "What on earth are you doing?" She knew he'd become a bit eccentric since his accident – but now the ex-racing driver from Aberdeen was floating fully *two metres* in the air without the use of wires!

Kris and Shakia, on the other hand, were really enjoying it. They knew Merdyn's true identity, but the reveal to the rest of the world was proving even more dramatic than they'd expected. If they hadn't run out of sweets, the moment would have been perfect.

"Sit down, Martin!" Rose's mum continued to implore. "You're making a fool of yourself!"

"MY NAME IS MERDYN THE WILD!" Merdyn announced with great gravitas. **"THE GREATEST WARLOCK WHO EVER LIVETH!"**

"Who?" said Jerabo flippantly. From the stage, he still couldn't see the volunteer as the bright theatre lights shone in his face. "Do I know you, mate?"

"Oh thou knowest me, all right!" Merdyn continued as he floated towards the stage.

"AND THOSE WHO KNOWETH ME DO BOW DOWN BEFORE ME!"

The audience began to think Merdyn was part of the show, like the gamekeeper. But they were pretty unimpressed with his flying.

"Ugh, he's so slow," said one spoiled child. They had, after all, just seen an eagle zipping around the room faster than a jet fighter.

Rose couldn't look. She caught her mum staring at her though.

"Did *you* know Uncle Martin could fly?" Suzy asked angrily.

From the stage, Jerabo the Great could finally make out the figure of the scruffy warlock floating slowly towards him. He could hardly believe his eyes. He wondered if it was a rival magician come to torment him. "Call security," he whispered in a panic to a technician at the side of the stage.

Moments later, Merdyn landed gently beside the performing magician. Ever the professional, Jerabo smiled at the crowd. "A big round of applause for Mervin, er . . . what was your name again, pal?"

"Do not pretend thou don't knoweth me, thou coxcomb! Thou crook-nosed rakefire! Thou snake with two faces!" bellowed Merdyn.

Jerabo had experienced weird volunteers before, but this one was the full fruit-and-nutcake. He looked anxiously to the side of the stage again. To his relief, he saw two burly security guards waiting for his signal.

"Thou will suffer for what thou has done to me, thou piece of caffledecack*!" spat Merdyn.

All right, enough's enough, thought Jerabo the Great. And he nodded to the security team.

When the two burly guards rushed on to the stage, Rose knew what was coming next. Sure enough, Merdyn turned on his heels, waved Thundarian through the air in a figure of eight and cried,

"GELIDA GLACIA FROSTORA!"

---

*Well, it means poo, what more can I say?

Quick as a flash, he trapped the guards inside solid blocks of ice. *ZZZFRING!* The poor guards were frozen in a running position, which made them look like cartoon characters. Rose could just make out their terrified eyes darting from side to side, wondering what on earth had just happened.

The crowd gasped like they'd never gasped before. Whether this was part of the show or not, it was brilliant!

"What's he doing now?" cried Suzy.

"Would you like me to call for back-up?" asked Sergeant Murray. "Turning people into solid blocks of ice is *definitely* a crime under section 34 of the Grievous Bodily Harm Act."

Rose's mum didn't know what to say. She'd never had a member of the family encase someone inside a block of ice before.

"We need to get on to the stage!" Rose said. "NOW!"

Rose and her mum started shuffling their way along the row of seats. It wasn't easy. By now, the entire audience were holding their phones in their outstretched arms, recording the spectacle onstage.

The crowd's enthusiasm was not shared by Jerabo the Great. "I . . . I don't know who you think I am," he stammered as Merdyn strode menacingly towards him, "but I'm a black belt in karate. If you come any nearer, I'll be forced into attack mode . . ." He held up his hands in a karate pose. The magician's words rang hollow, however, as everybody could see his hands were shaking like leaves on a very blustery day.

Suddenly two more security men rushed on from the other side of the stage, but were stopped in their tracks as Merdyn unleashed TWO ENORMOUS, GLOWING FIREBALLS from his fingertips. POW! POW! The guards ducked behind a props table, which the fireballs then hit, incinerating a top hat, a dozen packs of cards and a bunch of fake plastic flowers. Kris and Shakia, who had stayed in their seats, were having the time of their lives.

"I *told* you he could do fireballs!" enthused Kris.

Finding himself alone and with his security guards out of action, Jerabo the Great abandoned his karate charade and decided to make a run for it. He figured diving into the audience was the wisest thing to do, as he could get lost in the crowd and Merdyn might accidentally hit a member of the public instead of him.

He ran full pelt toward the front of the stage. But Merdyn was too quick for him. He pointed Thundarian and shouted, **"ANIMA CHICKATIS!"**

Electricity crackled through the air and in the blink of an eye Jerabo turned into . . .

A chicken. CLUCK CLUCK CLUUUUUCK!

Not known for its flying abilities, the chicken flapped and squawked at the stage front, trapped by the footlights. The audience went ballistic. They'd never seen anything like this before.

The chicken flapped for the side curtains. Merdyn quickly cast another spell.

"ANIMA CHELONOIDIS TORTILLA!"

The squawking chicken turned into a giant tortoise and thudded on to the stage. THUMP! You could tell it was still trying to get away from Merdyn as its little scaly feet scrabbled desperately for traction against the smooth stage floor, but of course it was too slow – which was exactly

why Merdyn had chosen that particular animal.

The enraged warlock strode up to the tortoise and placed his staff upon its shell.

"ANIMA HOMINUM!" he chanted and WHUMPH! the tortoise changed back into (a very discombobulated) Jerabo the Great, now sprawled on the floor.

"Where is thy spellbook?" Merdyn demanded.

"I don't know what you're talking about!" Jerabo squirmed in terror.

"Thy spellbook with the Rivers of Time spell. 'Tis where?"

"I don't have a spellbook!"

Merdyn pulled a little brown bottle out of the pouch on his belt. "Thou might have made a Rivers of Time spell, but I have made something even more impressive! *This* is a disenchantment potion. It will take away thy magic powers for ever. I will give thee one chance to tell me where thy spellbook is before I make thee drinketh it!"

The audience were on the edge of their seats. They had come out for a night of magic, but were instead being treated to the best conjuring show ever, combined with a medieval soap opera.

"I'll be happy to drink that!" said Jerabo the Great. "If it means you'll leave me alone. I'm just a stage magician, mate. I'd never have auditioned for *Britain's Got Talented People* if I'd know it was going to get me into THIS much trouble! This is all fake, phoney trickery!"

The audience all looked at each other. Then why was he charging fifty quid a head?

Merdyn was surprised by Jerabo's tactic too, for very different reasons. The man he knew would never admit to being a fake. It must be a trick.

"Thou lieth! Thy spellbook. Last chance. Tell me or DIE!"

He thrust his hand towards Jerabo. Lightning bolts crackled from the end of his fingers. The electric tendrils licked at the stage magician's cheeks, ready to strike him dead.

Suddenly the audience felt the show had become a bit TOO REAL. Some of them started screaming to get out of the theatre. Others cowered behind their red velvet seats.

All was chaos, when a voice cut through the noise.

"He's telling the truth, Merdyn!"

The crazed warlock let his lightning bolts fizzle out. He turned to see Rose, now standing next to him onstage, with her mum and Sergeant Murray.

"This does not concerneth thee, Rose," said Merdyn angrily, and he turned his attention back to Jerabo, summoning the lightning from his fingers once again.

"We were wrong," Rose persisted. "He's not Jerabo. At least, not the Jerabo you remember. Believe me, I wish he was. But he just isn't."

"He must be! The spellbook. I needeth it . . ."

Rose reached out with both hands and grabbed the black drapes at the back of the stage. They quickly tore from the scaffold and fell to the stage floor, revealing, to Merdyn's astonishment . . .

A network of pulleys, ropes, wires and levers.

A couple of stagehands stared guiltily out at the crowd and waved. The actor who had played the gamekeeper was in the middle of getting changed into his next costume. He covered his bare bottom with a Roman centurion's helmet.

"I told you!" said the magician, almost relieved to have been exposed. "It's just tricks. I can't really fly! I can't catch a bullet in my teeth! I didn't even want to be a magician. I wanted to be an actor!"

Merdyn's lightning bolts fizzled out all together. He felt light-headed. To Rose, he suddenly looked old, frail even, as his eyes darted around the stage in confusion. "But . . . thou did summoneth me. The Magic Circle . . .?"

"The Magic Circle's just a club for magicians!" said Jerabo desperately. "Anyone can join! As long as they don't reveal their secrets. Which I don't . . . usually."

Merdyn's head spun. "Then thou art not Jeremiah Jerabo of Albion, who did sendeth me through the Rivers of Time?"

"No! My real name's Julian Smith! And I don't know where Albion is, but I'm from Winchester!" cried the stage magician, sensing for the first time that he might not die today after all. "Jerabo's just an old family name I thought sounded good!"

Merdyn sank to his knees. Tears filled his sad, bright blue eyes. "But if thou art not Jerabo of Albion, then . . .

how do I getteth home? How do I returneth to Evanhart?"

Rose suddenly saw that Merdyn held the rock with Evanhart's face carved into it. He'd been holding it like a comfort blanket the whole time.

She walked up to him and patted the back of his cloak. "I'm so sorry, Merdyn," she said gently.

Sensing that the drama had finally ended, the riveted audience (those who hadn't run out screaming already, that is) rose up from behind their seats and gave the players a standing ovation.

And Suzy fixed her daughter with a hostile glower. "This isn't Uncle Martin, is it, Rose?"

Oh, Mum, they spun
you a load of rot,
for Uncle Martin
this is not…

CHAPTER TWENTY-THREE

DREAMS KILLED AND HEARTS SPILLED

They all flew home in silence. The helicopter landed in Daffodil Close and Suzy asked if Sergeant Murray could drop Shakia at home in a police car which, of course, he sorted immediately. Rose's mum was so angry, she didn't even let Kris blow Shakia a kiss goodbye.

"I could arrest this Merdyn gentleman," offered Sergeant Murray as Shakia climbed into his squad car. "I could charge him for Impersonating a Relative. It's not strictly speaking a crime, but then neither is turning people into zoo animals, and he should be arrested for that an' all, if you ask me."

Suzy thanked Sergeant Murray but declined the offer. She would deal with this situation in her own way. He kissed her hand and bid her farewell.

Inside the house, Mum told Merdyn that he couldn't

live in the shed any more. He would have to find somewhere else tomorrow. Merdyn simply nodded.

"As thee wish, mistress," he said.

The evening's events had taken their toll on the ancient warlock, and he opened the back door and trudged silently to the shed. Rose was less muted. She tried to explain that Merdyn had travelled forward in time and she was just trying to help him get home, but her protestations fell on deaf ears.

"You can't just kick him out, Mum!" Rose cried.

"Yeah! Where's he going to live?" complained Kris, supporting his sister for a change.

"Not my problem," replied their mum sternly. "You both lied to me. You *knew* he wasn't your dad's brother all this time, and you let me keep thinking he was. I can't have a complete stranger living in the shed. And that's that!"

"But he's not a stranger to me," said Rose sadly. "He's my friend. He can be selfish and a little rude sometimes, but I think he has a good heart."

"And look at all the things he can do!" said Kris.

"Like throwing fireballs and freezing people into

blocks of ice?" Suzy countered. "By the time they were defrosted, those men had frostbite. Not to mention the damage to the theatre! I won't have my children put in danger. No thank you!"

"He did get a bit fast and loose with the fireballs, but he thought he was battling his arch-enemy! He can do nice things too, Mum," said Rose. "Like he made us all *invisible* and made us *float* and made Bubbles *talk* and—"

"And he made Sergeant Murray fall in love with you, with a love potion!" said Kris impulsively.

As soon as these words left his mouth, he wished he could hoover them back up again. He even did a sharp little intake of breath to see if it was possible. But alas – as any sensible reader knows – once words are said, they cannot be unsaid.

Suzy looked at the pair of them. If Merdyn could have made a spell to make her eyes speak, they would have screamed "DISAPPOINTMENT!" After letting her children squirm with guilt for fully seven seconds (which is a long time in guilt-world) she said only, "Go to your rooms. Merdyn will be leaving tomorrow."

After they'd gone, Suzy went to a drawer in the kitchen and pulled it open. Inside were a dozen framed photos of Barry, Rose's dad. She picked one out. It was her favourite photo from their honeymoon in Corfu. They had taken a selfie. It was in the days before camera phones, so it was a bit wonky. But there they were, love's young dream, their cheeks pressed together, eyes wide and happy, huge toothy grins spread across their faces, their young 'just married' hair blowing in the breeze against the bright blue sky.

It wasn't the discovery that Sergeant Murray didn't REALLY love her that upset her. It wasn't even the fact that her children had lied to her. It was that in Merdyn, she thought she'd found a connection to the kind, curly-brown-haired dreamer in the photo. Merdyn's eyes were bright blue, just like Barry's. Bright blue like sapphires. While she had thought Merdyn was Barry's brother, a little piece of him was close to her again. But Merdyn wasn't Barry's brother. He wasn't even born within a thousand years of Barry, if her children were to be believed.

Suzy put the dusty framed photo back in the drawer with the others, dropped on to the sofa and reached for a box of chocolate Congratulations. Outside in the hall, peering through the crack between the door and the wall, Rose swallowed a sob and ran up the stairs.

Back in her room, Rose gave Bubbles his food and water and filled him in sadly on the evening's drama.

"I did try to tell you that magic shows were rubbish," said Bubbles.

"You were right. Remind me to listen to you more in the future." Rose went to shut her bedroom curtains when – OH MY GOD! She jumped out of her skin.

"Is it a fox?" squealed Bubbles.

It wasn't a fox. It was Merdyn, hovering outside the window like something out of a horror film.

"May I come in?" he asked politely, his voice muffled by the double glazing.

Rose opened the window and Merdyn climbed in. Although it was easier said than done. The window was really too small for him, and he had to squeeze, turn, squirm – and eventually ask Rose to pull him in. She tugged at his arms until he popped through the frame like a champagne cork, tumbling over Rose's bed into her bookcase, sending a pile of books and her lamp crashing on to his head.

"OW!"

Rose looked at the saddened warlock lying on her floor. "You OK, Merdyn?"

"Rose. If I am to be in this land for ever, there's something I wanteth thee to know." Merdyn scrabbled through the books that had fallen around him until he found what he was looking for: *Witches, Wizards and Warlocks of Auld*, the book Rose had taken from the library that day.

"Thou once did asketh me why I chose the path of darkness," he said, leafing through the book.

"Merdyn, you've had a tough day, you don't have to—"

"No!" Merdyn interrupted. "I wanteth to show thee. The great war I did telleth thee about. It was against this fellow, Vanheldon."

He pointed to a drawing in the book. To Rose, the man looked like the lead singer of a death metal band. He wore black animal skins and leather. He had a necklace adorned with bears' teeth, a big black beard and a studded bull-horn helmet on his head. He grinned viciously out at her. She shuddered.

"A Viking?" she said, before remembering her history class. "Wait, Vikings didn't come 'til the ninth century or something, did they?"

"I have never heard of these *Vi-kings*," said Merdyn. "Vanheldon was King of the Vandals."

"Ooh," said Rose, excited. "We have that word. A *vandal* is someone who destroys something for no good reason."

Merdyn laughed darkly. "Could not be a more accurate description. They did cometh from Germania and cutteth a swathe through all of Albion. They did killeth men, women, children, horses, dogs, cats; anything that got in their way – and plenty that didn't. I fought hard for my King and country, but alas, I was captured in the battle of Alderly Forest.

"As I was W-blood, the Vandals did keepeth me as their slave, putting me in a cage for months and feeding me nought but scraps. Then one day I did overheareth Vanheldon talking. They were close to victory. They had the castle surrounded and were to attack in the morning. Vanheldon did taketh particular delight in describing how they would kill the King. But first he said they would . . ."

Merdyn faltered. Rose took his hand and squeezed it, nodding for him to carry on.

". . . but first they would kill the King's daughter, Evanhart. For nought but larks. Well, an anger did groweth inside me that was so hot it could have burned the forests of the earth. The Vandals had taken Thundarian from me, so I could not destroy them that way. However, I realised suddenly that beneath my cage did groweth wild grasses. I gathered five varieties: bearded darnel, cocksfoot, clover, pendulous sedge and witches grass. Vanheldon had a watchful eye on me at all times, but that night he had left for town to stock up on supplies. 'Twas then I did chanteth the stone spell . . . *Holcus stonerata!*

"I did casteth the spell through the whole battalion of Vandals. Every single one of them turned to stone that night. There it should have ended – but it did not." The warlock lowered his head woefully. "My anger was still burning so bright that next I did breaketh from my now unguarded cage to trigger . . . an oblivion spell."

"What's an oblivion spell?" asked Rose cautiously.

"It turneth stone to ash, and sendeth it into the clouds for ever," said Merdyn forlornly. "Vanheldon came back to findeth his entire army turned to dust and blown away in the wind. He did runneth back to Germania before I could do the same to him."

Merdyn paused.

"I did destroy them all, Rose," he said. "Some of those soldiers were not much older than thee. Once I had calmed down and realised the true horror of what I had done, I decided that I would care for no one but myself henceforth. For look what happened when I did careth. When I did tryeth to do good."

The warlock stared into the distance, as if reliving the horror. Even Bubbles stopped chewing for a moment, caught up in the tale.

"Listen, Merdyn," said Rose at last. "What you did back then? You were angry. They were going to hurt Evanhart, who you clearly love, FYI. I can understand how terrible you feel but I don't think that was the real you."

"Was it not?" Merdyn groaned, not even bothering to mention that he hadn't a clue what FYI meant. "Look what I did this night! I did nearly roasteth that poor charlatan like a chicken!"

"But you didn't," Rose reminded him. "Don't give up on the idea of doing good with your powers. Imagine how you could help people! It's not too late to make it into the history books."

Merdyn smiled at her. "Bless thee for saying so, child. But that sort of thing changeth a man. Maketh a man an island."

"Or a woman," Rose pointed out sadly. "That's what I did when my dad died, too. Shut people out. Life is very lonely that way, but at least you can't get hurt."

"Or hurt anyone else," added Merdyn thoughtfully. "Rose, I've been meaning to ask thee. What did happeneth to thy father?"

Rose wasn't expecting this question. But as Merdyn had been straight with her, she thought it only polite to answer, even though it made her feel uncomfortable.

"He . . . he had a rare heart condition," she stuttered. "It's complicated but, basically, his heart was kind of too big for him and one day it just . . . stopped."

"I am so sorry, Rose," said Merdyn. He meant it too.

"Anyway . . ." Rose continued, adopting an upbeat tone, "when he was alive, he was an inventor and he made some pretty cool stuff! He invented this in fact."

She took Bubbles out of his cage.

"What, guinea pigs?" yelped Bubbles, incredulously.

"Not you." Rose removed a tray from underneath the cage floor and showed Merdyn. The tray was full of poos. "Anyone who has a guinea pig knows their sawdust gets covered in poos mega quickly," she said. "So Dad invented a sub air system that pulls the poos through the bedding and safely into a tray below, leaving the sawdust above nice and clean. He called it a Poover." Rose smiled. "Get it? Poo hoover?"

"What be a hoover?" asked the warlock.

"I don't get it," said Bubbles.

". . . But I knoweth 'tis ingenious!" added Merdyn. "And in it, is thy father's spirit, I'll warrant."

"What do you mean?" asked Rose.

"Remember I toldeth thee that the earth is all one? Humans, animals, the grass, the trees, even *Poovers*. I tell thee, with this strange contraption, thy father is with thee always."

Rose thought about what Merdyn had just said then smiled. "Yeah. I like that. I like that a lot."

Merdyn nodded back, as if to say "of course you do, because it's true". Then he started to help Rose tidy up the books he'd knocked over.

Rose wasn't sure what would happen next. She'd keep trying to get Merdyn home, she guessed. By the looks of things with her mum, she needed that singing spell more than ever now. But at least she and Merdyn were in it together.

"Tomorrow we'd better find you somewhere else to live," she said as they finished tidying. "And you'll need to get a job."

"A job? Ugh! Heaven forfend," groaned Merdyn.

He floated up to the open window, banged his head a few times on the frame trying to get out, then drifted back towards the shed. Before she pulled the curtains, Rose watched as Merdyn shut the shed door behind him, and sighed.

In her head,
these words she said:
"I shall miss
the wizard in my shed."

CHAPTER TWENTY-FOUR

A FAILED HAM, AND A SANDWICH OF JAM

Julian Smith – aka Jerabo the Great – arrived back at his nice semi-detached house in Winchester (not far from Bashingford, actually) just after midnight. His wife, Carol, was waiting up for news of how the London show had gone. He had asked her not to come, as her watching him made him nervous. She was the only one who knew he didn't *really* want to be a magician. He wanted to be an actor, but had been rejected by the Royal Shakespeare Company more times than he cared to remember. They said he was too hammy. *Hammy?* What did that even mean? Idiots.

It didn't take Carol long to notice that her husband had had a bad night. It wasn't just the huffing and puffing and slamming of doors as he came in. It was the fact that he went straight into the kitchen and made himself a huge jam sandwich. He always made himself a big jam sandwich when he was feeling sad. He said it reminded him of his childhood, when life was more about Lego, trampolines and pet snails, and less about earning money, paying bills and being grown-up about stuff.

"How did it go?" she asked as Julian finally slumped into a chair by the fire and bit into the sweet snack.

"Terrible," he said, chewing. "My magic career is going the way of my acting one. Down the toilet."

He then spent half an hour ranting about how a madman had hijacked his show and nearly killed him. How he'd been forced to admit to the tricks of his trade, probably doing him out of a job for ever, even if it was a job he didn't like. How the crazy old fool that had ambushed his show – "He appeared to have REAL magical powers, by the way" – kept wittering on about a spellbook. Carol listened to the whole story wide-eyed with wonder, but it was the last bit that really caught her interest.

"Maybe he meant the spellbook your grandfather left you," she said.

"What spellbook? Which grandad?" Julian replied.

"Your mum's dad," said Carol. "He gave you a box of

stuff, remember? He said there was a spellbook in there, and you ought to *guard it with your life*."

Julian looked thoughtful. "Grandpa Jones? You sure?"

"Yes!" insisted Carol. "I remember him saying it because it was a *very* odd thing to say. And then two seconds later he died. I'm surprised you don't remember."

Julian squirmed. "Of course I remember! But Grandpa Jones was a hundred and two years old and as mad as a bag of wasps." He wracked his brain. "We still got this box?"

"It's in the attic." Carol yawned, kissed Julian on the forehead and went to bed.

Two hours later Julian had searched the attic from top to bottom. Nothing. Dammit! His heart had been racing. Maybe the book was worth some money. Or maybe, just *maybe*, it contained ACTUAL SPELLS. That madman who'd come up on the stage HAD performed real tricks, after all. Tricks that no one in their right mind could explain. Maybe this book would allow him to do real spells too.

Nonetheless, he was just about to give up when he stubbed his toe on a plastic Christmas tree from 1998.

"Stupid thing!" he yelled and kicked the tree across the attic. He plonked himself down on an old drum, pulled his jam sandwich from his cardigan pocket and munched for all he was worth. And when he looked up . . . there it was. The box his grandad had given him, covered in dust. It had been hiding behind the fake tree the whole time.

Julian set about rummaging through the box. Old bowling trophies, love letters from the war, trinkets and tokens from a long life were all thrown carelessly into the air. But then . . . right at the bottom of the box . . . a glimmer of GOLD. Julian lifted the object out, blew off the dust and took a closer look.

It was Jerabo's black and gold spellbook.

Why do I get
this smell in my nose
that this won't bode well
for poor Merdyn and Rose...?

CHAPTER TWENTY-FIVE

HOOKS, CROOKS AND SPELLBOOKS

Back in the Dark Ages, De Selby had been working day and night in the King's castle with his mono-cubal tracing machine to work out the exact date that Merdyn had landed after his journey through the Rivers of Time.

By now, oh great intelligent reader, I'm sure you've realised, De Selby had not been as successful as Merdyn and Rose supposed. On this, the seventy-second day of trying, De Selby was hard at work in his study as usual, tired and hungry.

Jeremiah Jerabo was just across the courtyard in his quarters, having a bath. Jerabo liked baths a lot. He had developed a spell to create bubbles in the bath, which had the effect of soothing his aching muscles. He could make a fortune if he patented it, he always thought. He would call it a jer-ach-soothy. No, a jach-oothy. No, a jacuzzi? That was it! A *jacuzzi!* He'd be rich!

Then he remembered that he didn't need an invention to make him rich, because he'd be King soon. Soothed even more by this thought, he dunked his face lazily into the bubbles – only to SNAP out of his daydream at the sound of De Selby shrieking.

He jumped up, grabbed his spellbook, pelted across the castle courtyard in his bare feet and burst through De Selby's door. He found the genius scientist in a state of great excitement.

"I have made a significant breakthrough!" the scientist began, before trailing off as he realised Jerabo was standing before him in just a towel.

But then . . . PARP PARP PARP! A trumpet sound emanated from the mono-cubal tracing machine. De Selby and Jerabo bent down together to look at the findings.

"He's in the twenty-first century!" said De Selby.

Then the pair danced happily about the room.

"Huzzah! This be it, De Selby!" said Jerabo.

"Yes, sire! This be it!" repeated the joyful scientist. "These readings are strong. Merdyn must have been using his staff liberally. It's almost as if he's been involved in a wizarding duel!"

"Ha!" said Jerabo. He put his spellbook on top of the tracing machine. "When I travelleth to the future, he'll get a duel all right. Now, do we have an exact date? I don't wanteth to go forward in time and be left hanging around for ever."

"Indeed," agreed De Selby. "But the readings are a still a little way off. Ideally, we would have another object which straddleth the centuries, with which to gain more precision. If only we had such a thing . . ."

No sooner had he said this than Jerabo's spellbook, which was still on top of the tracing machine, started vibrating. Both men noticed at once. Jerabo went to grab the book but De Selby stopped him:

"Wait! 'Tis picking up unusual vibrations."

Suddenly the book flew open. The pages started to flip this way and that.

"Extraordinary," mused the scientist. "'Tis as if someone is turning the pages elsewhere in time . . ."

"In the future?" asked the wicked wizard.

"Most certainly! It cannot be a coincidence. And with this new reading, we shall getteth a precise time coordinate soon. Down to the hour, maybe even the minute!"

Suddenly the pages stopped flicking. A strange red mark appeared in the corner of one of the pages, like a crimson shadow.

"What is that, De Selby?" whispered Jerabo, with awe in his voice. "'Tis . . . 'tis *blood*?"

De Selby examined the red stain carefully through his magnifying glass, then oddly, gave it a sniff. "No, sire. 'Tis . . ."

"I thinketh I'm right . . .
why yes, I am . . .
I do believe 'tis . . .
strawberry jam."

CHAPTER TWENTY-SIX

FROM LAME TO FAME – 'TIS A FUNNY OLD GAME!

Rose awoke on Sunday morning to yet another strange noise coming from the front garden. It sounded like someone was shouting. Was Sergeant Murray serenading her mum again? But then she heard more voices. *Many* more. It was like there was a football match going on outside.

On the landing, Rose bumped into her mum and brother, who had also woken up at the commotion outside. Together they shuffled half asleep to the front window to look. Then, let me tell you, they woke up pretty sharpish. For what they saw out of the window was a crowd of thirty or forty NEWS REPORTERS, standing in front of their house. Sergeant Murray and a wall of police officers were having to stop the throng from storming the front door.

"Back! Everybody back!" the sergeant was shouting.

Dion was trying to stop journalists putting cups of

coffee on his beloved car. "Watch your cappuccinos!" he yelled. "Have you never heard of ring stains?"

Kris was already checking his phone to see what all the fuss was about.

"It's Merdyn," he gushed. "He's famous! That stuff he did at the theatre last night? It's gone viral!"

He showed Rose his screen. There were hundreds of posts on YouTube from people who had taken videos on their phones. Some of the posts had over a million hits already.

Rose peered at the crowd. It wasn't just journalists. There were fans too. Some were even *dressed* as Merdyn the Wild, in long flowing robes, pointy hats, false beards and dark eyeliner. They had catchphrases too. "I bow down before thee!" some were chanting. Others shouted, "I am the wildest warlock who ever liveth!"

"All right then," said Suzy wearily. "If it's Merdyn they want, they can have him."

Down in the shed, Merdyn was already up and packing his things to go, as Mum had instructed. He was blissfully unaware of what was going on outside. And he refused to look at the footage on Kris's phone, even when Kris shoved it under his nose. "I do not desire to be hypnotised by thy startfoam, thank thee very much. 'Tis black magic."

"But, dude, you're famous!" Kris enthused. "You've made it!"

Rose was more cautious. "Merdyn, you don't have to talk to them if you don't feel like it."

"I am so pitch-kettled," said Merdyn. "Who is *they*?"

Kris couldn't believe Merdyn was being so blasé. "TV! NEWS! THE MEDIA. The world! That's who 'they' are."

As far as Suzy was concerned, fame meant fortune. And fortune meant this imposter could afford to move out of her shed. She ignored Rose's protests and ushered Merdyn through the house and out front to the baying crowd.

As soon as the press and his fans saw Merdyn emerging from the front door, they flew into a frenzy. They burst through the police line and thrust microphones, cameras and startfoams in his face.

"Merdyn, over here! Is it true you're a real wizard?" one yelled.

"Merdyn, *Bashingford Daily* here, we want an exclusive. Where are you from?" another babbled.

Then, "Is it natural? Or did you go to Hogwarts?"

The crowd guffawed at this, while someone else screamed for a selfie. Rose could hardly believe the madness. Cameras flashed like crazy. Merdyn just looked baffled.

Suddenly a handsome man in a tight blue suit and black, slicked-back hair thrust himself between the warlock and the microphones.

"Gentlemen, please! Merdyn will talk as soon as we see the green. No pay, no play. Now if you don't mind, I'd like a bit of privacy with my client, thank you and good day!" And the tight-suited man ushered Merdyn and the family back inside the house.

"Relax, team," he said, once everyone was in the kitchen.

"Who the heck are you?" asked Rose.

"I'm the one who just upped the fee fivefold for a moment with your wizard," he said with a wink, thrusting out his arm to shake Rose's hand. "Frederick Montague, agent to the stars. My mates call me Freddie. Or Monty. You choose. I prefer Freddie, FYI." He shook Merdyn's hand next. "Pleasure to meet you, big guy. You're a ledge. Total ledge, mate."

Merdyn looked to the others, confused.

"Legend," Kris explained helpfully.

"You just changed the entertainment industry overnight, buddy," said Freddie. "Those old-school magicians? They're phonies! They're history, my friend. See ya laterrrr! You are the future, Merds. Real magic rules. Sign with me today, I promise you a lot of money. Bank!"

That's right, reader. Freddie used the word 'bank' as a sort of punctuation. Rose had never heard it used this way before and she didn't like it. Kris hadn't heard it used this way either, and he LOVED it.

"I can get you on talk shows. Bank! Regional theatres. Bank! Stadium gigs. Bank! Endorsements. Adverts. Corporate gigs. Bank. Bank. BANK!"

"How about somewhere to live?" Suzy asked.

"Oh yeah, new homestead. Bank!" said Freddie. "I've

got you a beautiful penthouse suite in Clifton Towers, not far from here. It's got a jacuzzi, bank. It has a double refrigerator, bank. Ice machine. Soft-close doors. A tenpin-bowling lane. Bank."

"Ooh!" Merdyn was excited. "A bowling lane."

Rose looked at him, perplexed. "You've never even been bowling."

"No, but it soundeth fun."

"And fun it is!" said Freddie. "With a capital F. Look. I want to be your agent, Merds. But more than that. Me and you, Merds – we're gonna be great friends. What do you think?"

Rose pulled her warlock pal aside. "I'm not sure about this guy. My dad said never trust a man who wears shoes without socks."

Merdyn looked at Freddie. He DID look a little fopdoodly. A bit coxcomby too. His trousers were even tighter than the Top Boy ones Kris had made him wear. But what choice did he have?

"What am I to do, Rose?" he said, his frustration boiling up. "Thy mother hateth me, thanks to thy 'let's pretend I'm Uncle Martin' ruse. I have nowhere to live. And I'm stuck here for ever. Thou did sayeth thyself I should get a job. Well, Freddie's offering me one."

"But is this what you want? To be famous like this?" asked Rose.

Merdyn looked at Rose knowingly. "This from the girl whose goal in life is to win a singing competition?"

"That's different," Rose blurted out, a little stung. "I'm normal. You're W-blood! When we talked last night, you said you would use your powers for good!"

"No, Rose!" Merdyn snapped. "THOU did sayeth that. Not I!"

Rose almost jumped. Merdyn had never spoken to her like that before.

"I am not thy father!" Merdyn went on, his temper rising. "I am not a Mr Do-Good-in-his-Two-Shoes, as much as thou would liketh me to be!"

"Is it so bad to help people, rather than destroy them?" Rose volleyed back.

The two of them glared at each other angrily for a moment before Merdyn spun back towards Freddie. "The proposal thou just madeth. Run it past me again?"

Freddie beamed. "I want to be your agent, Merdster! What do thou sayest?"

"I sayeth . . . thou speaketh my language, Fred . . . ster. Thou art on."

Then Merdyn stormed out into the garden, leaving Rose fighting hard to keep the tears from spilling down her cheeks. She was sorry that she'd snapped at Merdyn, even though he'd started it. But maybe he was right. Maybe she had hoped he could fill the hole left by her father. She felt so silly now.

"Listen, Freddie, I could do with some work at the mo," said Kris suddenly. "And I'm kind of Merdyn's stylist, so can I have a job on the team? I'll sort his clothes, hair, the lot."

"Coolio! That's one stylist hired. Bank!"

"Bank!" repeated Kris and happily accepted Freddie's offer of a fist bump.

Rose watched all this, open-mouthed. Was she the only one who could see that the only BANK that would be getting full here was Freddie's? What was Kris doing, getting involved? Last night, she'd thought he was on her side. She'd thought they were finally on the same page. But now here he was, back to his old self.

Merdyn thundered back in with his meagre sack of belongings and Thundarian. He dipped into his money pouch and threw a pile of pebbles on the table.

"For thee, Mistress Suzy," he said. "By way of compensation for the nuisance I have caused."

"Some dirty stones? Great," said Mum.

"Come on, Freddie. Let's go," Merdyn hissed.

"But—" Rose began.

"Thou art going to ask about thy singing spell?" Merdyn snapped. "Do not worry. I will get it to thee. I supposeth I have my uses, after all, eh?" Then the warlock swept from the kitchen without a backward look.

Failing to read the room, Kris yelled, "Me too!" happily, before following Merdyn and the smarmy agent out. "Freddie, I'm going to need a sizable clothes budget, yeah?"

"Yeah, yeah, sure thing, Kris," Freddie reassured him before the front door slammed shut behind them all.

Rose and her mum stood in the kitchen in stunned silence.

"It's just life, Rose. It always lets you down one way or another," said Mum eventually. She headed back to the sofa, slumped in front of the TV and switched it on. "And after all you did for him! He didn't even say goodbye."

As if Rose hadn't already noticed.

Yes, wipe a tear
from your shining eye,
the thoughtless warlock
didn't even say goodbye.

CHAPTER TWENTY-SEVEN

OF WHAT FAME SMELLS AND PINECONE SPELLS

Oh dear, reader. I don't know whether you have ever had the misfortune to become famous, but there are three major pitfalls to avoid if you ever do. And here they are.

1. People do EVERYTHING for you. When you're famous, activities like making yourself a sandwich become a thing of the past. That sort of thing is done for you. And once things are done for you, then having to do those things yourself again can feel like a catastrophic failure. So if, for example, you had someone make your sandwiches for you for ten years, and then suddenly you had to make a sandwich for yourself – you'd HATE making that sandwich. All that effort. The butter. The fillings. Cutting

it into triangles. What a pain! Whereas before you were famous, you had no problem at all with making a sandwich.

2. You lose a sense of the value of money. When you have lots of money, you lose the joy in saving up for something special. Say you like fish and chips, and once a week you treat yourself to a nice big portion from your favourite fish and chip shop. It's a moment to be treasured and enjoyed, and you savour every delicious mouthful. But say you could afford to have fish and chips *every night of the week?* It wouldn't seem so special, would it? And soon you would end up HATING fish and chips.

3. You don't know who your true friends are. Being famous tends to increase the number of people that are around you at any one time. You might have an agent, a manager, a lawyer, a press person, a hair stylist, a wardrobe advisor,

a financial advisor, a diet advisor, a fitness trainer, a tenpin-bowling instructor, a driver, a biographer etc. You end up spending so much time with these people that you think they're your friends. So much so, that you forget who your *real* friends are.

Merdyn fell headlong into all three pits in a matter of days. It was oh so easy.

For a start, Freddie did EVERYTHING for him. Whereas before, Merdyn had insisted on collecting the herbs and plants for his spells from nature, now Freddie ordered them from Waitrose and the garden centre and had them delivered to the apartment. Rosemary, foxglove, mint, parsley and clover all came in little neat packets, ready to be crushed and powdered by Merdyn's personal assistants.

Merdyn started doing sell-out gigs in football stadiums, bringing in untold riches. Never mind going to a fish and chip shop; he BOUGHT the fish and chip shop and had it installed in his spare room.

As for Rose, she waited for Merdyn to bring her the singing spell he'd promised, but the days passed and he never came. She even tried to visit him at Clifton Towers but, once she'd got past all the screaming fans, she found herself blocked by Freddie the smarmy agent.

"Merds is just so busyrooney, freckle-face!"

Her brother was even worse. "No time, sis. It's tough at the top, you know."

If it hadn't been for his constant TV appearances on adverts, chat shows and variety events, she'd have forgotten what Merdyn looked like.

Rose was sad about how things had ended between them. But it all made sense. What had Merdyn said to her when first they met in the woods? "I am the greatest warlock who ever liveth!" How jealous was he of Harry Potter's fame? And Merlin? He hated them both for being more famous than him. Maybe fame was all Merdyn really cared about.

It must be, thought Rose. Because now he was getting fame in spades, she was nothing to him.

When she had met Merdyn, she'd felt that everything was going to get better. But instead, everything was worse.

For a start, school was terrible. She had thought that Tamsin would be her friend now, after all the fun they'd had. But on that first Monday back at school, she passed Tamsin in a corridor and Tamsin couldn't even look at her. Catrina had glared at Rose through her too-much-eyeliner eyes and Andie had crushed an apple with her fist in a weird show of strength (a waste of a good apple, in my mind) – but there was nothing from Tamsin. Rose hadn't expected a high five, but at least Tamsin might have said hello.

Rose was more of an island than ever.

She couldn't even talk to Bubbles any more. The pinecone spell had worn off again, and without Merdyn she couldn't renew it. Night after night she sat in her room with her notebook, trying to enchant the pinecone herself. She'd tried every combination of herb, plant and Latin word she'd captured in her notebook, but maybe she'd written everything down wrong. Primula vernum speakoutsideinside? Vibernum opuli? Aaaaaaargh!

Rose wasn't surprised she couldn't do it. She wasn't a W-blood. But she wasn't going to give up without trying.

As if all that wasn't bad enough, Suzy was even more depressed than before, especially now Kris had moved into Merdyn's apartment full-time. She didn't even get off the couch to go to bed now. She just fell asleep there, midway through a box of chocolates, woke up in the morning, switched the TV back on to documentaries about tragic singers and carried on. She didn't see Sergeant Murray any more either. The love potion had worn off, and he only had eyes for the police force again. Dion next door came around most days and offered to help out, but Mum just stared through him and popped another piece of confectionery into her mouth.

So in a nutshell, everyone was sadder than Sad Sadie McSadface on a wet Sadderday morning, but let's get back to the story, shall we? One night, Rose was cleaning out Bubbles's cage as usual. She was emptying her dad's Poover tray and marvelling once again at its brilliant engineering. Would she ever make him proud of her? She swallowed the giant lump in her throat and glanced up, catching sight of the calendar on her wall. It was the last week of the summer term, which meant . . . the last *Mountford's Got Talented People* heat was this Thursday, the day before the class trip to Stonehenge.

Rose had been so preoccupied with everything else, she had almost missed it. Suddenly her regret at how she had left things with Merdyn turned to anger. The least he could do was give her the singing spell he'd promised her! It was the only way left she could see to make everything all right again. She would go to Clifton Towers tomorrow before school and demand to see Merdyn. And this time, she wouldn't give up.

She would barge past Kris,
and Freddie, that chancer!
This time she wouldn't take no
for an answer!

CHAPTER TWENTY-EIGHT

ENOUGH BLATHERING, STORM CLOUDS GATHERING

"Finally we have it!" cried De Selby, the genius scientist. "The exact year, month, hour, minute that Merdyn is in the future. What a triumph of science! What an achievement!"

"Well done indeed," agreed Jeremiah Jerabo. "Now I will goeth through the Rivers of Time, killeth Merdyn the Wild, returneth, marrieth Evanhart and becometh heir apparent, killeth the King and imprisoneth my wife for ever. Then I shall ruleth over all of Albion!"

Jerabo finished his little speech only to find De Selby staring at him in horror once again. "Oopseth," he said. "Did I say 'imprisoneth my wife for ever' at the end of the list of bad things I'm going to do?"

The scientist continued to stare.

"Sorry, De Selby." There was now a large trace of menace in Jerabo's eyes. "I'm afraid I have told thee too much."

"N . . . not necessarily," De Selby stammered quickly. "I don't remember hearing anything after 'killeth the King' which I did already knoweth about, so . . ."

"Really?" said the awful wizard, evidently toying with De Selby. "Thou did not hear me say *imprisoneth Evanhart*?"

"Nope," said De Selby firmly.

"But thou did heareth that when I said it just then?"

"Heareth what?"

"That I would imprisoneth Evanhart!"

"Oh that!" said De Selby. "I could forget I heard that. I am a very forgetful person, sometimes I forgetteth my own . . ."

SHWANG!

De Selby hadn't even finished his sentence before Jerabo turned him into a tiny bird and locked him in a little cage.

"Me and my big mouth," said the wizard-villain to no one. He hadn't let his plan to imprison Evanhart slip at all, of course. He had *always* meant to get rid of De Selby as soon as he had Merdyn's exact location. But you knew that already, didn't you? Shame De Selby didn't. Jerabo opened his spellbook and smiled.

He flipped the pages
with his thumbs.
Watch out, future,
here the wicked wizard comes!

CHAPTER TWENTY-NINE

SPELLS UNWISE AND MERCHANDISE

Rose went to Clifton Towers the morning of the final *Mountford's Got Talented People* heat and refused to move until she saw Merdyn.

"You listen to *me*, greasylocks," she started as soon as Freddie answered the intercom buzzer. (Between you and me it was true, Freddie did put too much grease in his hair.) "Tell Merdyn I want my singing spell and I'm not leaving until I have it. It's the competition today!"

"Fine, I'll ask him," Freddie conceded, hugely offended. "If only to stop you bugging me."

Upstairs in the penthouse suite Freddie released the intercom buzzer and went to find Merdyn. This was no easy feat, such was the size of the place. It looked more like a busy office or factory than a home. The kitchen was full of people in white jumpsuits grinding herbs and flowers into powders and decanting them into labelled bottles, which they then put into a giant refrigerator.

Merdyn was in the sitting-room area. His appearance had changed a lot since we last saw him. His beard was clean and silky, his eyes weren't caked in mud and his robes smelled less like drains and more like lavender. On the sofa next to him was Rose's brother, and they were talking about the new range of Merdyn the Wild merchandise. There were bathrobes, hats, mugs, T-shirts and a magic set. There was even a Merdyn the Wild doll which, when you pulled its string, said: "*I am the greatest warlock who ever liveth! Bow down before me!*" Kris was particularly proud of this one.

"I think we should get the doll out for Christmas, Merds," he was enthusing as Freddie came into the lounge area looking flustered.

"Ah, Freddie," Merdyn said. "Who was at the door – *bleurgh*!" He spat out the tea he'd just been given. "Too sugary. Take it away, fool!" he bellowed to one of his assistants. "Before I turneth thee into a toad!"

"It's that girl again," moaned Freddie as the

trembling minion scurried off to fetch a new cup of tea for Merdyn. "Rose."

Merdyn waved Thundarian over a batch of bracelets that Kris was thrusting in his face, imbuing them with good fortune. "Who?"

"Do you mean my sister Rose?" Kris piped up, slapping a hundred-pound price sticker on the nearest 'lucky bracelet' and tossing it into a crate.

"That's the one," said Freddie. "She wants a singing spell or something?"

"She won't give up, Merds," warned Kris. "Take it from me. She's like a dog with a bone when she gets a bee in her bonnet."

Merdyn didn't have a clue what Kris was on about, but he felt a twinge of guilt. He hadn't given Rose a moment's thought in the past week.

"We've got no time for her, Merds!" insisted Freddie. "We've got a whirly-bird waiting on the roof to take us to the *Lazy Ladies* studio."

"All right. Let me getteth the spell for her at least," said Merdyn. "Kris, thou can take it down."

"Me?" protested Kris. "You need me to dress you."

"He's dressed already, you muppet!" barked Freddie.

Merdyn crossed to the kitchen. One of the jumpsuited underlings saw him coming, and passed him a small brown bottle.

"What be this, girl?" the celebrity warlock snapped impatiently.

"Your howling wolf spell, sir. For *Lazy Ladies*."

"Ah yes." Merdyn opened the fridge and peered inside. "And where are the singing spells? Why don't these bottles have labels? Thou fopdoodle!"

"Sorry, sir." The girl trembled. "Haven't had time today. Top right."

"Merds, let's go!" Freddie said.

Merdyn grabbed the singing spell bottle from the fridge. He paused as his conscience twinged once more. But then he shook himself firmly, tossed the singing spell to Kris, popped the howling wolf spell in his pocket and ran to join Freddie on the steps to the roof, where the whirly-bird was waiting.

Minutes later, Kris opened the ground-floor apartment

block door and handed Rose the bottle.

"One singing spell," he said. "Merdyn sends his apols but, you know. He's busy busy busy." He pointed at the helicopter rising into the clouds from the roof twenty-three storeys up.

Rose sighed at the sight of the fleeing Merdyn, but she had other concerns just then. Like why Kris was wearing such oversized sunglasses. His baseball cap was the wrong way round as well. She looked him in the eye. Or tried to. "Are you OK?"

Kris shrugged nonchalantly. "Yeah. Why?"

"Because I can't see your face, for a start. Why are you wearing those ridiculous sunglasses?"

"Because if I don't, they'll go craaazeee." Kris pointed to the crowd of Merdyn fans and paparazzi behind Rose.

"Why?" Rose was perplexed. "You're not the famous one."

"No. But I *am* the good-looking one."

It was clear to Rose that Kris had finally got so vain that his brain had exploded. "What on earth are you talking about?" she said.

"Check this out." Kris whipped off his glasses and hat and directed a kilowatt smile at the crowd outside. Suddenly they all went crazy. Grown girls and boys screamed and wailed like he was a pop star. The paparazzi snapped like crocodiles in a feeding frenzy. One teenage boy even started crying.

Rose looked closely at Kris's face. It WAS different. His cheekbones seemed higher, his eyes bigger, his nose smaller. His eyebrows looked like they'd been plucked by the gods and he glowed like he had a lightbulb where his brain should have been.

"See?" Kris said, beaming from ear to ear as he put his glasses and hat back on.

"Merdyn gave you a handsome spell, didn't he?" Rose guessed, horrified.

"For all my hard work. Great, isn't it?"

Rose didn't know what to say. So, as always, she plumped for honesty. "No, Kris. It isn't great. You look like a human Barbie doll! What does Shakia think?"

"She . . . doesn't like it, actually," Kris admitted. "She preferred it when I was just really good looking, as opposed to really, really, *really* good looking."

For a moment, Rose could see the old Kris in his saddened eyes behind the glasses, but then he turned to go. "One last thing, Kris," she said. "Would you give Merdyn this?"

She dug into her school bag and handed over a pinecone. Her brother looked at it quizzically.

"I need him to enchant it," said Rose. "To make Bubbles speak again. There's a note inside. Make sure he gets it, will you? Don't just put it in the bin."

"As if I would!" Kris said. Then he disappeared back inside the doors.

Rose walked away. Slowly at first, but then she started striding, faster and faster. Fine. If Merdyn didn't want to see her again, that was just *fine*. At least she'd got the singing spell. Now it was up to her.

Kris's handsome spell
was something tragic,
but if it gets her what she wants
why shouldn't Rose use magic!

CHAPTER THIRTY

LIGHTNING STRIKES TWICE, THIS WIZARD'S NOT NICE

It had been a tough few weeks for Jim and Alan. First there was the mayhem caused by Merdyn the Wild as he conjured Thundarian from deep within the old well. Then there was the subsequent dematerialisation act of the warlock and three kids. What a business that had been.

The Oldwell Shopping Centre management had given them both some time off for therapy, which they'd found very valuable. Now they were back guarding the ornamental garden and all was well. It was a quiet morning. There was no trouble in sight, and the traumatic events of Merdyn the Wild were firmly behind them. They could even laugh about it now.

"Do you remember that song he sang?" Jim reminisced in a jolly tone.

Alan laughed. "The one about herbs and

plants and things?"

"That's the one. You know he's released it as a record now?" said Jim.

"I did not know that," said Alan. "So, he wasn't just trying to pull the wool over our eyes?"

"Well he was *then*," said Jim. "But now he's a famous magician and stuff, so he's cashing in with a novelty record. My therapist said I shouldn't let it bother me, but let it be a lesson instead."

"What lesson's that?"

"To expect the unexpected," Jim said triumphantly.

Right on cue, a shining green light appeared behind them. A familiar feeling of dread pulsed through Jim and Alan's beating hearts. They turned their heads slowly.

The light was coming from the fake grass in the ornamental garden. Suddenly the ground opened up as if someone was pulling an enormous zip. The sides parted to reveal a huge dark mouth, which spat out . . .

A man.

As soon as it had deposited the man WHUMP! the mouth slammed shut and zipped back up again.

The morning shoppers barely noticed. They were all busy shopping or texting on their phones. But Jim and Alan's eyes were like wagon wheels, and their mouths like Pez dispensers.

Oddly, the new arrival looked exactly like the fellow who'd won *Britain's Most Talented People* recently: all quiffy blond hair, narrow eyes and thin lips. Except THIS version wore an ornate black and gold tunic, tights and a cape. His eyes adjusted to the light and he looked around in wonder. Finally, his gaze settled on the stunned security guards.

"Thou there!" he ordered. "What century be this?"

"Er, twentieth?" said Jim, in a shaky voice.

"Twenty-first," Alan corrected. It's an easy mistake for those much older than you to make.

"*Gooooooood!*" said Jeremiah Jerabo – because that's who it was, of course, though I'm sure YOU already realised that. He turned his attention properly to Jim and Alan. What strange clothes these future people wore. Uniforms of sorts?

"And who might thou be?" Jerabo demanded. "Important keepers of the Rivers of Time, perhaps?"

Alan remembered his counselling. *Don't let anyone undermine you. YOU are in charge, Alan,* he said to himself. "We're people you don't wanna mess with," he declared out loud.

Jim took his lead from Alan. No more Mr Nice Guy. "Yeah! Mess with us and we'll teach you a lesson you'll never forget," he added.

Jerabo proceeded with caution. Who knew how advanced magic had become in the future? How far humans had come in harnessing the awesome power of nature? "Art thou wizards?" he asked the dumbfounded pair. "Warlocks? Speak!"

"That's right, mate. We're wizards," Alan quipped. "And as soon as we say the magic words '*You're under arrest*', you, my friend, will *magically* go straight to jail!"

Jim thought that was a brilliant line from Alan. They both gave a self-satisfied chuckle.

Jerabo couldn't risk going to jail. It would be terrible for his plans. He decided to call their bluff. "Very well, future wizards," he said. "Let us have a wizard battle and settle this quickly."

"Do w-what?" asked Jim. But the words had hardly left his lips when . . .

"ANIMA PORCINEUS-PIGGUS!"

Jerabo chanted a spell from his book and SHWONG! turned Jim into a pig.

Alan looked in horror at his now porcine friend. He reached for his pepper spray and unclipped his truncheon, both of which he held toward the wizard in a threatening manner.

"Is that all thou have?" Jerabo scoffed.

"Erm, yeah," said Alan. "We're not allowed guns or even tasers at our level."

SHWONG! In a trice, Jerabo turned Alan into a pig too. Both porkers took off down the mall, squealing and weaving in and out of startled shoppers.

The evil sixth-century wizard stepped out of the ornamental garden and walked through the shopping centre, taking in his new surroundings. There were lots of bright colours. Flashing lights. But where was the nature?

The people were *weak*, Jerabo concluded. Enslaved to the small black tablets in their hands. Some had even plugged their *ears* into them. It was clear they knew no magic, had no nature. This was going to be EASY.

But Jerabo's itinerary was thrown into disarray when he saw Merdyn's face right in front of him. He was only five minutes in this new world and he had already found his foe, here in this brightly coloured market!

Merdyn seemed to be talking to some painted ladies. They were all sitting, shrunken, in a little box inside one of the market stalls.

Jerabo decided to vanquish Merdyn on the spot. He pulled his sword from under his cloak and shouted, "Prepare to meet thy death, you cur!"

Then he ran at full speed towards his foe and . . . WHUMP! . . . ran straight into the window of the TV shop.

What a strange place, thought the evil wizard as a kindly old lady helped him up off the floor. Maybe there was magic here after all.

"Are you all right, dear?" the elderly lady asked.

"Yes. Thank you, old hag," said Jerabo, a little dazed.

The woman was wondering if he'd really just called

her an 'old hag' when she was distracted by his face. "Hey, it's you!" she said. "You're Jerabo the Great."

Jerabo was flattered that his fame had travelled fifteen hundred years into the future. "I am he," he announced grandly.

"That Merdyn fellow certainly gave you a good hiding," the old lady said, puncturing the moment. "You recovered yet?"

Jerabo thought he must be dreaming. "What meanest thou? Merdyn the Wild, get the better of *me*? Never."

The woman got her phone out to show him otherwise.

The wizard's mind was promptly blown. The little theatre inside the tablet was *tiny*. And there was someone in it who looked exactly like him.

"What be this depiction?" he enquired frantically. "This be happening now?"

"This was about a month ago," said the lady. She frowned. "I heard you took it badly, but this is ridiculous."

Realisation dawned on Jerabo. "This is not me," he said. "Why, it must be my offspring! My progeny! That's who was leafing through my spellbook! He's the one who liketh strawberry jam! Tell me, can thou direct me to this youngling's abode?"

"You mean where does he live?" the kindly granny said. "I don't know."

"I desperately need to find him!" cried Jerabo. "You see, he is my great grandson!"

The old lady stared at him quizzically. "His real name's Julian Smith, I know that. You could look him up in the phone book, I suppose."

"The foam-book?" Jerabo repeated, in that way that people from the sixth century do. Apparently.

"*Phone* book!" she shouted, in case he was a bit deaf. "Should have his address in there, I would have thought!"

Jerabo's eyes filled with tears. He was an unsentimental fellow, but even he felt overwhelmed at the thought of meeting his great

great great great great great great great great grandson.

"Very well. I shall findeth him in this foambook," he said. "Then my descendant and I will killeth Merdyn together. It can be a family outing!" He had to bite his own fist, such was the emotion coursing through his veins.

"You're going to do what?" said the old lady.

"Many thanks for thy help, old hag." Jerabo dipped his hand into his purse and threw some dirty stones at her. "Here. For thy time."

Realising now that she *hadn't* misheard the words 'old hag' first time round, the woman began thwacking him repeatedly over the head with her handbag.

Maybe not all of them are weak,
Jerabo's inner voice said . . .
as the handbag pummelled
him over the head.

CHAPTER THIRTY-ONE

THE TRICKS MIX

Lazy Ladies was a TV talkshow where a panel of laid-back women talked to guests about anything and everything, usually touching on something they wished to promote. Merdyn was plugging his huge new shows at Wembley stadium and a new line of "Thundarian" magic staffs (a bargain at £34.99) so Freddie had figured *Lazy Ladies* was perfect.

At the same time, Rose was standing backstage in the school assembly hall, getting ready for her performance for the *Mountford's Got Talented People* heat. She'd chosen "Beautiful" by Christina Aguilera. It was a song she knew inside out and she liked its message of positivity. All she needed was the pipes to sing it – and Merdyn had, finally, provided those. She held the bottle tightly in her hand and unscrewed the lid.

She was about to take a swig when she saw Tamsin coming towards her.

"Hey, Rose," Tamsin said a little nervously. "I just wanted to wish you good luck. But for what it's worth, I don't think you need this."

Rose was confused. "What do you mean?"

"I just think you're so much better than you think you are," said Tamsin. "Just be you, Rose."

Rose glowered. "That's rich. You can't even 'be you' enough to say hello to me in the halls!"

"And now," boomed the tannoy suddenly, "please welcome back . . . Rose Falvey!"

Rose pushed past Tamsin into the wings. What did Tamsin know anyway? Winning this competition and becoming a star would solve everything. Her mum would get off the couch. Kris would respect her. She'd finally be the special person her dad always told her she'd be, and she'd finally make him proud. Everything would make sense. She'd tried being herself, just the way she was, and it hadn't worked. This was the only way!

Rose took a deep breath, gulped down the foul-tasting singing spell and strode confidently on to the stage.

Meanwhile, on *Lazy Ladies*, Merdyn had been asked to show off one of his spells. Merdyn faked surprise, although this had of course been planned all along.

"All right. Which of thee ladies would liketh to howl like a wolf?" Merdyn asked.

The women all giggled before one of them, Linda, bravely volunteered.

"I warneth thou," said Merdyn. "For nigh on five cock-crows* thou shall not speaketh a word. The only sound that will leaveth thy mouth will be the *howl of a wolf*."

"Don't call your husband, then!" said another Lazy Lady, improvising.

"He probably won't even notice!" Linda bantered back, and they and the studio audience laughed like hyenas.

Merdyn opened the little brown bottle and offered it

---

*Nearly five minutes – remember this, it's important to the story, any moment now ...

to Linda. Linda took a sip, smiled nervously, then opened her mouth to talk.

BUT . . .

Instead of howling like a wolf, she SANG like an angel. In fact, everything she said came out in beautifully pitched operatic notes.

"*I harrrdly feel any differrrrrrent,*" Linda thrust a hand over her mouth, then opened it again and sang, "*Wait a minute. I thought I was meant to howl like a wolf. This sounds beautifuuuuul!*"

The crowd went wild. They stood up and applauded, thinking it was part of the act. Merdyn laughed along. But this wasn't the plan at all. What had happened?

Then he remembered how much of a rush he'd been in, leaving the penthouse earlier. How he'd given Kris a singing spell to pass to Rose and put the howling spell in his pocket. A terrible thought was released into the neural pathways of Merdyn's brain.

But if THIS was the *singing* spell, then . . . Then what did Rose have?

The audience at *Mountford's Got Talented People* fell silent. Tamsin took her seat next to Catrina and Andie.

"Where've you been?" hissed Andie.

"You better not have been talking to Rose," Catrina whispered. "I've told you, it's either *her* or *us*."

"Relax. I just went to the loo," lied Tamsin.

Rose made her way out to the centre of the stage and the music began. *This is it*, she thought. This was the moment her life came into focus. The great mystery of what her dad thought she'd be great at would finally be solved. It wasn't even a question of practice. It was going to be magic! Get a load of this voice, world!

Rose opened her mouth and . . .

"*Howoooowoowooowooowooowl!*" came the sound, like something out of a horror film. The audience's mouths fell open. Rose wondered if she'd heard her own voice wrongly. That didn't sound like good singing. It sounded like . . . a howling wolf.

She tried again.

"You're beautifuoooooooowoowooowoooooooowl!"

Nope. It was no mistake. She sounded like a wolf all right. Worse than a wolf, if anything. More like fingernails on a chalkboard.

"Hoooowwooooooooooooooowl!"

There it was again.

There was a moment's pause. Then the WHOLE

SCHOOL burst out laughing.

"HA HA HA HA HA!"

Catrina and Andie were laughing loudest of all. "HA HA HA HA HAHAAAAA!" But Tamsin wasn't.

"It's funny, Tam! Laugh!" Catrina demanded, laughing so hard her lipstick smudged into her cheeks.

"Yeah, get with the programme!" Andie demanded in her deep, strong voice.

Tamsin forced a snort.

Rose saw everyone laughing at her, now including Tamsin. If this had been the animal impression Olympics, Rose would have won a gold medal. But it wasn't. Instead, it was the worst moment of her life. In fact, of all the many worst moments in her life, this one felt like the *worst* worst of them all. Humiliated again. In front of the whole school.

Rose burst out crying and ran from the stage as fast as her legs could carry her.

"Well, that was a *howling* success!" Rose heard one of the judges say through a microphone as she sprinted out of the theatre, out of the school and through the school gates. How could Merdyn do this to her? Had he done it on purpose? She'd once said that she thought Merdyn was good at heart. But now, as she pounded the pavement, crying all the way home, she wondered how black the devious warlock's heart could get.

"I hate you, Merdyn!" she screamed.
"I wish we'd never MET!"

CHAPTER THIRTY-TWO

THE ASCENDANCE OF THE DESCENDANTS

Julian Smith (formerly Jerabo the Great) sat down every day and night by the fire and read out spells from the black and gold book he'd found in the attic on the night of his humiliation at the hands of Merdyn the Wild. But alas he couldn't conjure up a single bit of real magic. To add insult to injury, he'd had to watch Merdyn become a global superstar while his own star waned terribly.

He was about to give up when he received a visit from his great grandfather.

The real Jeremiah Jerabo had found Julian's house that afternoon and had been watching him from outside the window for some time.

"My progeny!" he whispered proudly as Julian got angrier and angrier with each failed spell. "How he looketh like me! How handsome he is. Such fine hair!"

But now, the time had come to meet. Jerabo performed a dematerialisation spell and passed through the window so that he was in the same room as Julian at last.

"Hello, grandson!" he announced.

Julian leaped off the sofa, grabbed a poker from the fireplace and shook it at the hooded intruder. "Who the heck are you? What do you want? I don't have any money! Who are you?"

"My child," said Jerabo softly. "My offspring. 'Tis I."

"Who?" said Julian.

"Why, thy great great great great great great great great great great great great great (seriously? *Every time*?) great grandfather."

Jerabo stepped into the light and pulled his hood down. Julian could scarcely believe his eyes. "Wow!" he said. "You look just like me. So handsome. Such fine hair!"

"Of course I looketh like thee!" enthused Jerabo. "Or should I say *thou* looketh like *me*. I am thy ancestor from long ago, travelled forward in time to visit thee. Thou art my progeny!"

"OK. So . . . nice to meet you, great great great great blah blah grandfather," said Julian slowly, unsure how to take the news. He remembered something. "How long are you going to stay actually? Because I'll have to ask my wife, Carol. And we're decorating the spare room so you'll have to sleep on the couch."

"Young Jerabo!" Jeremiah boomed, slightly angrily.

"Actually, my name's Julian," Julian corrected him.

"Ju-LION!" boomed Jerabo less *slightly* and more *actually* angrily. "I'm not sure thou art completely grasping the enormity of what has happened here. Sit down."

Jerabo then explained the situation to his (great times thirty-six) grandson as speedily as he could. He told him how he had travelled through the Rivers of Time to destroy Merdyn. Then how he was going to go back to the Dark Ages and claim the throne for the family name. He decided *not* to tell Julian about killing the King and imprisoning his wife, just in case he wasn't into that sort of thing.

When Jerabo had finished, Julian paced up and down in front of the fire pinching the bridge of his nose. "OK," he said. "I'm into this plan. Really into it. Finish Merdyn, blah blah blah. I mean I hate him. But after it's done, you go back, become King or whatever, while muggins here is still left with no career and no money. What I'm saying, is . . . what's in it for me, Great Etcetera Grandad?"

Jerabo looked at Julian with tears in his eyes. "Ah *Ju-lion*!" he said proudly. "Thou art truly a Jerabo. Don't thou understandeth? If I becometh King in the past, then THOU shall likely becometh King in the future. Now."

"Hm, yeah," said Julian. "But being King isn't what it used to be. The prime minister runs the country now."

Jerabo rolled his eyes. Wow, his progeny was annoying. "I shall teach thou how to use thy spellbook, how about that? Then thou can rule over this *prime minister* too. And anyone else thou wanteth to. THOU shall be King of this pathetic world without magic. THOU, my child."

"Now we're talking. That WOULD be cool." Julian was excited. To become a magician so powerful that he ruled not just the country but the world? Wouldn't that be something! Wouldn't that teach those fools at the Royal Shakespeare Company a thing or two? He could take over the whole blooming theatre and play all the parts himself!

"But first," said Jerabo, getting down to business. "We must deal with Merdyn the Wild. He is the only one who can stop us. But it won't be easy. He will not just rolleth over and giveth in to us. We need to be cunning. Trappeth him somehow . . . Merdyn playeth the heart of stone, but really he is a sentimental fool. Tell me, has he struck up any kinships while here? Who does he care for? If we can get to them, we can make Merdyn do whatever we desireth."

A smile started to play across Julian's thin lips. "There is someone he cares for actually. She was there that night at the theatre. A little girl with fuzzy hair and glasses."

"A little girl with fizzy hair and gasses?" repeated Jerabo, mishearing but still liking the sound of this.

Julian nodded. "A little, pointless sort of girl. And her name was . . ." He scratched his head and pulled his nose.

"I seem to remember
her name was . . . Rose."

CHAPTER THIRTY-THREE

LOOK WHO'S WALKING, LOOK WHO'S TALKING!

In the helicopter after his *Lazy Ladies* triumph, Merdyn asked the time.

"Three-thirty, mate," said Freddie.

"So schools are still open or . . .?"

"Schools are out by three-thirty. Why?"

"Nothing," said Merdyn, and he looked back out of the window. Since realising his potion mix-up, he'd had a strange feeling in his stomach that he couldn't fathom. "Methinks I might take the night off, Freddie," he said now. "I'm feeling a little unwell."

When he got back to his penthouse suite, Merdyn's stomach was aching so much he threw everybody out. He threw out the personal assistants. He threw out the people who bottled his potions. He threw out Kris.

"Where am I supposed to go?" Kris asked.

"Go and see thy love, Shakia," said Merdyn. "Do not be a fool and letteth her slip from thy fingers, thou loiter-sack*."

So Kris headed to Shakia's, even though she had said she didn't want to see him again until he WASN'T the best-looking boy on the planet. (How many girls are brave enough to say that?)

Merdyn even threw out his agent.

"Merds!" Freddie pleaded. "What's your beef, buddy?"

"I needeth some space, thou rakefire!" Merdyn hissed, though he wasn't sure what beef had to do with it.

Then Merdyn ordered seven portions of fish and chips from his personal fish and chip shop, and sent the chef home too. He rolled a few balls in his personal tenpin-bowling lane. He'd got pretty good at bowling lately. He got a strike every time. But even this didn't make him feel any better. Then he threw himself on to his sofa and watched the entire Harry Potter franchise back-to-back. He remembered how he'd seen the first film with Rose

---

*This literally means someone who loiters (lies around) in their sack (old word for bed) all day. So next time your mum or dad calls you a lazybones for staying in bed, say "You mean '*loiter-sack*'." This will be sure to improve their mood! (It won't.)

and her family at their house that night. He recalled how they'd all laughed as he'd kept complaining about magical and historical inaccuracies.

He fell asleep during *Harry Potter and the Deathly Hallows (Part 2)* and awoke the next morning with a battered cod stuck to his face.

Merdyn still felt the aching in his stomach. He realised that he'd fallen asleep clutching the stone with Evanhart's likeness etched into it, and he looked at her beautiful face and sighed, "Oh Evanhart, if only thou were here. Thou would telleth me what aileth me."

Then, to his astonishment he heard a voice.

"I'll telleth thee what aileth thee, thou fusty-lugged coxcomb*!"

Merdyn sat up and looked at his beloved's face in the stone again. "Evanhart?" He gasped.

"Does this soundeth like Evanhart's voice, thou fopdoodle?"

It didn't sound anything like Evanhart. It was a male voice, for a start. Also, not human. It was more nasal, beaky . . . bird-like, even? Whoever it was, they were

---

*Hard of hearing show-off. That's not very nice, is it?

being quite rude.

"Over here!" piped up the voice again. "In the rubble bucket!"

Merdyn's eyes darted around until they fell upon Thundarian, propped upside down against a wall with its top end in a wastepaper basket. He quickly scrambled across the fish-and-chip-strewn carpet and plucked his beloved staff from the bin. Its head was covered in battered fish skin, bits of paper and, incongruously, a pinecone. Merdyn wiped the rubbish off and stared into the face of the noble eagle carving.

"Was that thee, great eagle? Thundarian, did thou speak?"

Nothing. Merdyn blinked. Had he imagined it? Then he looked down at the pinecone he'd discarded at his feet. He noticed now that it had a folded piece of paper wedged in between its scales. He pulled it out and opened it. It said simply: I tried but couldn't do it, can you please? – R.

What did it mean? Was this some kind of strange code?

I think you'll agree that Merdyn was being particularly

stupid this morning. It was probably all those chips the night before, but gradually the cogs of his brain started to whirr. Pinecone? Strange talking . . .? Could it possibly be . . .? Slowly, he placed the pinecone against the eagle's head and . . . It sprang back into life.

"At last. The fool gets it!" squawked the wooden bird.

"I do?" said Merdyn.

"Now, where was I?" Thundarian spoke in a haughty yet authoritative voice, like a stern but fair headteacher. "Ah yes. I'll telleth thee what aileth thee, Merdyn the Wild. Thou feeleth so dire because thou did letteth that poor girl down so *abysmally*."

"Girl?" repeated Merdyn. "Thou meanest Rose? I feel bad because of . . . Rose?"

"Yes, thou cloth-eared nincompoop!" said Thundarian. "Because thou knoweth in thy heart that she was right about thee. Thou should be using thy powers for good. She could see that somewhere inside that foolish heart of thine is a wizard, not a warlock. And she could see it because the pitiful girl did looketh up to thee. Not as a father, but a father *figure*. A friend, even. And what did thou do? Thou did mocketh her like a cold-hearted jester, and abandoneth her in her hour of need."

"I was—" Merdyn started to protest.

"Thou were what? Too busy?" The wooden eagle interrupted. "Busy doing what? Being famous? Having your ego massaged? Being a HUFTY TUFTY? Look at what thou have become in such a short space of time! Thou have divorced nature! A refrigerator full of spells that servants bottleth for thee? A fish and chip shop in thy house? That *feeling* in thy belly, Merdyn the Wild, is *shame*. Shame that thou have let down someone thou loveth."

These words sank in. "Zounds, thou art right!" Merdyn gasped. "I do care for Rose. I careth as if she were mine own child. It's Rose! That's why I feeleth so bad . . ."

"Finally, the bell ringeth for the dunderhead!" the staff hollered.

"But wait, Thundarian," said Merdyn. "There is still one thing I do not understandeth. Who did enchant the pinecone? 'Twas not me."

"*Look at the note*, thou ninnyhammer*!"

---

* *Ninny* is a word you may know meaning idiot. *Hammer* was added to *hammer* it home, so to speak. So Thundarian meant Merdyn was a complete idiot. Now, what are you doing down here? Get back to the action, you *ninnyhammer*!

Merdyn read it again slowly. *I tried but couldn't do it, can you please? – R.*

'R' . . . that could be Rose! Hang on . . .

Merdyn had a lightbulb moment at last. "She did tryeth and she DID do it!" he cried. "Rose did this! *Rose* is W-blood! And she doesn't even knoweth it!"

"Finally," said Thundarian. "Yes. Rose be a good witch all along."

"This is wonderful news! Come, come, Thundarian!" Merdyn tucked the pinecone in his pocket and headed out the lift door, clutching his wise staff. "Thou art very clever, Thundarian. Rose a W-blood? Who knew?"

I did, thought Thundarian, but he couldn't say it because Merdyn had taken the pinecone away from his head and put it in his pocket.

"Ah well," the staff said, to deaf ears.
"I suppose that's me quiet again
for another two thousand years..."

CHAPTER THIRTY-FOUR

TROUBLE DOUBLES FOR ROSE AND BUBBLES

Rose was nothing if not a brave and hardy soul. Many pupils, perhaps even you, dear reader (certainly this writer), would have taken the day off following a howling-wolf-related humiliation in front of the whole school.

But for Rose, staying home was even worse. Her mum was riveted to the couch and barely speaking to her. Besides, today was the day of the school trip to Stonehenge, and Rose wanted to see it for herself. Most of all, she wanted to check out the mystery of the missing stone. Because perhaps the gods were right. Perhaps mankind *had* been cursed when the stone was taken, like Mr Onetone had said. It certainly felt that way to Rose at this moment.

The school coach left at 8 a.m. and Rose sat on her own somewhere in the middle. She'd never felt so lost and alone. She had finally let go of her singing dream. She was useless at it, just like she was useless at everything else. Her dad was wrong. The only thing she'd ever be great at was being a loser. At that, she was world champion.

She checked on Bubbles, who she'd tucked into her school bag that morning. She knew he couldn't talk any more, but she liked to know he was there. After all, he was her only friend left in the world.

The CATs, of course, were sitting at the back of the coach, having commandeered all five seats for themselves. Tamsin kept trying to get Rose's attention when the others weren't looking, but Rose wasn't interested. She just stared stubbornly out of the window.

Finally, the coach pulled up at Stonehenge and the children spilled out.

Despite her misery, Rose was amazed by Stonehenge in the distance. It stole the air from her lungs as soon as she laid eyes on the circle of huge, imposing stones fully four metres high, seven feet wide and as thick and as heavy as a car. She suddenly found she was nearly as excited as Mr Onetone himself.

The teacher hurried the class past a souvenir shop

where an artist was selling scale models of Stonehenge, heading for the stone circle itself.

"Maybe on your way back then?" the artist called after them sarcastically, as not one child had expressed a modicum of interest in his lovingly crafted models.

It was a long walk to the stone circle. Once there, the class followed the protective rope pegged around the stones as they walked past the monument, listening to Mr Onetone's drone.

"Radiocarbon technology puts the date of the stones at around 3000 BC. Which means they have stood here for nearly five thousand years. So, er . . . if you thought your nan was old . . ." It was meant to be a joke, but because Mr Onetone didn't change his inflection to indicate this, no one laughed, apart from Rose who sniggered out of politeness. Mr Onetone was her partner for the trip, after all, since no one else wanted to pair with her.

The CATs nudged each other.

"Teacher's pet," hissed Catrina.

"Yeah, and that pet's a wolf!" quipped Andrea. Tamsin just looked awkward.

"That doesn't mean to say that the formation of the stones hasn't changed," Mr Onetone continued as they reached the far side of the monument. "Here is the space for the *famous missing stone* on the east side, which was removed around fifteen hundred years ago."

Rose looked curiously at the space on top of two giant pillars, like two giant goalposts missing a crossbar.

"Who has breached the perimeter ropes?" Mr Onetone said suddenly.

A quick head count revealed that the whole class was present. But someone WAS walking inside the stone circle itself. In fact, now it looked like there were *two* people running between the stones.

"Hello?" Mr Onetone called out. "You're not allowed to breach the perimeter ropage. I shall have to call security."

"Go ahead," came a voice from the centre of the stones. "See if I care."

Rose felt there was something familiar about the voice. And then, out from behind a stone, stepped Julian Smith, aka Jerabo the Great. What was HE doing here?

Then things got even weirder. *Another* man walked

out from behind a different stone. A man who looked exactly like Julian, but was dressed in black and gold and looking like he was from Merdyn's time. Rose felt her breath escaping her lungs in one big whoosh. Was this . . . could this be . . . the original Jeremiah Jerabo?

The two identical men strutted toward the middle of the circle and climbed on to the central altar stone.

"We've come for Rose Falvey!" declared Julian.

Everybody looked at Rose. Rose just grinned nervously.

"Hand her over and there will be no blood spilled at this great Magic Circle today," added the other-Julian-or-maybe-Jerabo in black and gold.

"Er . . . I should certainly hope that there won't be any blood spilled *anywhere* here today, *mister man*," said Mr Onetone, raising his voice an octave. "I'm going to call security."

Then Rose watched in horror as probably-Jerabo opened his black and gold spellbook and chanted mellifluously, **"HOLCUS STONERATA!"**

Rose recognised the enchantment at once. "The

stone spell!" she blurted.

No sooner had the words left her lips than SHWINK! Mr Onetone turned to stone.

The schoolchildren gasped. Someone screamed. A few tourists felt dizzy.

Hysterically, Catrina pointed her finger at Rose. "I told you she was a witch!"

Julian spun to look where Catrina was pointing, scanning the children's faces. "There she is, Great Etcetera Grandad!" he said suddenly, also pointing at Rose. "With the frizzy hair and glasses!"

Jerabo strode across the grass towards Rose, causing the other children to run to a safe distance.

"So *thou* art Rose Falvey?" he said. "Allow me to introduce myself. I am Jerabo. The ORIGINAL Jerabo. Thou may have heard Merdyn speak of me."

Rose tried to run too.

"Young Ju-lion," said Jerabo. "A chance to use your new powers. Perform the treacle spell."

An excited Julian flipped open his spellbook, chanted loudly, "**ANIMA CHICKATIS!**" – and promptly turned himself into a chicken. Jeremiah rolled his eyes.

"Sorry, Great Etcetera Grandad!" squawked Julian.

"Worry not, my progeny," Jerabo said, turning him back into a human. "You will learn. Eventually." Then he performed the treacle spell himself.

Suddenly the ground beneath Rose's feet turned to *treacle.* Literally. Not only could she not move her feet, she could feel the sugary syrup soaking through her shoes.

"HUMANA GIGANTICUS!"

Jerabo chanted.

As Rose flailed about in the sickly sludge, she saw her shaken fellow pupils staring over her shoulder in fresh horror. She swivelled round to look as best she could in all the goo.

Uh oh.

Whatever fresh spell Jeremiah had performed, he was now twenty metres tall and still growing. As Rose watched, his blond quiff poked an unsuspecting goose in the backside as it migrated across the sky.

A broad smile spread over the wicked wizard's huge

face as he saw Rose's terror. He took a step towards her – BOOM. The world around them shuddered when his giant foot hit the ground. Rose began struggling afresh in the treacly mush, like a fly in a spider's web. HEAVE! TWIST! But Jerabo just laughed. The noise was so loud that the windows on the souvenir shop shattered, over a mile away. Then he reached out his gargantuan hand and . . .

With a twist
of his wrist,
he picked Rose up
in his giant fist.

CHAPTER THIRTY-FIVE

ONE BIG SURPRISE AND NO MORE LIES

Merdyn was running as fast as he could to Rose's house. Even he had accepted by now that this was faster than his flying spell. He *needed* to apologise to Rose. He hadn't wanted to see her before because he couldn't admit the truth about – well, everything. She was a wise head on young shoulders and he wanted to say sorry with a capital S.

He passed Dion, tinkering with his Pontiac. "Don't touch my car!" the postman shouted instinctively as Merdyn drew level. But the warlock ran straight past him and banged on the front door of the Falvey household.

He was expecting Rose or her mum to answer. What he was NOT expecting was a carbon copy of himself.

For as the door slowly opened, Merdyn saw a man standing before him that was like his own reflection in a pond. The man had the same wide, piercing blue eyes, the same slender nose and the same thick, dark hair and beard. The only difference was their clothes. Merdyn was in his warlock's robes and this other Merdyn was in jeans and a biker jacket.

The two men stared at each other. As if looking in a mirror, they then started blinking and squinting and touching their own faces to see if their eyes were deceiving them.

"You must be Merdyn the Wild?" the other Merdyn said eventually.

"Aye," said Merdyn, wondering what on earth was going on. "And who art thou, sire?"

"I'm Martin, Rose's uncle. Her dad's brother," said the other Merdyn. "I just arrived on the overnight train from Scotland."

Uncle Martin carried on talking as several cogs and pulleys whirred in the washing machine of Merdyn's brain.

". . . you see, I got this strange message on my answering machine from Suzy when I got home the other day. I'd been on a week-long fishing trip, didn't take my phone, I'm not one for technology . . ."

But Merdyn wasn't listening. His thoughts were beginning to add up like some complex mathematical equation. It went thusly . . .

Merdyn's theory of relativity: I am from here + Rose is from here + Rose's dad and brother are from here + Rose is W-blood + Rose's dad's brother looks exactly *like me* = . . .

Every muscle in Merdyn's face spasmed with joy and he embraced Martin suddenly. "We are family!" he cried. "THOU art my descendant! Rose is my great great great great lots-of-times-great granddaughter! I am her ancestor! THAT'S how she is W-blood!"

Martin was just hearing words he didn't understand, but he liked a good hug as much as the next man, so he didn't mind.

"Where is Rose? I must see Rose and tell her the good news!" cried Merdyn, almost bursting with joy.

"Everyone wants to see Rose this morning," said Uncle Martin. "Join the queue, pal."

"What do thou mean?" asked the warlock, pitch-kettled.

"We had this weird magician here just before you arrived," Rose's uncle explained. "Jerabo the Great or something?"

"What did he wanteth?" Merdyn asked, not liking the sound of this.

"It wasn't as much what *he* wanted," Martin said. "But his twin brother."

"His twin brother?" said Merdyn, *really* not liking the sound of this.

"Yeah. He was with a fellow who looked the spitting image of him," Martin explained. "Except he wore weird clothes. A bit like you, but black with gold tassels and stuff."

"And what did he sayeth? What was his business?" Merdyn asked, his pulse quickening.

"He wanted to know where Rose was."

If Merdyn had had an early-warning alarm system fitted in his ears, it would have been ringing very loudly just then. Was it possible? Had Jerabo come here?

Of course it was possible. *Jerabo has the spellbook.*

There was a sudden scream from the front room of the house. Merdyn and Uncle Martin rushed inside, with

Dion – who had also heard the scream – close behind them.

In the front room, they found Suzy pointing at the TV news with fear in her eyes. They all watched in horror as live footage of Rose at Stonehenge filled the screen. She was scared. She was squirming. And she was being held in the huge fist of Jeremiah Jerabo – who was looking, frankly, very giant-like. It reminded Dion of a famous scene from the film *King Kong*.

"The Magic Circle!" hissed Merdyn breathlessly. "'Tis still here?"

"BRING ME MERDYN THE WILD!" boomed the giant Jerabo as news helicopters flew around his head like bees. "BRING ME MERDYN AND I WILL LETTETH THE GIRL GO!"

A news reporter flashed up on the screen, standing near Stonehenge and explaining that the Prime Minister had asked the army to be on standby for this most unusual national emergency.

"No!' yelled Merdyn. "They must not calleth in the army. Jerabo will destroyeth them all, including Rose. It's me he wanteth. I have to get there!"

But it was Rose's mum who was the most dumbstruck. A sudden shock like this can do strange things, reader, as I'm sure you know. It can clutter the mind with confusion OR it can bring great clarity. I am pleased to tell you that this shock had the latter effect on Suzy. At that moment, she realised that for the past couple of years, she'd been living her life all wrong. Yes, her lovely husband had died far too young, and that was about the worst thing you could think of. But she still had two wonderful children, and she loved them, and they loved her. *What an idiot I've been*, she thought. And she sprang into ACTION MUM mode.

"Right. Dion," said Suzy. "Can we borrow your car?"

Dion groaned. He'd only just fixed his car up and, if he was reading the room right, now it was going to be used in a life-or-death race to confront an angry giant. What could possibly go wrong?

"Er . . ." he said.

"Good," said Mum. "Martin, can you still drive?"

"Well," Martin said, looking worried. "It's been a while . . ."

"That's two yeses then," said Suzy firmly. "Let's go!"

Rose's mum, Merdyn, Martin and Dion ran out of the house and jumped into Dion's car. Martin started it up, put his expert foot on the accelerator, slammed the car into gear and sent the Pontiac Firebird wheel-spinning out of Daffodil Close.

With the twin turbos pumping
like they'd been lit by fires.
And a cloud of smoke rising
from the burning tyres!

CHAPTER THIRTY-SIX

REVENGE AT THE HENGE! (AKA THE GROANS BETWIXT THE STONES)

All hell was breaking loose at Stonehenge. The whole place was teeming with police and soldiers, but they couldn't touch the giant Jeremiah Jerabo. The Prime Minister had sent fighter jets and attack helicopters, but Jerabo was too big and powerful to overcome.

Meanwhile, Julian was getting the hang of his spellbook. It was a little hit and miss, but he'd done at least one ice spell and summoned lightning from his fingertips.

"Ha ha! Look at me, Great great etcetera Grandad! I'm like Darth Vader!" he shouted as he zapped a nearby tree.

"Good work, son. Is Darth Vader one of the good guys, like us?" boomed Giant Jerabo, swatting away fighter jets with his giant hand as if they were paper aeroplanes.

"Erm, kind of," replied Julian.

Rose rolled her eyes. She'd given up trying to squirm out of Jerabo's big fist and had settled for giving him the occasional bite instead. Not that he was taking much notice. So she was very relieved when she looked up to see the welcome sight of Dion's big American car hurtling towards the police cordon with her mum in the front passenger seat.

Uncle Martin screeched to a halt next to the line of army soldiers.

"Sorry sir, this area is in lockdown," said a diligent officer.

Mum wound the window down. "Let us through!" she screamed. "That's my daughter up there in that monster's hand!"

But the soldier shook his head. "Move along, madam," he said instead, rather threateningly.

"I WILL NOT!" cried Suzy.

"Then I shall have to arrest you, ma'am."

"Stand down, soldier!" said a firm voice suddenly.

Suzy looked about for her saviour. It was none other than . . . Sergeant Murray.

"Let this fine woman through," said the sergeant.

"Sir, yes, sir!" saluted the solider, and he stepped aside to let the Firebird pass.

Uncle Martin sped through the police cordon, past the souvenir shop with its broken windows, along the path towards the monument, round Rose's scared schoolmates, between terrified tourists, and stopped just outside the ancient circle of stones.

Merdyn staggered out of the back seat (he'd been throwing up the WHOLE way) and stumbled to the centre of Stonehenge. He looked up at the huge face of the Giant Jerabo, some twenty metres above him.

"Here I am!" cried Merdyn. "Now let my great great many times granddaughter go!"

"Be careful, Merdyn!" cried Rose. Then: "Hang on – we're *related*?"

"Aye," said the warlock tenderly. "I had hoped to tell thee under slightly better circumstances but yes, I am thy ancestor, and I'm so so sorry for how I have treated you of late."

"So you DIDN'T give me the wrong spell

on purpose?"

"Of course not!" Merdyn was appalled. "But I *was* careless. Please forgive me?"

"All right. As long as you get me out of here!" yelled Rose.

"Worry thee not, child. Everything will be *oookaaay!*"

Jerabo laughed. "I did knoweth you'd be foolish enough to come, Merdyn the Idiot," he boomed. He lowered Rose to the ground and scooped up the warlock in her place.

Suzy rushed to Rose's side and hugged her tight. It was a hug that meant a thousand words and phrases. *I'm sorry, Rose. I'll be there for you from now on. You're special to me, Rose, just as you are. You can count on me!* And Rose heard every word, loud and clear. It seemed like a long time since they'd felt like a proper mum and daughter, and boy had Rose missed it.

Meanwhile, held high in the giant Jerabo's hand like one of his own merchandising dolls, Merdyn noticed the Royal Engagement Ring on his enemy's finger. Jerabo watched Merdyn's face fall.

"Oh yes, thou don't knoweth, do thou?" Jerabo said. "Evanhart and I are to be married. Isn't that wonderful? It didn't taketh her long to forget about thee . . ."

"I don't believeth thee!"

"It doesn't matter if thou believeth me. Thou art going to die now anyway."

The evil wizard tightened his grip on the good warlock (confusing, isn't it?) and prepared to crush him like an ant. But Merdyn's anger was now at boiling point. He wasn't giving up without a fight.

He thumped Thundarian against Jerabo's palm. **"ANIMATUM GIGANTICUS!"** he yelled.

And seconds later, he burst out of Jerabo's fist and thumped his feet on to the ground. WHUMP! WHUMP! Now Merdyn was twenty metres tall too.

"I AM MERDYN THE WILD! DESTROYER OF ENEMIES! BOW DOWN BEFORE ME!" he boomed.

Not to be outdone, Jeremiah boomed back: "AND I AM JEREMIAH JERABO! BRINGER

OF JUSTICE! AND I WILL NEVER BOWETH TO THEE!" It was as loud as a jumbo jet.

"And I am Julian Smith! The best actor who ever lived!" squeaked Julian from the ground below. "But, er . . . carry on."

And so the two giants from the year 511 stood toe to toe in the middle of Stonehenge while news crews pointed their cameras and beamed the image around the world. In houses and pubs and workplaces around the globe, people gathered about their televisions to watch the spectacle unfold. In Buckingham Palace, the Queen was gripped. In the White House, the President was enthralled. In the Vatican, the Pope was praying.

People in Europe, America, China, Russia, Australia, Tanzania, Indonesia, New Zealand, India, everywhere all looked on in disbelief as the ancient pair traded magical blows in a supernatural battle royale. And they didn't even know yet how much the fate of their world rested on this battle. After all, if Merdyn lost, Julian Smith would be in charge.

Jerabo threw a lightning bolt CRACK-ACK-ACK! It missed Merdyn and hit one of the army trucks. The truck burst into flames and soldiers spilled out.

Julian laughed. "Oops-a-daisy!"

"No!" shouted Merdyn. "Don't hurt them!"

"What?" Giant Jerabo bellowed in disbelief. "Thou actually CARETH about these people? Thou CARETH about these weak, insipid, magicless creatures?"

"There are good people here," said Merdyn. "I have seen more goodness in them than I have ever seen in THOU!"

But Jerabo was in no mood to chat.

WHOOSH!

He threw a fireball at Merdyn.

DOUBLE-WHOOSH!

Merdyn threw one right back. Jerabo summoned a shield spell, however, and the fireball rebounded towards Merdyn, setting the end of his beard ablaze. The evil wizard slapped his thighs guffawingly, and the sound reverberated like thunderclaps across the landscape.

Merdyn was not cowed though. He spun, brandished

Thundarian boldly, and hurled an ice spell at the chuckling Jerabo.

"GELIDA GLACIA FROSTORA!"

✶FFFFFRING!!✦ Suddenly Jerabo was encased in an oversized block of ice. He looked like an iceberg.

Rose whooped. In homes and pubs and offices across the planet, people cheered. In the White House, the President sent a direct order to the Pentagon. "Someone bring me some popcorn! This is gonna be a heck of a show!"

Not one to miss a party, at this moment Freddie arrived at Stonehenge shouting, "Hi, I'm Merdyn's agent. For personal appearances please call this number," and handing out business cards to anyone who would take one. He threw a thumbs up to Merdyn, "Keep going, Merds, this is great publicity. BANK!"

But Jerabo wasn't finished just yet. Suddenly, he burst out from within his frozen prison, scattering shards of ice into the air that plummeted into the landscape like darts in a dart board. Then . . . he disappeared.

Merdyn looked around desperately. Where had the villainous giant gone?

CRACK!

The blow came out of nowhere. Merdyn flew sideways. WHACK! Merdyn had just got back up when he was knocked on to his backside. BONK! SMACK! HOOF!

Two could play at that game.

"BARBARIUM INVISIBLATIS!" Merdyn roared.

Now Merdyn was also invisible. The two magicians wrestled and grappled loudly – and invisibly – until they realised that this meant neither held an advantage any more. They reappeared, looking significantly more battered and bruised, much to the watching crowd's delight.

In a sudden dastardly move, Jerabo plucked one of the rounder Stonehenge rocks from where it had stood for five thousand years and bowled it along the floor at Merdyn. The nimble warlock jumped, so the rock tumbled past and hit three other giant boulders, sending them spinning into the air like bowling pins.

"Nice roll, Great Etcetera Grandad!" shouted Julian.

But this gave Merdyn an EXCELLENT idea. He whispered a new spell he'd invented only a few days earlier, when cheating at tenpin-bowling against Kris and Freddie.

"TRANSFORMUS BOWLUS BALLUS!"

Rose, her family and the world watched in amazement as Merdyn began to transform. At first, his body folded forward. Then it tucked inward and scrunched into . . . a ball. By the time the change was complete, there was a giant, shiny, purple-patched bowling ball resting on the grass, with a pointy hat sitting on top. The ball hurtled towards the bamboozled Jerabo at speeds beyond comprehension: a purple blur, skittling him and the rest of the Stonehenge rocks in all directions.

"Striiiike!!" cried the Queen from Buckingham Palace.

A roar of delight went up the world over as Jerabo landed in a broken heap among the heavy stones. Rose jumped so high with relief she pulled a muscle in her gluteous maximus (bottom). In the little souvenir shop, the

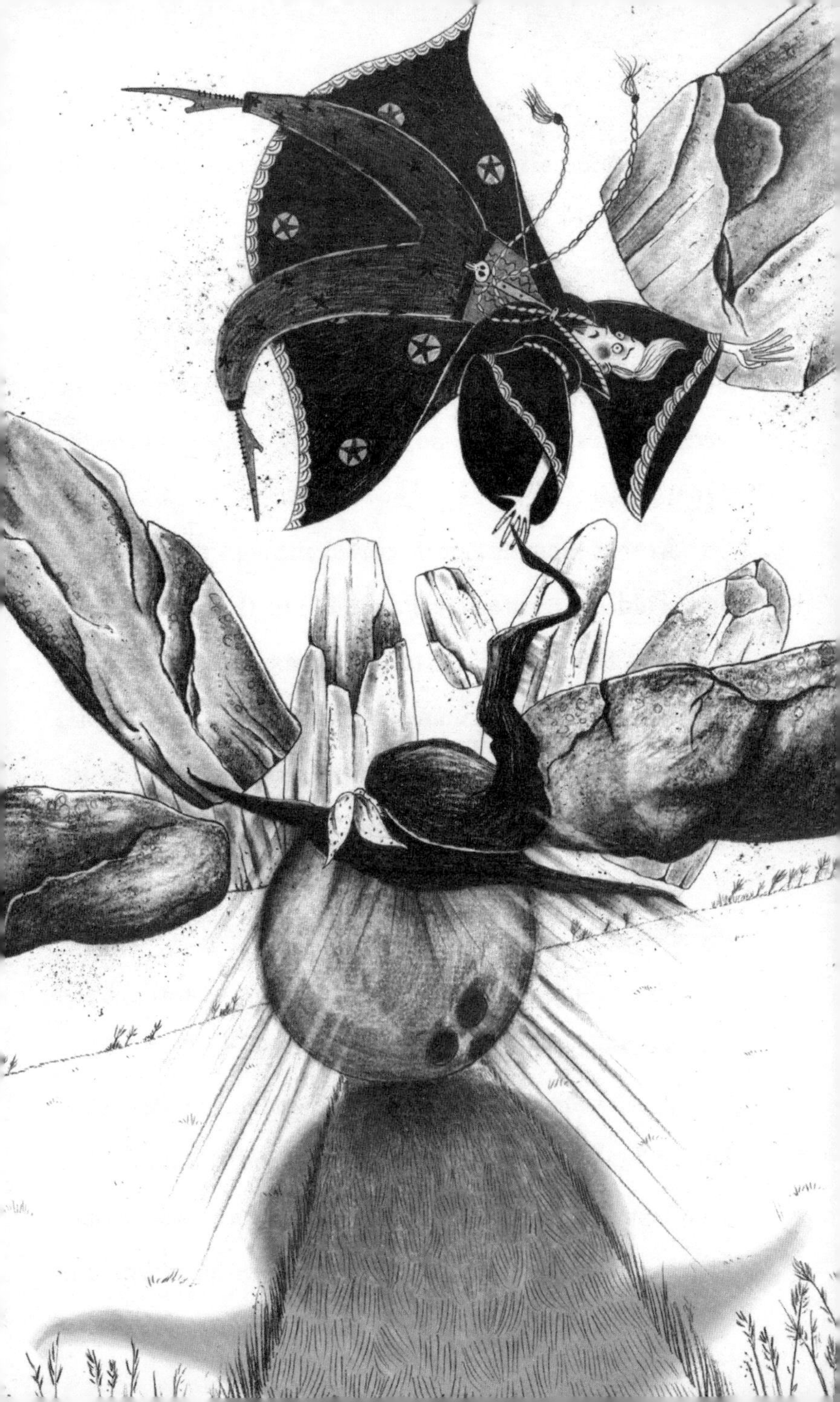

scale-model artist burst into tears, picked up his beloved works of art – which no longer matched – and smashed them on the ground.

Merdyn the Wild turned back into the giant version of himself and stood over the stricken Jerabo. "And now perhaps a drink?" he said, producing the brown bottle from his belt.

At that moment, a car weaved through the wreckage and skidded to a stop in the middle of the site formerly known as Stonehenge. Kris and Shakia climbed out.

"Rose! Rose, where are you? Where's my sister?" Kris shouted frantically. "You may be embarrassing but I still love you! I'm here to rescue you!"

"Kris, I'm here, I'm OK!" Rose shouted from where she stood with her mum.

Her brother spun around but could see nothing but toppled stones, smoke and police helicopters.

Julian's devious mind started whirring. "Kris, over here! I'll take you to your sister!" he cooed.

"Thanks!" said Kris in relief. And before Shakia could stop him, he jogged blithely towards the ex-magician.

"Noooo!" cried Rose. She let go of her helpless mum and ran towards her brother.

"Rose, stay back!" Merdyn shouted.

But it was too late. As Rose and her brother converged on each other and came within Julian's grasp, Julian grabbed his spellbook, muttered something desperately and . . .

FRRRISHH!

Rose and Kris were encased in another block of ice.

Suzy howled. Uncle Martin and Shakia had to hold her back from running over and putting herself in danger too.

"Ha!" Julian crowed. "And they told me I couldn't act! Take *that*, Royal Shakespeare Company!" He turned to Merdyn. "Now let my great blah blah grandfather go, or these kids are burnt toast." He crackled some lightning from his fingertips and laughed an evil laugh. (I think the Royal Shakespeare Company were right. He WAS a bit hammy.)

Merdyn backed away. He couldn't risk any harm coming to Rose and Kris.

"Great Etcetera Grandad!" shouted Julian. "That brown bottle in Merdyn's hand. It's a disenchantment potion. It will take away your powers. He tried to use it on me at the theatre!"

Jerabo pulled himself back on to his giant feet and looked at Merdyn, reluctantly impressed. "'Tis true?" he asked. "Thou has perfected the disenchantment potion? In that case, how about a bargain?"

"I will not bargaineth with THEE!" cried Merdyn.

"Really?" said Jerabo. "We have thine precious Rose and her idiot brother thou carest so much about."

From inside the ice Rose tried to wriggle free. God it was cold in there.

"But what if we did goeth back in time together and liveth in peace, me and thou, leaving everyone here unharmed?" Jerabo continued. "Thou can marry Evanhart. Everybody's happy."

"And what do thou wanteth in return?" asked Merdyn suspiciously.

"To be King."

Merdyn laughed.

"I jesteth not," said Jerabo. "I shall overthroweth King Paul, and thou will letteth me."

"But I would NEVER let thee do such a thing! My powers are too much for thee," Merdyn rasped indignantly.

"I knoweth this." Jerabo paused for dramatic effect, knowing he had Rose, her class, the police, the army, the President, the Queen, the whole world hanging on his next words. "Which is why THOU art going to drink the contents of that bottle and lose thy powers for ever instead."

The watching world gasped.

"If you keepeth fighting, you will loseth," Jerabo said. "There art two of us, after all. And when thou loseth, thou will dieth without descendants, and these two children will disappeareth from the face of the earth. For ever."

"Like in *Back to the Future*," whispered Dion to Rose's mum.

"This is no time to talk about films, Dion!" Suzy shrieked.

"No, listen. If Merdyn doesn't go back and live out his life as planned, Rose and Kris will never have existed."

"Or me," said Martin. He checked his arm to see if he was already disappearing.

Jerabo smiled meanly. "I'm offering you a way to guarantee your progeny, Merdyn," he said. "Drink the bottle and we all goeth safely home."

Rose could hear all this from inside the ice. She was nearly blue with cold, but silently screaming for Merdyn NOT to drink the spell. She didn't trust Jerabo one bit.

But Merdyn knew Jerabo was right. If he lost this fight, then Rose and Kris were doomed. "Set them free first," he said, gesturing towards the ice.

"Do as he sayeth, my many-times-great-grandson," ordered Jerabo.

Julian threw a fireball at Rose and Kris. They fell, soaking wet, from their melted icy tomb.

"Don't trust him, Merdyn!" cried Rose through shivering lips.

"I must ensure your safety, youngling." Merdyn looked at Rose and Kris and smiled bravely. Then, with a heavy heart, he lifted the bottle to his lips – and drank the disenchantment potion. GULP!

"Nooooooo!" screamed Rose as Merdyn shrank back to his normal size. The light in his bright blue eyes went out, and they became grey-black.

"Excellent." Jerabo kicked Thundarian aside. He picked up the weakened Merdyn between his finger and thumb and dropped him on to the altar in the middle of the ruined stone monument.

"What are you doing?" shouted Rose.

"Me? Oh. I am going to kill Merdyn, of course," said Jerabo casually. "You were quite right. 'Twas a trick. Merdyn really should know better than to trust me. Now I shall go back and rule my world, Ju-lion shall rule this one and the only person who could have stopped us has been rendered powerless.

"I just loveth it when a plan comes together."

The world, the Pope,
the President and Queen
all prayed for a hero
to undo what they'd just seen.

CHAPTER THIRTY-SEVEN

FORTUNES SWITCH AND AN UNLIKELY WITCH

Even as Jerabo spoke, Rose noticed with shock that she was slowly disappearing. This wasn't like turning invisible – she'd been able to feel her toes then. But now where her toes had once been was just air, and there was a definite sense of absence. Merdyn wasn't going home, she realised, so she was being erased from time before her very own eyes!

She looked at her brother. "Kris! Your face!"

Kris checked himself in his phone. His beautiful face was turning see-through!

Uncle Martin's arm was gone too. "We're *backtothefuturing*!" he muttered to himself, almost certainly inventing a new word.

Jerabo didn't care about any of this. As he towered over the normal-sized Merdyn, he turned to the news cameras to make his victory speech to the world.

"Hear this!" he bellowed. "After I killeth this pathetic wretch, I will be leaving this natureless world. And when I am gone, my progeny, Ju-lion—"

"Ahem, it's Julian, actually," said Julian.

"Oh. Sorry, yes. *Julian* will becometh thy leader. Consider him a good guy. You know, like Darth Vader." Julian smiled and waved for the cameras. "Thou will doeth as HE says!" Jerabo went on. "Defy him at thy peril!"

As Jerabo ranted, Rose was desperately trying to think of a way to save Merdyn. She looked at him for help, but he only dug his hand into his robe pocket, pulled out a pinecone and threw it at her.

"Thou did doeth it," he whispered weakly.

Rose picked the pinecone up. What did Merdyn mean?

Everybody around her had lost their heads. Her mum was crying hysterically. Her brother and Uncle Martin had almost completely disappeared now, as had much of her own bottom half. The remaining onlookers were shaking with fear. But as the pieces fell into place – her heritage, the familiar pinecone in her hand, Merdyn's words – she suddenly understood.

She grabbed her bag, pulled out Bubbles and attached the pinecone to his collar.

Unaware of the gravity of the situation, Bubbles immediately crawled out of Rose's arms to nibble at the grass under her feet. "Hm. Hm. Nice grass here. So varied. Hm. Bearded darnel, my favourite . . ." he said.

I did it . . . I made the pinecone work again! Rose thought. *Of course! I'm related to Merdyn. I'm W-blood. That means I can do magic too!* But did that mean she – Rose the loser – was now the world's only hope?

She looked at Bubbles. He was too busy eating to come to her aid. Fat lot of use he was in the world's time of need. Then something Bubbles had just said stirred a memory. *Bearded darnel?* . . . Where had she heard that before?

Yes! She remembered now. When Merdyn had told the story of his capture by Vanheldon and the Vandal army, he'd made a stone spell from the grass that grew beneath his cage. If she could remember the ingredients, maybe she could conjure the stone spell herself. Bearded darnel, cocksfoot, clover, *something, something* . . .

Rose turned to her schoolmates. They had been cowering behind the fallen stones all this time. "Listen, everyone!" she whisper-shouted, trying not to alert Jerabo (who was *still* making his speech). "I know some of you think I'm weird. And you don't know how right you are. I've just found out I'm an actual witch." *Oh, witches grass*, she remembered. Bearded darnel, cocksfoot, clover, witches grass and . . .

"I always said you were!" sneered Catrina.

"Pendulous sedge!" Rose said, to everyone's surprise. That was the fifth grass! "Listen. With your help, I can stop this! But we don't have long!"

Her classmates looked at her – well, what was left of her – in silence. Just as Rose was about to give up all hope, a voice piped up.

"What do you need?"

It was Tamsin. She broke from the pack and linked arms with Rose. "I'm sorry," she whispered.

Shakia joined her sister with an approving wink, linking arms with Rose on the other side.

Catrina and Andie were horrified. "Tams?" they yelled in unison.

"Oh, shut up, you two shallow cretins!" Tamsin snapped.

Shakia backed Tamsin up. "You want to spend your life being ruled by that blond buffoon?" She pointed at Julian, who was preening himself like a peacock as his great great whatever grandfather made his speech.

"No," they conceded.

"Then listen the heck up!" said Tamsin, warming to her emancipated self. "She's our only chance. Go ahead, Rose."

Rose forgave Tamsin everything in that second and threw her a grateful smile. Then she leaped into action. "I need five ingredients to make a stone spell and STOP THAT LUNATIC," she whispered. "Five types of grass, actually."

"Grass?" said Catrina. "Boring. Shouldn't it be, like, frogs' legs and spiders' webs and stuff?"

"Who says grass is boring?" squeaked Bubbles indignantly. "There are twenty types right under our feet as we speak!"

Ordinarily, being told off by a guinea pig would have blown their minds. But the class had just witnessed a fight between two twenty-metre-high wizards, so they took it pretty well.

"All right, all right. Fine. Grass is cool," admitted Catrina.

"We need bearded darnel, cocksfoot, clover, pendulous sedge and witches grass," said Rose. "Get looking."

"I want to help too!" said another kid.

"And me!"

"Me too!"

As they got to work, Jerabo was finally finishing up his rambling speech.

". . . and so I shall leaveth my great great great etcetera grandson in charge. Obey him or die. I hope thou will remembereth me fondly. And now to put an end to my old friend, *Merdyn the Wild*!"

Jerabo curled his giant hand into a clenched fist and lifted it high above Merdyn's limp body, which was laid out on the altar like a sacrificial lamb.

Rose clawed frantically at the ground, trying to ignore her increasingly absent knees. Everyone was looking up the different grasses on their phones and checking them against the plants underfoot. They had bearded darnel, cocksfoot, clover and pendulous sedge, but they still needed witches grass. It was too late though. Jerabo was bringing down his giant fist. Any minute now, Rose's friend and great-ish grandpa would be flattened . . .

But suddenly the evil wizard stopped. He wanted to say one last thing.

"If thou would liketh to erect a statue of me when I'm gone, that would be nice. It's up to thou, though. I do not wanteth to tell thou what to do but, just a thought. Now, where was I?"

Little did he realise that his excessive grandstanding had given Rose and her friends just enough time to find the missing ingredient.

"I've got it! Witches grass!" Catrina

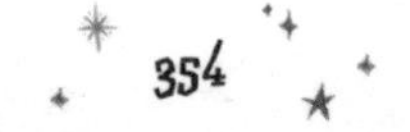

hissed jubilantly. But she couldn't pull it out. Its roots were too long and twisted, like witches' fingers, hence the name!

Andie came to the rescue. She gripped the stalk with her sausage fingers and pulled it loose in one go. She threw it to Rose, who caught it and rushed towards Jerabo on her increasingly see-through feet, crushing the grasses in her hand. Was she too late?

As Jerabo brought his giant fist down on Merdyn as hard as he could, Rose hurled the mixed grasses into the air towards the evil wizard and his annoying grandson.

"HOLCUS STONERATA!" she shouted.

Jerabo's fist was inches away from squishing Merdyn when – * SHWINK! * The giant fist turned to stone.

His spellbook, which he'd been holding all this time, shrank to its normal size and fell safely to the ground, where Rose quickly picked it up. With this Merdyn could get home and all would be well! She could already feel her feet rematerialising.

"No! NOOOOOO!" cried Jerabo as he watched his giant arm turn to stone, then his giant shoulder, his body, his legs, his neck, and finally his . . .

"NOOOOOOO!"

SHWINK His giant lips and head turned to stone and there was silence.

Julian looked very sheepish now Jerabo was incapacitated. He was just trying to slink away when –

"HOLCUS STONERATA!" SHWINK!

– Rose turned him to stone too.

The police, the army and the millions watching on television around the world all cheered and jumped for joy.

"Hey, I never did get that popcorn!" complained the President in the White House.

"Bravo!" said the Queen from Buckingham Palace. "When is this on again?"

Rose's schoolmates leaped up and down with glee too, as only children who've just saved the world using plain old grass can. Then they all hugged Rose. Then Rose hugged her brother, and they both hugged their mum, who pulled Uncle Martin and Dion into the hug too. Even Shakia joined in, relieved to see that not only was Kris whole again, but even better, he had his normal face back.

"So nice to be just really good looking again!"

Kris exclaimed happily.

Rose finally extricated herself from the group hug. She and Tamsin ran to the altar to help Merdyn up. Merdyn smiled weakly.

"Well done, Rose. Thou did saveth us all."

Rose didn't feel like celebrating. "But Merdyn, your magic has gone. I wish there was something we could do . . ."

"So do I," said Freddie, appearing at her shoulder. "A magicless wizard is sooo not bank."

"I've got an idea," said Tamsin. "That spell has only been in his stomach five minutes, right?" Rose nodded. "Then let's get it out."

But how?

"Leave that to me,
I've just the thing,"
said Uncle Martin
with a knowing grin.

CHAPTER THIRTY-EIGHT

ALL'S WELL THAT ENDS WITH A SPELL

Thirty seconds later, Merdyn the Wild was in the back of Dion's car with Uncle Martin driving, expertly and at full speed, in tight circles. Merdyn, of course, threw up the entire contents of his stomach. At last, the Firebird's wheels spun to a stop and the pale green warlock fell from the back seat on to the grass in a dizzy heap.

"What a day!" he moaned.

"Has it worked?" Rose asked. "See if you can magic Mr Onetone back?"

Everybody looked towards the silent Mr Onetone. Most of the kids had forgotten that their monotone teacher had been turned to stone.

Rose handed Merdyn his beloved staff. He pointed Thundarian at Mr Onetone and chanted:

"REVENTIM HOLCUS STONERATA!"

Everyone waited breathlessly for Mr Onetone to turn back to normal. But nothing happened.

"The disenchantment potion must have dissolved too far into my blood," said Merdyn sadly.

Rose was crestfallen. What a sacrifice the great warlock had made for her.

But then . . .

"Look!" shrieked Tamsin. "Mr Onetone is cracking!"

Rose looked back at Mr Onetone quickly. It was true. Slowly but surely, the history teacher WAS cracking, turning from stone back to flesh and blood.

". . . I shall call security!" he droned automatically as he completed his transformation. Then he looked around at the carnage. "Did I miss something?"

"It did worketh!" cried Merdyn. The bright blue light was coming back into his eyes as Rose beamed with joy. "Thank thee, Martin! I did never thinketh I would be so pleased that someone did maketh me sick."

"What should we do with these two?" said Rose, and she gestured to the stone statues of Jerabo and Julian.

"I had better take Jerabo back to the Dark Ages with

me. But first I will clippeth both their wings," Merdyn answered.

He poured what was left of the disenchantment potion into both stone mouths, then turned them back to normal. Sergeant Murray thought he'd do Merdyn a favour, and clamped some handcuffs on both their wrists too.

"Just while that spell does its work," he said with a wink and a wiggle of his moustache.

Just then, Freddie ran up to Merdyn. "What am I gonna do without you, Merds? You're my best client! You're my ONLY client!"

Merdyn gestured to the distraught Julian. "There's a fellow over there that could do with some helpeth. His only crime was being led astrayeth by his wicked ancestor."

Freddie put his arm around Julian's shoulders. "Don't worry, mate, there's no such thing as bad publicity. You ever considered acting lessons?"

Jerabo burst into floods of tears. "I'm a normal! A normal human! 'Tis the end of days! Whatever shall I doeth?"

"Worry thee not," said Merdyn. "Evanhart and I will

findeth thee a job. Cleaning the castle toilets, perchance? Now, the spellbook please, Rose."

Rose handed over Jerabo's black and gold spellbook. Merdyn could finally go home. But looking around, Merdyn realised he had one more job to do before he went.

He pointed Thundarian at one of the giant rocks that had been skittled like a bowling pin during his epic brawl with Jerabo. Then he performed a levitation spell. The rock creaked upwards, as if lifted by an invisible hand. Merdyn moved it carefully through the air and put it back in its rightful place.

The TV cameras were still filming. Around the world, people watched in awe as, one by one, Merdyn put ALL the displaced giant rocks back in their correct positions.

With one exception.

Merdyn reached into his pocket. He took out the shrunken stone that he had stolen hundreds of years earlier, on to which he had carved Evanhart's face. With a flick of his wrist, he magicked it back to its original size and zapped it back to the place he had taken it from.

Rose couldn't believe it. "YOU took the missing

rock?" she said to Merdyn, appalled. "Your people must have been very cross with you!"

"Why do you think they did wanteth rid of me?" Merdyn chortled.

When Mr Onetone saw the rock float back into its rightful place, his voice finally broke into an excited shriek.

"*The missing stone*!" he squeaked. "The world is saved!"

And if only that were so, dear reader. But it saddens me to say that the druids were wrong. There is no miracle cure for the world's ills. But let me tell you this. With the entire planet watching this extraordinary spectacle on TV, everyone had become just that little bit more aware that we are more than a collection of separate countries and races. We are all connected. We are all one. We are nature and nature is us. All bumbling along together, trying to live our best lives. And all we need to make that a tiny bit easier is a little magic in our lives.

And I'll add one more thing. Everyone was a little nicer to each other from that moment on. Well, for a while anyway.

The one person who was not so pleased with the

day's events was the souvenir-shop artist. He had just finished his first model of the *new* Stonehenge, with the stones scattered around the circle. Now he looked out of the window and saw it was back to normal. "Make up your minds!" he bellowed before smashing the new model to pieces.

Merdyn started his goodbyes. First to Suzy, who had by now forgiven him for everything. Merdyn slipped her a little potion bottle as she gave him a hug.

"A singing spell," he whispered. "Just in case you want to start again."

Then Merdyn said goodbye to Dion, Uncle Martin, Kris, Shakia, Tamsin and even Bubbles. "Who are you?" said Bubbles, guinea pigs not being known for their long-term memories.

Now there was only one person left.

"Do you have to go?" Rose asked, her bottom lip quivering already.

"Oh, Rose, thou knoweth I do," Merdyn replied

gently. "I don't belongeth here. And I have much good to do. But I shall thinketh of you every day. I shall misseth you very much."

They looked at each other. Very soon, fifteen hundred years – twenty *lifetimes* – would separate them once again. Rose threw her tiny arms around Merdyn's broad shoulders and sobbed her heart out. Her tears misted her glasses, forming two wet circles on the shoulder of his old purple cloak.

How she would remember this crazy man who had changed her life FOR EVER.

When at last they pulled apart, Merdyn wiped the tears from Rose's freckly cheeks with his thumb. "My descendant," he said, with the tenderness of a butterfly landing on a lily.

"My great great great great great great . . ." Rose trailed off. "Could we just say Grandad?" she finished shyly.

"I liketh Grandad very much." Merdyn smiled. "I'm so proud of thee, Rose. Thy father would have been proud too."

Rose knew it was true. And as he said this, Rose could fleetingly see Merdyn's resemblance to her dad, it was something about the warm glint in his eyes and quirk in his smile. Almost as if, just for a moment, her father was standing before her one last time saying, "It's OK, Rose. Don't worry. You're going to be OK." Then a second later, Merdyn's face returned unmistakeably to his own.

"Have a wonderful rest of thy life," the once-warlock said finally.

Rose smiled bravely. "You too, Merdyn."

Then Merdyn opened the black and gold spellbook and read out the Rivers of Time spell. **"FRANDALIN BUGANTI RIVERO. CLOCKASHOCK!"**

The ground opened up in a green blaze like a giant emerald mouth. It swallowed up Merdyn and the sorrowful Jerabo, before slamming shut again with an almighty

THWACK!

The world watched in silence.
It was done . . .
Merdyn the Wild
was truly gone.

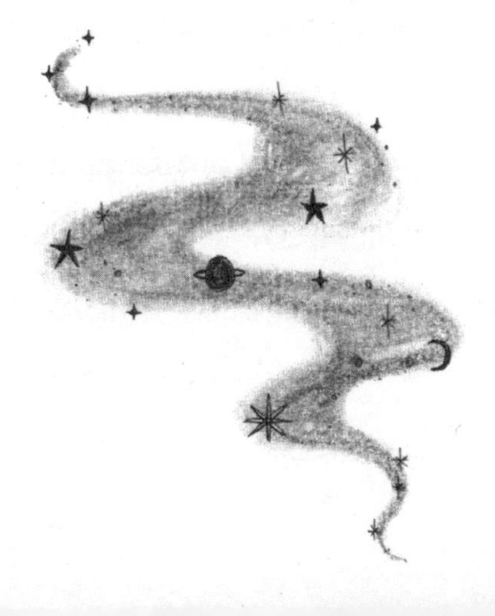

CHAPTER THIRTY-NINE

VETS, PETS AND UNLIKELY DUETS

Merdyn was gone, yes. But a long, hard school term had ended and Rose had the summer holidays to look forward to, and some new friends to enjoy it with. She used the time wisely.

Rose, Tamsin, Catrina and Andie set up the Merdyn the Wild Hospital for Animals in the shed in the garden. People came from miles around to have their pets' most unusual problems diagnosed. With the help of her magic pinecone, Rose could talk to any animal to ascertain exactly what was wrong, however odd.

"I think I'm allergic to carrots," a rabbit with a rash would say. Or "ALL the neighbours on my street feed me," an overweight cat would admit guiltily. "I eat fourteen meals a day!" Or even: "I stole four bars of chocolate from the fridge while my owner wasn't looking, and everyone knows chocolate and canines don't mix!" a poisoned dog would confess with his head hanging in shame. One of Rose's friends would then write a note for the owner to take to the vet, who found the letters VERY useful when treating the animals for their ills.

Rose's mum spruced the house up before taking the old family photos and proudly hanging them back on the walls. She even brought one of Rose's dad's inventions in from the shed and put it in the kitchen. It was "The Mean Bean Machine", a coffee-making device similar to modern machines except it was three times the size and three times noisier, but it made coffee three times better too.

Suzy had also started singing again. One night Rose, Kris, Shakia and Dion went to see her at the Frog and Bucket in town. She sang like a goddess, and had several record companies trying to sign her. She turned them all down. Rose assumed she'd taken Merdyn's singing spell. But all the while she sang, Suzy had Merdyn's singing spell in her back pocket, the lid untouched. She didn't need it, but it was nice to have it, just in case.

Dion drove them home afterwards. On the way

he turned to Suzy and said awkwardly, "That was . . . I was . . . erm. You're . . . er . . ."

Rose couldn't take it any longer. She grabbed the enchanted pinecone from around Bubbles's neck and pressed it against Dion's head. Suddenly ALL his inner thoughts came spilling out in a stream of consciousness.

"I think you're the most incredible woman I've ever met I love you from the tip of your head to the toes in your feet the only reason I stand outside polishing my car all day is to get to see or talk to you but I never do talk to you because I once asked a girl out and she laughed at me but if you want me to I'll love you until we're both old and grey."

Rose removed the pinecone. Dion looked embarrassed. Then he pulled himself together and declared, "By which I mean to say, would you like to go to dinner tomorrow?"

"Yes," Suzy said, glowing red. "I'd love to."

The whole family had a holiday too, in Corfu. How did they afford it? It was the strangest thing. One day Kris was mowing the lawn when the rotor blade hit a bunch of dirty-looking stones. When he went to pick them up, he noticed one of them glinting in the sunlight. He rubbed it on his jeans – and what do you know? It wasn't a dirty pebble at all, but *pure gold.* ALL the dirty pebbles were.

When Kris showed them to Rose, she knew instantly what they were. "So Merdyn *did* have money all along." She laughed.

And somewhere in the Cotswolds, two pigs turned back into the security guards Jim and Alan. The farmer, who had been rather pleased that he'd somehow acquired two new pigs without paying for them, looked at them quizzically as they walked away from their sty.

"I rather liked being a pig actually," said a dazed Alan, covered in mud.

"Easier than being a security guard," agreed Jim.

And so, as you may have guessed from the lack of pages left to turn in this book, we are almost at the end of our remarkable tale. I have just one more thing to tell you though, before I go. One night, Rose was emptying the

Poover beneath Bubbles's cage, listening, as usual, to the guinea pig wittering away.

"I want to try this thing called an *aubergine*," he said. "Do you know *aubergine?* I've heard people talking about *aubergines*. Can I have an *aubergine*?"

"Sure," said Rose, lifting some books on to her shelf. "But I don't think you'll like it."

"How do you know?" Bubbles retorted. "You don't know me. You think you do, but you don't."

Rose tutted and shoved the books to one side of the bookshelf. But as she did so, one of them fell off. "Oh drat!"

"You deserved that," said Bubbles, and went back to nibbling on a carrot.

As Rose picked up the book, she glimpsed the title. It rang a loud bell in her memory box. *Wizards, Witches and Warlocks of Auld*. It was the book she and Merdyn had looked at in the library. Rose chuckled at the memory.

For old times' sake, she flicked through it. There was the illustration of Vanheldon the Vandal in all his evil glory. And there was the picture of Merlin that had so driven Merdyn crazy. But when Rose looked at the illustration again, something caught her attention.

The drawing was exactly the same as when she'd previously looked at it. But now, somehow, she saw it in a different light. There was something very familiar about Merlin's eyes . . . They were *bright blue*, just like Merdyn's. And Merlin's hair? Why, if Merdyn were a little older and combed and washed his own hair, wouldn't it look just like this? Even his purple robes were very similar, just cleaner. In fact, if you'd taken the Merdyn Rose knew and given him a complete makeover, say, by the hand of a loving wife, wouldn't he look exactly like Merlin?

Rose's heart was racing. What else hadn't she noticed about the picture? Well, she hadn't noticed that standing in the background of the illustration, so distant you could almost miss her, was a beautiful woman with red hair and freckles very much like Rose's. Could this be Evanhart? It must be! Her great great great etcetera grandmother!

It was all becoming clear. Merdyn must have gone home, become good and wise, and used his powers for the benefit of others as he'd promised. In fact, he had become, perhaps through some misspelling over time, the man we now know as . . . Merlin.

"Good for you, Merdyn!" Rose cried out loud, bursting with pride.

"Just remember. *Au-ber-gine*," said Bubbles, never one to miss an opportunity to misjudge an occasion.

Rose grabbed a magnifying glass and studied the illustration before her even more closely. There was one more thing, the Latin inscription on the sword Merdyn was holding – she'd noticed it in the library but hadn't had time to translate it. it read: *Gratium Autem Rosa Est.*

Rose scrambled for her phone and carefully tapped in the Latin words inscribed on the sword, before pressing "translate to English". As the translation popped up on her screen her heart leaped and a feeling of great joy spread from the top of her head to the tips of her toes.

For the inscription on the sword read:

Thanks Be To Rose

Grasses – a guide

– they're really awesome!

Bet you think Merdyn was making it all up, well, think again... Meet the superheroes of the grass world!

← BEARDED DARNEL – also known as "mimic grass" because it looks like wheat, but it has one big difference – if eaten it causes dizziness or even death. Hence its other nickname: "wheat's evil twin"!

COCKSFOOT – so called because the clumped flowers and seed heads look like a cockerel's foot. It was thought to be a magic plant by farmers of old because it appeared to need no water to survive, it was so hardy. →

PENDULOUS SEDGE – known as the "Hercules of the grass" as it's so strong you can make rope and even clothes out of it.

Although I'm not sure what I'd look like in a pair of grass shorts!

An old rhyme to help tell grass types apart goes like this:

Sedges have edges, rushes are round,
and grasses are hollow right up from the ground.

What do you think, could this be MC Warlock's next hit record?

WITCHES GRASS - so called because its panicle (leaf cluster) looks like a witch's broom! It was thought to reverse curses and hexes. What's that? Your pencil sharpener keeps mysteriously disappearing when you most want it? You need . . . witches grass!

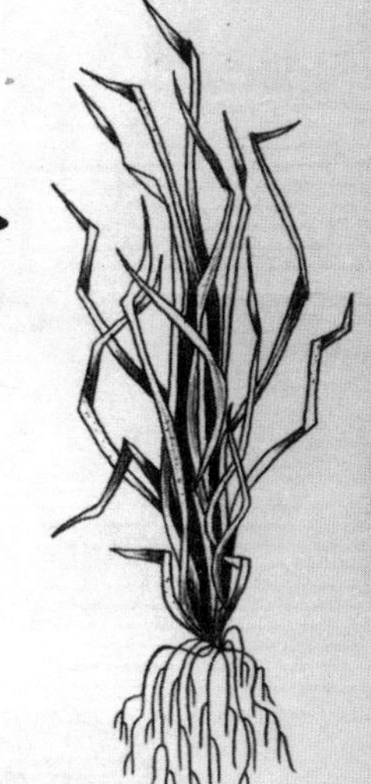

CLOVER – thought to be sacred as its three leaves represent the holy trinity (father, son and Holy Ghost). A four-leaf clover is said to bring good luck to those who find one. Problem is, they're incredibly rare. So good luck finding one!

COMING SOON!

Join Merdyn, Rose and Bubbles on their next madcap adventure – in the **DARK AGES!**

Vanheldon the Vandal has kidnapped Kris and only they can rescue him.

It will involve time travel, **MAGIC** and a lot of guinea pig poo.